Recipe for Disaster

RECIPE FOR DISASTER

A MEN OF THE SECRET SERVICE ROMANCE

TRACY SOLHEIM

TULE
PUBLISHING

DEDICATION

This one is for Meredith, my best girl. Thanks for being my fashion guru. Love you more!

CHAPTER ONE

T HE SPRINGTIME SUN was slipping past the horizon as a line of government vans and black SUVs quietly snaked their way through the New Jersey industrial park. Most of the one-story buildings were deserted for the night, but light from a few of the offices bathed areas of the parking lot with a soft glow. Civilian casualties weren't something Secret Service Agent Griffin Keller wanted to contemplate right now. Not when he was so close to capturing the man who had eluded him for nearly two years. A man, known only as The Artist, who was responsible for flooding the world's monetary system with nearly fifty million dollars in counterfeit one hundred dollar bills.

Griffin fidgeted in the front seat of the Chevy Tahoe, an SRG rifle on his lap and a lump in his throat. Any one of those occupied offices could be housing a lookout who might alert their prey to the incoming visitors. They needed to get the strike team in place before that happened. The intel he'd received earlier in the day indicated the group was preparing to relocate. Possibly overseas. Griffin would be damned if he let the counterfeit ring slip away from his grasp. He hadn't played nice with the FBI for all these months just to lose the biggest collar of his career.

"Subject on the move." The voice of one of the agents staking out the warehouse whispered through his earpiece.

"Damn it! Let's move in," Griffin shouted into his radio transmitter. "I don't want that son of a bitch getting away!"

Agents from the Secret Service and the FBI quickly slipped out of the vans, their bodies forming a wide circle around a darkened office/warehouse unit at the end of one of the buildings. Their dark battle dress uniforms and sleek black helmets equipped with night vision goggles made them look like a bunch of cockroaches fanning out in a kitchen after dark.

"Hey, Agent Keller, let's not forget who's in charge here," Leslie Morgan's husky voice floated through his earpiece. "No one enters that building until I give the go order."

Louis Silva, the driver of the SUV, chuckled next to Griffin. "Damn. That woman loves her position of power," Silva said. "I'll bet she's like that in bed."

At Silva's comments, Griffin felt himself go hard. Leslie *was* like that in bed; constantly trying to dominate her partner. Sex with the FBI Special Agent always turned into a sweaty wrestling match. One Griffin never let her win. He frequently wondered if Leslie's need to best him was what kept her coming back for more. Not that he minded. Their relationship—if it could be called that—was about blowing off steam. Nothing more.

Griffin didn't bother sharing this information with Silva, though. "Get your mind out of the locker room and back into the op, Silva," he commanded before jumping out of the car.

Leslie had her team of agents in place just outside the bay doors leading into the warehouse. Griffin's team positioned themselves along the perimeter of the building, blocking all the possible escape routes. Based on the intel they'd gathered from the agents manning the stakeout, there was only one person inside. Presumably, he was packing up the printing presses, ink, and specialty paper to move to their next site.

"Okay, team, let's see who's at home."

Leslie had no sooner gotten the words out when one of the garage doors opened. A rental box truck, its engine running, filled the warehouse bay. Sitting in the driver's seat of the truck, a young man, wearing a Yankees baseball cap, stared wide-eyed at the twenty assault rifles trained on him.

"Federal agents," Leslie called out to him. "Come out of the truck slowly with your hands where we can see them."

Griffin watched the driver's mouth turn up in a sneer as he reached for the gear shift.

"I'm going to disable the vehicle!" Griffin shouted while he aimed his rifle at the truck's front tire. "I want this guy alive."

The windshield exploded before Griffin could get the shot off, however. The box truck never moved, its engine quietly idling. Through the shattered glass, Griffin could see the driver leaning against the blood-spattered back wall of the cab, his eyes still wide and a perfect black hole in the Yankee emblem of his baseball cap. Chaos followed as Griffin swore violently.

"Damn it! Who the hell took that shot? I'll have your ass fired tonight!"

Leslie was yelling for the strike force to check the perimeter rooftops as sirens peeled in the background. All Griffin could hear was the roaring in his ears. He took two steps toward the truck before Silva grabbed him, pulling him behind the line of vans.

"Stay back, Keller," he said. "We need to check the area for explosives."

Fuck. Not only was his best lead dead, but all the evidence could be blown to bits, as well. Two agents dressed in explosive ordinance disposal clothing exited one of the FBI vans, each with a dog by his side. The agents slowly circled the truck as the dogs danced around the chassis, sniffing for explosives. Like the dogs, Griffin was filled with his own nervous energy, pacing as the agents and their canine partners seemed to take their time inspecting the truck.

"The shot came from a rooftop two buildings away, Agent Morgan," a voice said over the transmitter. "The shooter got away."

Griffin ripped his receiver from his ear and let it dangle down over his shoulder as he swore viciously again. He didn't want to hear about anyone escaping. Not tonight when he'd been so close to breaking the case wide open. His gut had been right about someone else watching the place. Whoever it was, they hadn't bothered warning the kid in the truck. They simply silenced him instead.

"Can we make this go any faster?" He practically growled the question at Leslie who'd come up to stand beside him.

Griffin was impatient to get inside that truck to see if the gang had left any clues to their identity. Specifically, clues that would lead him to The Artist. Not that he believed he'd find anything, but there was always a chance the black hats had slipped up. Griffin didn't want to stand around with his hands in his pockets while potential leads slipped away.

Leslie shot him a sympathetic look, but that was the only thing soft about her. "I won't jeopardize the safety of anyone on this team, Agent Keller."

She was right, of course. Busting into the truck would have to wait until the area was secure. Her ability to keep cool under fire was one of the things Griffin respected about the FBI Special Agent. Griffin had a tendency to act first and think later. A trait that bugged the crap out of his parents when he was a teenager, followed by every supervisor he'd ever had. He shoved his earpiece back in and continued his pacing.

"The lobby area is clear, Agent Morgan," a voice said.

"Copy that," Leslie said. "As soon as the bomb squad gives the all clear, forensics can go in and sweep."

He ceased pacing and stood to watch as one of the bomb squad agents carefully opened the driver's door. Griffin held his breath as the agent slowly turned the key, killing the ignition. He then checked the driver's pulse before shaking his head, telling those assembled what they already knew. The guy would be heading to the morgue rather than an interrogation room. Griffin swore in frustration.

"The dogs aren't picking up anything," one of the bomb squad agents relayed through the transmitter. "I'm going to do a quick X-ray of the truck's container just to be sure."

"Ten-four, Agent Oswald," Leslie replied.

Not wanting to wait any longer, Griffin sought out the two Secret Service agents he'd had staking out the warehouse. Mark Phillips trotted out from one of the nearby buildings, presumably the one where the sniper had fired his fatal shot.

Phillips shook his head when he saw Griffin. "Nothing. Not even a gum wrapper up there. I cordoned it off anyway. Maybe the forensics team can find something that will help." Phillips dragged in a lungful of the night air. "That wasn't an easy shot to make," he said. "Whoever pulled the trigger was a trained sniper. A damn good one."

Griffin made a mental note to check with his buddy from their days at West Point, Adam Lockett, a former army sniper who now served as a commander on the Secret Service Counter Assault Team. It was Adam's job to know who and where the best shots in the world were. Keeping tabs on his competition was a source of pride for Adam who considered himself to be at the top of that list of the world's best shots.

"I still can't figure out why the shooter didn't take more people out," Phillips said. "Hell, he could have decimated the New York field offices of both the Secret Service and the FBI in one round."

Griffin stared at the warehouse where the bomb-sniffing dogs sat at attention while their handlers x-rayed the truck with handheld machines. "That wasn't his mission. This group is arrogant. Whatever we find in that truck will be sterile as the day it came from the factory. The tools can be replaced. As long as they have The Artist, they can set up shop somewhere else." He kicked at a lamppost in disgust.

Two black sedans with sirens flashing rounded the corner and came to an abrupt stop in front of Griffin. He blew out a heavy breath, having no doubt each car contained the director of both agency's field offices. Steve Kass, the Secret Service field director of the New York office, alighted from his car first.

"What the hell happened, Keller?" he demanded as the FBI field director made his way out of his car and over to where Leslie was still trying to keep charge of the scene. "You told me this was as close to a sure thing as it gets. I'd assumed we would arrive in time to see you leading out counterfeiters in handcuffs."

"It would seem someone didn't want to leave behind anything that could incriminate the rest of the gang," Griffin said. "Including the driver."

"The truck is clean, Agent Morgan," the bomb squad agent relayed thru Griffin's earpiece.

"If there were something in that truck that could lead us to The Artist or this group, we'd be sifting through shrapnel right now," Griffin told his boss. He gestured to the crowd forming at the back of the parking lot. Apparently, there were more people working late in the industrial park than he'd counted on. "Phillips, take Silva and whomever else you can grab and start interviewing those people. I want to know what they saw and heard. After you get their names, forward them to the joint operations center in DC for cross-check. Let's make sure everyone is who they say they are."

"You think our shooter might not have left?" Director Kass quietly asked when Phillips walked off.

"At this point, I don't know what to think anymore," Griffin responded. "But I'm not taking any chances. Let's go see what's in the truck."

Just as Griffin suspected, the truck contained boxes of ink and linen paper used for printing money. A high-pressure intaglio printing press, carefully wrapped on shipping pallets, sat at the rear of the truck, seemingly mocking Griffin. While this kind of printing press was expensive and difficult to come by, the group had proved they could get any and all materials they needed to successfully make fake money. The Artist's talents for creating bills that were nearly indistinguishable from the real thing were the component of their operation that was priceless.

Leslie came up beside Griffin and discreetly touched his arm. She knew how important solving this case was to him. "We'll take the truck back to the lab and dust it for prints."

"The only prints you'll likely find will be that guy's."
Griffin gestured to the kid who'd been driving the truck,
now stretched out on a gurney, awaiting a body bag.

"Still, it's worth a shot." She gave his arm a squeeze and
went to talk to her team.

Griffin wandered over to the gurney and stared down at
the deceased driver whose license identified him as twenty-
year-old Jamal Issacs, from Freehold, if in fact that was his
real ID. Griffin wondered how a kid from Springsteen's
hometown got mixed up with a counterfeit gang made up
of crooks based in Greece.

"Whoever took that shot must have been a Red Sox
fan," the medical examiner joked from behind him. With
his gloved hand, he reached around Griffin and lifted off
the baseball cap, gesturing to bullet hole before dropping it
into an evidence bag. Having grown up in Boston, Griffin
came from a long line of Sox fans, but the sight of the
desecrated Yankee cap didn't alleviate any of his disgust
over the current situation.

"He had this in the front seat with him," the medical
examiner continued. "Must not have wanted it rolling
around in the back." He pulled out a three-foot-long
cardboard tube; the kind used to carry blueprints.

Griffin's interest was immediately piqued. He grabbed
a pair of latex gloves out of the evidence kit and pulled
them over his fingers. Gingerly, he took the tube from the
medical examiner and pried the plastic cap off one end.

"They look like paintings." Griffin gently drew the
rolled-up canvases out of the tube. Leslie made her way

over, and Griffin handed her the tube while he spread the paintings out on a table at the back of the bay.

"So, our artist actually *is* an artist," she said.

"Not unless our artist is the reincarnation of Jean Paul Monet." Griffin shuffled the canvases. "Or Paul Cezanne."

"A forger, then?" Director Kass asked.

Griffin looked up to see both field directors had joined Leslie and him at the table.

"Most likely. That's probably how he got drafted into designing 'forged' money," Griffin said. But something wasn't sitting right. Something about these paintings seemed familiar.

Leslie fingered the corner of one of the cut canvases. "I never figured you for an art enthusiast. How do you know who painted them?"

"My mom's an art teacher. She'd bribe me with hockey tickets if I'd go to a museum with her." He smiled at the memory. "The best Mother's Day gift I ever gave her was a private tour of the White House with the curator..." His voice trailed off, and a chill ran down his spine. Griffin suddenly remembered why these paintings looked so familiar. He'd seen them all hanging in the White House.

He sorted through the canvases again, checking their backs. "Holy shit," he murmured. "It can't be."

"Can't be what, Agent Keller?" Director Kass demanded.

"I don't think these are forged," Griffin said. "I think they're the originals. And I'm pretty sure they were stolen from the White House."

Everyone around him started talking at once.

"Are you sure about this?"

"How could someone get inside the White House and steal a painting without anyone noticing?"

"Aren't these things rigged with some sort of alarm?"

All their questions were valid, but there was a bigger question that consumed Griffin. "How many others are missing?"

"Agent Keller, we still don't know definitively that these aren't forgeries," Director Kass said. "Before we jump to any conclusions, why don't you take these down to the forensics lab at DC headquarters and have an expert check them out. With any luck, they might be able to grab a fingerprint from these. Agent Morgan and the FBI can keep working the case from here."

Griffin hesitated. He didn't want Leslie and her team grabbing his collar. But this gang of counterfeiters had been methodical and thorough so far. His gut was telling him Leslie wouldn't find anything of use in the truck. The paintings, on the other hand, just might lead to something. The Secret Service forensics lab was the best in the country at finding trace evidence on an item—fake money, in particular. The director was right; it was worth a shot. If nothing else, while he was back in DC, he could grab a beer with Adam and check out the sniper angle.

"I'll drive down tonight." He rolled up the paintings and carefully slid them back into the tube, except he couldn't quite make them fit the way they had before. Griffin pulled the paintings back out and laid them on the table before turning the tube upside down and shaking it. A white cloth fell to the floor.

"What's that?" Leslie asked.

Griffin reached down and carefully picked it up, shaking it out as he did so.

"It's a dish towel." His gut clenched when he caught sight of the monogram on the towel. "From the White House kitchen."

The group was somber as Griffin shoved the towel into an evidence bag. "I'll head out now if you don't mind, Director," he said.

"Be sure and brief the agency director first thing," Director Kass said.

Nodding to the field office director, Griffin headed for the SUV he and Silva had arrived in forty-five minutes earlier.

"Agent Kellar," Leslie called after him.

He stopped in his tracks and turned to face the FBI agent who was his sometimes lover. The stark contrast of the bright lights of the warehouse bay against the dark night left her in silhouette so that he couldn't make out her expression.

"Don't forget to brief me as well," she commanded, hands on her hips.

He was pretty sure that was code for "call me." Griffin wasn't in the habit of calling any woman except his mother. And despite a few exerting nights in bed, Leslie didn't warrant being added to his phone log. It seemed a trip to DC couldn't have come at a more strategic time.

CHAPTER TWO

"I T'S NOT EVEN seven a.m., and you're already on your way to work?" Marin Chevalier tried not to cringe at her cousin Ava's condescending tone. "You really need to get a life."

Marin stepped off the escalator at the Farragut North metro station wishing her cousin had called a few minutes earlier. That way she would still have been deep in the tunnel, and the call would have gone straight to voicemail. She didn't normally avoid her family, but, with Ava's wedding a little over a week away, her cousin was more cranky than usual.

"I have a busy few days ahead of me, Ava, and you know I do my best work when the kitchens are quiet. Besides, if you're up, it can't be that early."

Looking both ways, she crossed K Street and headed into Farragut Park, mingling in with the line of federal workers trudging toward their offices. The sun rose over the Washington Monument, making it look like a giant pinwheel.

"I'm headed to spin class, Oompa Loompa," Ava said. "Something you'd have time for if you got out of the kitchen once in a while."

Waiting for the light to cross I Street, Marin checked her exercise tracker on her wrist. She suddenly regretted skipping the added steps that walking the entire way from her condo in Dupont Circle would have given her. Ava always had a way of making Marin feel inferior. It didn't help that her cousin had called her by the childhood name their grandfather had dubbed Marin when she was a pudgy adolescent; one who would rather spend time in the kitchens of her family's hotels than by the pool with her much prettier—and always more popular—cousin.

"You can't fight genetics," her grandfather would say, patting his formidable belly. "You've got the Chevalier genes, Oompa Loompa. Blonde hair, blue eyes, and a build that, when you are older, men will call statuesque, while your cousin got her mother's dark, beauty-queen genes. Let's just hope Ava didn't inherit the woman's cheating ways," he'd always add with a disappointed whisper. Aunt Vanessa had left Uncle Clay and the family compound in the Garden District of New Orleans when Ava was just seven. Marin couldn't remember whether her former aunt was on husband number three or four.

"Is your mother coming to your wedding?" The words slipped out of Marin's mouth without forethought as she passed the Hay-Adams Hotel and waited to cross H Street. It wasn't like her to antagonize Ava. As hateful as her cousin was to Marin sometimes, she always took the high road. Not because she was more forgiving than Ava, but because Marin didn't have the patience to argue with her domineering cousin. It was always easier just to let Ava have her way.

The light changed and she walked along the sidewalk bordering Lafayette Park. Ava was quiet on the other end of the phone and a sliver of guilt wormed its way up Marin's spine. Her cousin's childhood hadn't been unhappy by any means, but her relationship with her estranged mother was always a source of tension.

"She hasn't responded yet," Ava finally said. "But that's why I'm calling. I'm working on the seating chart, and you haven't let me know if you're a plus-one."

Marin sighed as she passed the statue of French General Rochambeau, pointing with his right hand in the direction she was walking. Ava's wedding was destined to be the society event of the year. Over three hundred guests were expected to attend the nuptials at their family's flagship hotel in New Orleans's French Quarter.

"I'll be extremely busy that weekend working on the wedding cake." Marin crossed Pennsylvania Avenue and followed two West Wing staffers through the metal detectors of the White House's northwest gate. She gave the officer from the Uniformed Division of the Secret Service a smile as he scanned her ID. "I don't think it's fair to bring a date when I'll just end up neglecting him."

The officer winked at her. "I'd be okay with you neglecting me on a date," he whispered as she passed by him.

Marin blushed furiously, but her confidence received a much-needed boost after her cousin's comments.

"What you mean to say is that you don't *want* to bring a date, so, as usual, you're using your status as White

House pastry chef as an excuse not to," Ava said. "Well, Rich and I don't really care about the wedding cake, so let me take that off your very broad shoulders. I'll have one of the chefs here prepare it. Everyone else in the wedding party will have a plus-one. I need you to do the same so that the aesthetics at the head table aren't off. Do you think you can manage that?"

Ava's words stopped Marin in her tracks, which was a good thing. She was about to pass through Stonehenge—the area of the White House lawn between the driveway and the press briefing room where networks set up their cameras on tripods for live broadcasts. Several of the cameras had their lights shining on reporters who were likely on-air with the morning news programs. The last thing Marin needed to do was have a meltdown on the phone with her cousin while passing in front of the cameras broadcasting to half the kitchens in America.

"You can't do that. It's my gift to you and Rich," she protested. "Every bride wants a gorgeous wedding cake. At least they ought to. And who cares about the aesthetics of the bridal party's dinner table?"

"I do," Ava snapped. "So please, if you want to contribute something to my wedding day, you'll bring a date." And with that, her cousin hung up.

Stunned, Marin stared at her phone. Had Ava—the woman who was practically her sister—just said that to her? Tears stung the back of her eyes and Marin wasn't sure if they were due to anger or hurt feelings. Not that it made a difference. Ava never cared about other people's feelings.

She shoved her phone into her purse and—checking the television cameras—trudged up the driveway toward the north portico of the White House.

"Hey, you!"

Marin looked up to see Diego Ruiz, her sous chef, heading toward her from the opposite end of the driveway. "You keep stomping like that and someone might mistake you for one of the nut jobs crashing the building," he joked. "This place is a magnet for psychos, you know."

Her friend's teasing had the desired effect, calming Marin so her steps became less forceful and her shoulders relaxed. "Sorry. The only psycho is my cousin. I'm afraid she's become a bit of a bridezilla. Now she's insisting that I bring a date to her wedding. Or else."

They passed under the covered part of the driveway and climbed the steps. "The nerve of that wench," Diego said. "Insisting that you bring someone to dance with, get tipsy with, and possibly get naked with. Nope, not a good time at all."

Marin laughed at the face Diego made. She stopped briefly to rub the soft ear of one of the dogs that routinely patrolled the grounds of the White House. Otto was a favorite of Marin's. The dog wasn't technically on duty any longer; he'd been retired for a couple of months. His handler was in charge of training the new dogs and he often brought Otto to work with him to use as a model for the canine recruits. The big Belgian Malinois sat quietly next to the entranceway, his body on guard, but an ever-present twinkle in his whiskey-colored eyes.

"Good boy, Otto," she whispered as they passed. "What are you doing here so early anyway, Diego? It's rare to see you at the House before nine."

"Just between you and me, my boss is a bit of a pastryzilla. She has me making hundreds of marzipan bunnies for Monday's Easter egg hunt." He playfully nudged her shoulder with his as they entered the wide entrance hall.

"Good morning, Miss Chevalier. Mr. Ruiz." The chief usher nodded to them both as he exited the usher's office on their right. "What's this about the Easter egg hunt? All is proceeding according to plans, I assume?"

"The pastry kitchen won't let you down, Admiral," Marin said. It was her first Easter at the White House, and she was determined that the desserts and centerpieces would be better than they ever had been. Of course, she could manage to create several hundred marzipan figures, thousands of mini-cakes and cookies, but she couldn't find the time to meet an eligible bachelor to take to her cousin's stupid wedding. Irony was a bitch.

"See that no one is let down, Chef." With a brisk nod, the chief usher headed past them and climbed the main staircase to the second floor, presumably for his morning meeting with the First Lady.

"That guy gives me the heebie-jeebies," Diego whispered.

"That's because you still think you're in the navy and he can have you swabbing decks or whatever it is you sailors do."

Diego shot her a bemused look. "I spent four years in

the Navy Mess downstairs," he said. "The only water I ever saw was the swimming pool in the West Wing. And that was just fine by me." He gestured toward the stairs the chief usher had just ascended. "I didn't think I'd still be answering to an admiral when I got out."

Admiral Sedgewick had retired from the navy to take the position as chief usher two years ago when President Manning's term began. As such, he was in charge of the executive mansion and its staff, including Marin and Diego. Running the White House was similar to running a ship, Marin supposed. Aside from his formal manner, she had no complaints about her boss.

"Speaking of the Navy Mess," Diego said, "I came in early to catch up with a friend still working there. He's having a bit of a hard time. Do you mind if I swing by the West Wing for a few minutes? I promise my marzipan menagerie will be finished on time."

"Go ahead. I'm headed upstairs to the pastry kitchen to whip up some sugar cookie dough for this afternoon. I promised Arabelle I'd help her make some bunny cookies for her preschool class."

Diego grinned at her. "The President's granddaughter has you wrapped around her cute little finger. It's no wonder you don't have a life."

Marin halted in her tracks and stared at him. "You too, Diego?"

"Hey, I just call 'em like I see 'em." He gave her a jaunty salute before taking the steps, two at a time, down to the ground floor.

Turning on her heel, Marin headed in the opposite direction, passing by the Red Room before cutting through the majestic State Dining Room. Even after working in the White House for nine months, Marin was still awed by the history that surrounded her every day. Normally, she would stop and spend a few minutes daydreaming about the men and women who had dined in this room, wondering what they had eaten and what they had worn to dinner. Or she'd glance at the stunning portrait of a pensive President Lincoln that hung above the room's marble fireplace, trying to guess what the man was thinking.

Today, however, she kept her head down, pondering her life—or lack thereof. Unlike her two brothers and three cousins, she'd eschewed a career in the family hotel business, preferring a pastry kitchen to a boardroom. At twenty-seven, Marin had studied with some of the best chefs in the world, including two years in Switzerland at the Richemont Centre. When First Lady Harriet Manning, Marin's godmother, asked if she would come to Washington to work at the White House, Marin jumped at the opportunity.

Little did she know how challenging and demanding the job would be. In the months since she'd arrived in DC, she'd yet to meet her neighbors much less anyone to hang out with. Her circle of friends included Otto, the guard dog; Diego, her gay sous chef; and Arabelle, an adorable five-year-old with a tendency to suck her thumb when she thought no one was looking. Still, Marin loved it here at the White House.

Rounding the corner into the butler's pantry, Marin bypassed the elevator that would take her to the third-floor office she shared with the executive chef of the large White House kitchen. Instead, she headed for the spiral staircase that led to her domain; the pastry kitchen tucked away on a mezzanine floor just above the pantry. She would start on the cookie dough while she pondered her dilemma.

"Oh—" She cried out when she collided with a man hurrying down the narrows stairs. "I'm so sorry. I wasn't looking where I was going."

Marin was surprised to confront anyone this early in the morning. The only people who used these stairs were the kitchen chefs, an occasional usher or housemaid. The man staring down at her from two steps above was unfamiliar to her. At first glance, he appeared to be one of the contractors who delivered the food to the White House. Deliveries of supplies to the pastry kitchen were normally made via the dumbwaiters, but it wasn't unusual for the heavier items to be carried up by contractor staff. With the Easter egg hunt days away, the chefs had been ordering a multitude of supplies.

With the stranger's sudden appearance, it dawned on Marin that among the nearly five hundred staff working in the mansion, there had to be dozens of eligible men around. She didn't need to scour Washington DC for a wedding date. All she had to do was interact with some of the men working in the White House.

Starting with this guy.

She studied him carefully. Dressed in dark chinos, a

navy windbreaker and a dark ball cap adorned with an obscure logo, she guessed he was good-looking—if one liked guys with finely chiseled features arranged in a cold sort of way. Still, Marin treated him to the five-thousand-dollar smile her parents had paid for when she was thirteen.

"Good morning? Are you lost?" Wishing she'd paid more attention to how Ava attracted men like bees to honey, she hoped her teasing sounded flirtatious.

His lips formed a tight line as he slowly shook his head. Without a word, he pressed his slender frame against the railing and gestured for her to proceed up the stairs.

"Oh," Marin said, the giddiness at her plan fading. "Um, okay."

The close confines of the winding staircase forced her to pass within inches of him. The odor of cabbage and beetroot wafted off of him and Marin cursed her keen sense of smell. Their eyes met when she slid past him. Marin had the feeling of walking over someone's grave when she peered into his icy blue gaze. His pupils looked so empty and devoid of any emotion that Marin was happy to put some distance between them when she climbed a few steps farther.

"Have a nice day," she called out, unable to suppress the manners two years of cotillion had drilled into her.

He hesitated briefly as if wanting to say something, before he quickly turned. His gloved hands shifted his messenger bag on his shoulder and he disappeared down the stairs.

"He doesn't count," Marin mumbled to herself as she

climbed the last few circular steps. "He's obviously painfully shy. Not to mention a little creepy. Surely, there's at least one half-decent guy somewhere in this big house."

Spirits buoyed, she hurried into the pastry kitchen only to let out a squeal when she nearly collided with yet another unexpected person. At least this time it was someone she knew. Bita Ranjbar, Arabelle's maternal grandmother, was standing in front of the glass cabinets housing an assortment of marzipan and sugar figures. The woman's rich perfume permeated the narrow, low-ceilinged room.

Bita was a frequent guest of the Manning family at the White House, usually when the First Lady had a busy travel schedule. The president's son, Clark, Arabelle's father, was enrolled in a demanding neurological fellowship program at the Washington Institutes of Health. Clark and his wife, Farrah, lived with Arabelle on the third floor of the mansion. As far as Marin could tell, Farrah wasn't much into motherhood. The former fashion model chafed at the "Mommy and Me" circuit, preferring instead to run around with her jet-set friends, much to the dismay of the president and his wife. It was left to Bita and Harriet Manning to raise their granddaughter, along with a doting White House staff. Not that Marin minded spending time with the little girl.

Marin leaned against one of the long counters in front of a bank of ovens trying to get her heart to settle into a normal rhythm. At five-foot-eight without her hat, she always felt a little claustrophobic in the room carved out between two floors. Right now, though, she felt as if the kitchen was closing in on her. "That's the second time in less than five minutes someone has scared the bejesus out of me."

Bita arched a perfectly made-up eyebrow at her. "Second time?"

The woman's thick Persian accent always reminded Marin of the housekeeping supervisor in her family's hotel in Constantinople. Not that she could picture Bita vacuuming or dusting. She'd never seen the older woman looking less than perfect. Her jet-black hair was always stylishly coiffed; her makeup was impeccable, and her clothing, designer. It was quite a feat to look that good at seven-twenty in the morning. Marin looked down at her baggy black uniform pants, her sensible Skechers, and her turquoise T-shirt from The Gap in disgust.

No wonder that guy didn't even want to make eye contact.

"Yeah." Marin pulled out her key and stowed her backpack and jacket in the small locker in the walk-in pantry next to the spiral staircase. "I nearly took out some unsuspecting man on the stairs just now."

"On the stairs, you say? A stranger?" Bita's voice held a trace of panic. "Should we alert the guards?"

Marin bit back a smile. She and Diego always chuckled at the way Bita referred to the White House as though it were a palace.

"He was just a delivery guy sent up from the kitchen," Marin said to calm the easily excitable woman. "Neither of us expected to see anyone else in this part of the house so early. We both startled one another, that's all." After adjusting her ponytail, Marin set her tall, pleated toque on her head and pulled on her chef's jacket. There. Sufficiently armored, she felt ready to face the day. A day that was already proving to be unsettling. "What can I do for you this morning, Bita? Everything is well with Arabelle, I hope."

"Oh, my little princess is fine." Bita clapped her manicured hands with excitement. "I came here to remind you about the cookie baking this afternoon. Arabelle is very anxious this morning that she have cookies for her friends before the family leaves for Camp David tomorrow night. Today is still good, yes?"

"Of course we are still on," Marin said.

The little girl must be really excited this morning if Bita had come down to the small hidey-hole of a kitchen herself to confirm Arabelle's visit. Usually, the Secret Service simply called. She mentally shrugged. Apparently, it was going to be one of those days where nothing made sense.

"Does three o'clock work?"

"Splendid," Bita said with another clap of her hands. "You are so kind, Chef Marin."

"Trust me. It will be the highlight of my day." Given how this morning had gone so far, Marin didn't doubt her own words.

CHAPTER THREE

G RIFFIN GLANCED DISCREETLY around the corner
before exiting the curator's office. The center hall of
the White House basement level was empty except for two
ushers setting up the folding screens that would keep the
visitors from wandering where they shouldn't once the
mansion opened up to guided tours.

"Dude, she isn't likely to come down here before
noon," Adam Lockett said from beside him. "You don't
need to be on the lookout."

They walked the ten yards down the hall to the office
of the White House Secret Service Director, Steve Worcester, and stepped into the reception area.

"I'm not looking for anyone," Griffin told his friend.
"Except a thief. And now, it seems, a White House curator
who is AWOL."

Adam shot him a speaking look, but wisely let the subject drop. "Do you think it's a coincidence that you found
those paintings two nights ago and our curator hasn't
shown up for work since?"

"You know as well as I do that in our business, there's
no such thing as a coincidence." He acknowledged the
director's secretary with a vague smile.

A flush crept up her neck to her cheeks in response. The young woman always reacted that way at the sight of Griffin. Hell, most women did. His sister jokingly referred to women's reactions to him as the "Dimple Phenomenon."

Griffin sighed and continued their conversation. "With the missing curator, it looks like I'll be in town longer than I thought. Can I bunk in my old room at the townhouse?"

Adam shook his head sheepishly. "Dawson's been squatting there for the past three months. Much as Ben and I'd rather shoot hoops with you, the guy's pretty low right now, and we can't kick him out."

"Dawson? Why isn't he living with his wife and three kids?" Griffin asked, even though he could guess what Adam's answer would be.

"Because *they* are living with an orthodontist in Rockville. One with normal working hours who doesn't miss every major holiday. Or bring home a gun."

The two men shared an empathetic look. Both had witnessed the toll a career in the Secret Service had on family life. Griffin would never subject a woman to such an unstable relationship. Even with that mythical thing called love, it was never enough. Thankfully his career provided all the fulfillment he needed.

Griffin rapped on the director's open door. Both men made their way into his office just as Director Worcester was slamming down the phone.

"The admiral—excuse me, chief usher—will see us in his office in five minutes," the director said with a grimace.

An inherent power struggle between the Secret Service and the usher's office had always existed. But tensions had ratcheted up a notch with an admiral occupying the chief usher post. Clearly, it rankled the director to have play the subordinate.

"Still no word from the curator?"

Griffin shook his head. "According to his secretary, he usually doesn't wander in until well after nine." All three men glanced at their watches. It was nine-twenty.

"Lockett, sit outside his office," the director ordered as he stood up and pulled on his suit jacket. "If there's no sign of him by nine-thirty, buddy up and go check out his residence. I want to know where this guy is."

"Got it, boss." Adam slapped Griffin on the shoulder. "Welcome back to the Big Show, Griff. Try not to break any more hearts than usual while you're here."

Griffin shot his friend a menacing look. "When you're done with your comedy routine, maybe you can email with those sniper profiles I asked you about?"

"I still don't think anyone else besides me could have made that shot, but I'll humor you and send you a list anyway," Adam joked as he headed back down the hall.

The director and Griffin went in the opposite direction, taking the stairs up two flights to the chief usher's private office in the old clock room on the mezzanine level. The admiral was waiting for them at the top of the stairs.

"We just received a call from the Falls Church Police Department," he said without preamble. "They've found our curator."

One look at the admiral's face told them everything.

"How did he die?" Griffin asked as they followed him into his office.

"Wes hung himself." The admiral gestured for them to take a seat at the conference table. Director Worcester was already on his cell phone to Adam instructing him to coordinate with the police.

"Or at least it appears that way to the detectives. His housekeeper found him," the admiral continued, his expression pensive. "Wes was a pleasant guy. You wouldn't know from interacting with him that he was troubled. Or that he would resort to taking his life."

"Are we sure it was suicide?" Griffin asked. "Did he leave a note?"

The admiral studied Griffin for a long moment and then shook his head. "I'm not sure if part of me wishes it was or it wasn't." He scrubbed a hand down his face in frustration. "So now we've got a dead curator and three paintings stolen directly from their frames in this house."

"Three that we know of," Griffin added.

The admiral groaned. "Pretty ballsy of someone to take them from right under our noses."

"'Ballsy' is this group's middle name," Griffin said as the director ended his call. "They're also not afraid to leave a few bodies lying around."

"So, do we assume that Wes was in on it?" the admiral asked. "That would explain how the paintings got switched without anyone noticing."

"It all sounds too neat and easy," Director Worcester

said. "I'd like to go over every piece of art in this house and figure out if anything else is missing. Obviously, the curator would have been a big help in that area, but now I don't want to involve anyone in that office."

"Agreed. I've called in a team from the Smithsonian who specializes in this type of thing. I'll put the word out that we're conducting an audit of all White House property beginning with the artwork," the admiral explained. "They'll let me know privately whether we have any more forgeries in our midst. There will be questions from the media about the curator's death, but I want to keep the thefts quiet for as long as we can. I'll brief the president this afternoon."

"That's a sound plan," Director Worcester acknowledged. "We don't want to tip anyone off."

"That still leaves us with the kitchen staff," Griffin said.

"Agent Keller, do you know how many towels, napkins, and placeholders are stolen from the House each month?" the admiral asked. "Stolen by supposedly respectable guests? Hell, an Academy Award-winning actress posted a picture on social media of the hand towels—*plural*—she took from the women's lavatory outside the Oval Office. Do you think one dish towel holds the clue to our thief?"

"With all due respect, Admiral, I don't think it can be ignored," Griffin argued.

"None of this makes sense," the admiral said. "Why would a bunch of counterfeiters suddenly branch out to stealing artwork? Especially artwork that is so visible?"

"We'll never know if you don't let me follow this lead."

Griffin sat stoically, refusing to give up. There was a connection somewhere. Griffin was sure of it. He just needed the opportunity to find it.

Director Worcester let out a beleaguered sigh. "The results of the autopsy won't be back before Easter Monday. That gives you five days. I won't be able to justify keeping you here in DC much longer than that. And I don't have any extra agents to assign to help you with the questioning of the chefs. There are at least half a dozen, right Admiral?"

"Five full-time and three part-time," he replied.

"Then I'd better work fast," Griffin said.

The admiral pushed a pile of personal folders across the table. "Most of the kitchen staff has been here for more than five years. Some as long as twenty. But the two at the top are our most recent additions. Both of them work in the pastry kitchen. The sous chef transferred over from the Navy Mess about seven months ago. The executive pastry chef, Marin Chevalier, arrived last summer. They were both fully vetted via extensive background checks."

Griffin opened the first folder and nearly flinched at the wide, effervescent smile staring back at him. The image of the nubile pastry chef was about as sweet as the confections she was employed to create for White House guests. Cheerful, cornflower-blue eyes and full, rosy cheeks rounded out her wholesome look. But, as Griffin knew firsthand, wholesome didn't always mean innocent. He perused the pages of her file more deeply.

"She's Max Chevalier's granddaughter?" Griffin didn't bother hiding his astonishment.

The admiral leaned back in his chair. "One of his granddaughters, yes. The Chevaliers are good friends of the president and his wife. But that doesn't mean that Marin isn't extremely qualified for the position. Mrs. Manning is a big fan of the chef's inspired desserts."

Director Worcester studied Griffin. "Is there some sort of connection between the counterfeiters and the Chevalier hotel chain, Agent Keller?"

"Not that we've been able to prove. Yet." He gathered up the personnel folders and stood. Griffin needed to access his case files. Several of the Chevalier family's five-star hotels had been used as designated pick-up points for the counterfeit money, both in the United States and overseas. This was one of those coincidences that Griffin didn't believe in. "Admiral, do you mind if I take these down to the Secret Service lounge to study further?"

"As long as you keep them secure, I don't see any problem. But Agent Keller—" The admiral's voice had become steely. "Be very sure before you act on anything. As I said, the two families are close. And Marin is well liked around here. Upstairs and down."

Griffin gave him a brusque nod. He didn't care how adored the pastry chef was. It was his job to bust up a ring of counterfeiters. If the cherub in charge of the White House confections was somehow connected, he wouldn't hesitate to bring her down.

"I take it you plan to keep out of sight while you're here in the House?" Director Worcester asked after the two men left the chief usher's office and were taking the stairs back down to the ground floor.

"I think it's best, don't you?"

"Uh-huh. Just don't leave me another mess to clean up after our unsuspecting pastry chef comes in contact with your irresistible good looks," the director mumbled. "Although, if your dimples get the pastry chef to open up, by all means, use 'em."

Griffin shook his head. He'd been teased about his looks his entire life. It wasn't his fault women tended to throw themselves at him, though. Sure, he'd taken advantage of the situation on more than one occasion, but never in the workplace. Unfortunately, the president's daughter-in-law wasn't used to taking "no" for an answer from any man. Her unwanted advances had been what forced him to leave the president's protective detail. Not that life in New York City was bad. He was closer to his family in Boston, and Griffin got a thrill out of tracking down counterfeiters. Still, he resented having to uproot his life just because a woman was attracted to him.

He headed to the lounge located in the West Wing, directly beneath the Oval Office, to formulate a plan—preferably one that didn't involve his damn dimples.

MARIN RUSHED UP the spiral steps to the pastry kitchen. She'd spent most of the day in the small White House chocolate shop, tucked away on the mansion's basement floor. By concentrating on the delicate task of creating edible birds' nests for Diego's marzipan figures, she'd been able to avoid focusing on her cousin's wedding date ultimatum. Now, she had to hurry to get the kitchen ready to make cookies with Arabelle. She was looking forward to spending time with the little girl.

Unfortunately, when Marin stepped into the narrow workspace, she found her sanctuary invaded yet again. One of the main kitchen's assistant chefs, Lillie, loaded a tray of sticky buns into the oven at the far end of the room while she chatted animatedly with a man Marin didn't recognize. And she would definitely remember this guy had she seen him before.

Broad shoulders and a tall, athletic body perfectly filled out the gray suit he was wearing. The pin in his lapel identified him as a Secret Service agent, but the dark stubble along his jaw and the thick sable hair curling past his collar gave him a roguish demeanor so unlike the military look of the men who protected the first family. He murmured something to Lillie, and the rich, gravelly timbre of his voice brought goose bumps to Marin's skin. Then he did the unexpected and grinned—so slowly, it was mesmerizing. Two devastating dimples formed at either side of his lips. Marin swallowed a sigh just as the agent's gaze settled on her. Eyes that couldn't decide whether they were blue or green quickly sized Marin up before he murmured something soft to the other chef. Lillie's laugh was like a machine gun, piercing the room in small staccato bursts, startling Marin from her enthralled stance.

She ducked into the pantry, telling herself it was to

grab the plastic cookie cutters she'd brought from home, but she spent a long moment trying to get rid of the disappointment that Agent Hottie wasn't flirting with *her*. Not that she could blame the guy for his interest in Lillie. She was a petite, Asian woman with alluring eyes and delicate features. The total opposite of Marin whose daily runs were the only thing keeping her from being a plus-sized pastry chef. Glancing at herself in the small mirror that hung on the wall, she swiped at the hair that had escaped her ponytail and tucked it under her toque.

"Get real, Marin," she admonished herself. Guys like Agent Hottie didn't give Amazons like Marin the time of day. But it wouldn't be the first time that she wished they would.

"Have you heard?" Diego's quietly asked question startled Marin once again. Framed by the doorway of the pantry, his face was inexplicably drawn. His knuckles were white where his fingers gripped the doorjamb.

"About Wes?" she asked.

Diego nodded solemnly.

The chief usher's office had sent out an email an hour earlier announcing that the White House curator had died suddenly that morning. Marin was as shocked as Diego appeared to be when she read the news. Wes was—or had been—a jovial man with an inordinate amount of patience and knowledge. Since arriving at the White House, she'd enjoyed many afternoons strolling with the curator and listening to his enthusiastic descriptions of the artifacts displayed within the mansion.

"It's so sad," Marin said. "Folks downstairs were whispering that it was a suicide. Wes was such a sweet man. I just can't imagine him taking his life. He didn't seem the type."

"Not sure there is a type," Diego murmured. With a weary sigh, he dropped his hands and looked over his shoulder. "Hey, what are you doing hiding in here when there's a potential wedding date candidate hanging out in your kitchen? A very hot one, if I do say so myself."

"I think Lillie already has dibs," Marin mumbled as she dug through her backpack looking for the cookie cutters. "But I'm sure you can take him if you're that interested."

Diego's head snapped back around to stare at her disapprovingly. "Snarky doesn't suit you, Boss. First of all, that guy out there is not gay."

"How do you know this? Is there some secret code I'm missing?"

"And secondly," Diego continued, ignoring her question, "I have it on good authority that Lillie is very happily involved with one of the assistant ushers. So, stop hiding in the pantry and making excuses."

Marin wanted to argue that she was doing neither, but they'd both know she'd be lying. "Or we could make my life easier and you could come with me to the wedding?" she asked, a hint of pleading in her voice.

Reaching over to adjust her toque, Diego smiled softly. "This isn't a Lifetime movie, Marin, where the gay friend rides to the rescue. You have two choices here. Either stand up to your bridezilla cousin or find a date." He shook his head when Marin pointed at him. "A straight date."

Standing up to Ava required more stamina than Marin possessed at the moment—or any other moment in her twenty-seven years. She blew out a pained breath. "Or, I could always go with option number three and hire an escort. That worked out in a movie once."

Diego groaned in exasperation. "You don't need to hire a guy. Not when there are plenty to choose from here. Starting with the hot dude in the kitchen."

"That's just the point," Marin whispered. "That guy's a hottie. And I'm…" she gestured to herself "…a nottie. Men like that aren't interested in women like me."

"What do you mean '*women like me*'?" Diego asked.

"You know." She shot the sous chef an exasperated glare, angry she had to point out the obvious. "They prefer their women smaller. Like size zero smaller."

"Zero is *not* a size," Diego scoffed.

"Amen to that," Marin replied. "But guys like Agent Hottie out there don't go for big-boned girls with childbearing hips."

Diego threw his head back and mumbled something at the ceiling in Spanish. She steeled herself for more arguments, but when his eyes met hers again, they were wide with surprise. "Do you smell smoke?"

The scent reached her nose just as his words registered in her ears and they were both clamoring out of the pantry when the smoke detectors began screeching. Black smoke was billowing from the oven where Lillie had put the sticky buns in to bake minutes before. Agent Hottie yanked the oven door open just as flames began to fan to life inside of it.

"Shit!" Diego managed to yell before the word was swallowed up in a flurry of coughs. He gestured for Marin to get out of the kitchen, but she wasn't leaving her friend behind.

Heart racing, she snatched up a dish towel to use to beat the flames down when the entire oven suddenly erupted into a ball of fire. Agent Hottie jumped out of the way of the flames just in time, ducking onto his hands and knees. Diego grabbed the fire extinguisher and pulled its pin. Foam spewed all over Lillie's sticky buns, dousing the flames, but not before the thick smoke had engulfed the narrow, low-ceilinged room. Breathable air vanished. Marin began to gasp frantically.

Her eyes burned, and her head was spinning. *Fresh air.* They needed fresh air. There was a window in the hallway a few steps down the spiral staircase. Marin would go and open it. Holding the dish towel to her mouth, she pushed on the door, but it was jammed.

No! Not today!

The old door had a tendency to stick. Marin had meant to have one of the carpenters look at it for months. She pushed again, using her shoulder this time, but no luck. Marin's thoughts were beginning to scramble when Agent Hottie got to his feet and shoved her out of the way. Two swift kicks later, he had the door open. Marin didn't wait around to thank him. Instead, she scrambled down the steps to the small window. But, she was only able to slide the window an inch before it became as stuck as the door. Dropping the towel, she tried to pull it open with both hands, yet it still wouldn't budge. Marin opened her mouth to swear or scream, she wasn't sure, but she was overcome by a coughing spasm instead.

Tears of frustration and fear were running down her cheeks when suddenly, two hands gripped her own on the window. Together they tugged it wide open. Wheezing from the smoke, Marin thrust her head outside and gulped in a mouthful of fresh air. It wasn't until her lungs started to clear that she realized there was a hard body pressed up against hers from behind. She glanced to her left and nearly collided with Agent Hottie's cheek. From this close distance, she could see his eyes were the same blue color as the waters of the Caribbean. *Smooth and tempting.* He sucked in deep breaths of the fresh air and Marin could feel every expansion and contraction of his chest against her back. The shrill sound of the smoke alarm faded into the distance as they relaxed into one another as though their bodies were intimately familiar.

Their breathing was returning to normal when a line of people hurried up the stairs behind them. Rather than step back, the agent pressed closer into her. His palms were on the wall, bracketing her body, shielding her from being jostled by the agents and staff converging on the pastry kitchen.

"You okay?" he asked, so close, his breath fanned her ear.

Marin wasn't sure whether it was the effect of the fire

or his nearness that kept her speechless, but all she could do was nod.

"Good." He pushed away from the wall—and her body. "Stay."

Clearly, he was one of those men who thought his good looks gave him permission to dictate to others—women in particular. Except Marin wasn't like most women. He'd gone two steps before Marin finally found her voice. "Like hell I will," she choked out as she charged after him. "That's my kitchen."

He wisely refrained from issuing any more arrogant commands, but he wore a bemused expression when she slid by him on the narrow stairs. Neither of them got very far, however. The small room was crowded with members of the Secret Service's Emergency Response Team, an assistant usher, and Diego who was breathing into an oxygen mask one of the officers had brought with them.

"Diego, are you all right?" Marin shoved into the room and rushed to her friend's side.

"My sticky buns!" Lillie exclaimed when she stepped from the elevator. "What happened?"

"That's what I'd like to know," the admiral announced as he made his way into the room from the opposite direction.

Diego pulled the mask off his face. "What was in those damn buns?" he croaked.

"Nothing unusual. I just ran downstairs for a minute." Lillie's tone was a bit defensive. "I needed to check on the dinner preparations for the First Family." She glanced at

Agent Hottie. "You said you'd watch them."

The heads of everyone in the room turned to stare at him. His mouth was set in a grim line.

"Agent Keller?" the admiral asked.

"Everything happened pretty quickly." Agent Keller maneuvered between the assembled crowd and took a few steps toward the oven. "But I don't think it was the buns." He crouched down next to one of the other agents inspecting the charred oven. "The fire sparked to life too quickly and was too intense."

"It looks like it started in the circuitry," the other agent said, shining a flashlight on something at the back of the oven. "They build these appliances like little robots, nowadays. This one must have decided to go rogue on us."

"Lillie's sticky buns have that effect on men and machines," Diego joked before he doubled over with another coughing fit.

"That's it. Any investigating and cleanup can be handled by my staff. Chef Marin and Mr. Ruiz, I want you both in the physician's office immediately," the admiral commanded. He gestured to the assistant usher. "Peters, take them downstairs and don't let them leave until the doctor gives them the okay. You, too, Agent Keller."

Agent Keller hesitated, planting his hands on his hips. "Nothing gets cleaned up until Agent Seager from our forensic unit takes a look at that oven."

Marin watched in fascination at the nonverbal exchange between the Secret Service agent and the admiral. Since she'd arrived at the White House, she hadn't seen anyone countermand one of the admiral's orders so direct-ly. Clearly, Agent Hottie was an outsider. One who didn't mind committing career suicide. To her fascination, though, the admiral simply cocked an eyebrow at the agent, before nodding brusquely.

"How long will that take?" Marin interjected urgently. "I can't wait around for days. I need this room cleaned up as quickly as possible so I can prepare for Monday's Easter egg hunt."

Both men stared at her with identical looks of exaspera-tion.

"Chef Marin," the admiral said, his tone placating, "it will take several days to replace the oven if we are lucky. In the meantime, I will make every effort to ensure you have the proper equipment to perform your duties. Until then, I'd like you to report to the physician's office immediately. Please."

Swallowing an exasperated huff, Marin took Diego's arm and guided him toward the elevator. Peters held the door open for them both.

"Coming, Agent Keller?" she called out, matching her tone to his smug look.

The admiral nodded toward the elevator. The agent muttered something to one of the other agents before joining her. Diego's ragged cough filled the small chamber as they traveled down to the ground floor. When the doors slid open, Executive Chef Samuels was waiting to greet them.

"Jesus, Marin, if you didn't want Lillie invading your

turf, you could have just spoken up," he joked. His face blanched when Diego was overcome with another coughing fit, however.

"Help me get him across the hall to the doctor's office," Peters said to Chef Samuels.

They each took one of Diego's arms and led him away. Marin went to follow them when she was hit in the knees by thirty pounds of preschooler and one hundred and twenty pounds of Belgian Malinois.

"Chef Marin!" Arabelle cried as she wrapped her arms around Marin's legs. "Me and Otto were so worried. Grandma Bita said there was a fire. Was somebody playing with matches?"

Arabelle's big caramel eyes were wide with concern. Marin gave the little girl a reassuring smile. Brushing her hand over the wild dark curls that surrounded the child's face, Marin bit back a laugh. Everything was simple to a five-year-old.

While kitchen fires weren't a normal occurrence, Marin, like most cooking professionals, had been through her share and knew how to handle them. But most of those had been common grease fires caused by careless staff. Marin wasn't careless. Neither was Lillie or anyone else who worked in the White House kitchens. A faulty oven was something she hadn't expected to ever deal with. And the speed with which the fire spread was disconcerting.

Arabelle must have sensed Marin's unease because her arms shot up. "I think you need a hug."

Marin lifted the girl up. Arabelle wrapped her arms and

legs around her like a little monkey. Otto sat on Marin's foot. The weight of the child in her arms and the feel of the dog against her thigh went a long way in calming Marin.

Burying her face in Marin's neck, Arabelle squeezed tightly. "I'm so glad you didn't die," she whispered.

"Me, too." Had Diego or Agent Keller not been there, she might have been trapped in the kitchen until help arrived. The thought made her heart race again.

Arabelle pulled out of the embrace, her arms looped loosely around Marin's neck. "But now we can't bake cookies," she said, her bottom lip protruding out.

"Sure we can. I just need to check on Diego and change clothes. We can make cookies in the oven upstairs in the residence." Marin looked to Bita, who'd just joined them, for confirmation.

"That oven isn't going to blow up, too, is it?" Arabelle asked, her eyes wide again.

"No. That oven is a nice old-fashioned one without any circuits to go haywire."

Arabelle was reassured by Marin's words, but Bita's face was outlined in panic. Marin opened her mouth to soothe the grandmother's nerves, but Bita spoke first.

"Agent Keller," Bita hissed. "What are you doing here?"

Caught off guard by Bita's question, Marin looked over her shoulder at the agent who she'd forgotten was standing behind her. He was as rumpled and filthy as she likely was, but it did nothing to deter the rugged handsomeness he exuded. The guarded expression on his face was less than welcoming, however.

"Agent Keller is in the House for a few days on special assignment," Secret Service Director Worcester said from behind Bita. "And if you ladies will excuse him, I need to see him right away." He waved Agent Keller in the direction of his office.

"Bye," Arabelle said to the agent while her grandmother's eyes narrowed with what looked to Marin like suspicion.

Agent Keller gave Marin's elbow a gentle squeeze. "Make sure you have the doc look you over," he commanded quietly before following the director down the hall and into the Secret Service office.

And just like that, he was gone. Marin was mad he'd left her with yet another arrogant order. But she was even angrier at herself for not thanking the agent for potentially saving her life.

CHAPTER FOUR

GRIFFIN WEAVED BETWEEN the groups of tourists admiring the cherry blossoms on the trees that lined the National Mall. He was careful to keep his jog relaxed and steady, but far enough behind the pastry chef that she didn't notice him following her. She ran haphazardly, lacking the innate grace and rhythm of a natural runner. Instead, her pace was more like that of someone who didn't really want to be exercising, yet forced herself to anyway. Her efforts paid off, though; the chef's long legs were shapely and muscular in her pink running shorts. Griffin had noticed more than a few appreciative, lingering glances from males after she'd passed them by.

Since the fire the day before, Griffin had carefully gathered as much intel about the pastry chef as he could from her fellow White House staffers. The admiral had been right; she was well liked. But he knew from experience a pretty smile and a shapely body could mask all sorts of deviant intent. Until he found some other evidence, Marin Chevalier was high on his list of suspects in the White House art thefts. Yesterday's fire in her kitchen only made his gut even more suspicious. Because that fire was no accident. It had been deliberately set.

He'd spent much of the previous evening sifting through the soot covered pastry kitchen with his buddy, Ben Seager from the Secret Service forensics lab. Ben was one of those guys who was stupid smart. And Griffin should know. He wouldn't have passed any of his calculus classes at West Point if it weren't for his roommate Ben's help.

"It's not the wiring," Ben had concluded after only a few minutes of inspecting the oven. "My guess, based on the pattern made by the burn marks, is that there was an accelerant placed on the bottom of the oven. I won't know for sure until I run some chemical tests, but I am sure that's where the fire started. Probably when the oven was pre-heated. If it were the wiring that started this fire, there wouldn't have been anything left of the top of the oven or the tray of sticky buns."

They'd looked over at the charred tray where Lillie's pastries sat like petrified wood.

"An accelerant would explain the ball of fire and the huge amount of smoke," Griffin agreed. "Whoever planted it wanted this room—and everyone in it—incinerated because the door leading out of the kitchen was jammed and there was a splint in the window holding it closed."

"Sounds like you were in the wrong place at the right time to be a hero," Ben said. "Now you need to figure out who was supposed to be in that kitchen when the fire started."

From what Griffin could uncover, the only person scheduled to use the oven in the pastry kitchen that afternoon was Chef Marin. Half the staff knew she planned to bake cookies with the president's granddaughter. So why go to all the trouble of setting up an arson when she was the one who would be in its path? What if the agent accompanying Arabelle to the kitchen couldn't get the door open? It was quite a risk. And a preschooler as the target made no sense.

Unless there wasn't a target at all.

"What if no one was supposed to be in the pastry kitchen?" Griffin asked. "What if the fire was meant to be a distraction? Maybe it was a literal smoke screen for another heist. The arsonist couldn't have known that Lillie would be using that particular oven. Or that I would be up there snooping around. You said all that the perp needed to do was to preheat the oven and then leave."

"So why the jammed door and window?" Ben countered.

"To keep the fire going for as long as possible, while whoever was behind it stole whatever it was they intended to steal."

Ben shrugged. "It's as good a theory as any."

Right now, it was the only theory Griffin had. Which meant he was jogging fifty paces behind Marin Chevalier as she zigzagged her way along the Mall on her way back to the White House. Thanks to one of the staff from the Uniformed Division, he'd discovered she liked to jog after lunch most days. Griffin had spent thirty minutes this afternoon blending in with tourists while waiting outside the south entrance of the White House for her to emerge before his patience had eventually paid off. His plan was to catch up to her as she returned to the southeast gate and make his appearance seem unintentional. Thanks to the director's comments yesterday, she already knew he was in the White House on special assignment. The last thing he needed was for her to suspect that *she* was that special assignment.

She crossed Fourteenth Street and jogged to one of the walking paths in front of the Washington Monument. Griffin had to sprint to make the light so that he could keep her in his sights. Her pace hadn't slowed in the thirty minutes he'd been following her and Griffin had to admire her stamina. He wasn't the only one admiring Marin Chevalier, however.

A man wearing maroon nylon shorts and a gray muscle shirt had sped up to follow the pastry chef across the street, as well. With the fluid gait of a seasoned runner, the guy had been keeping pace with her from a discreet distance which meant he was about twenty feet in front of Griffin. The baseball cap the man wore bobbed along as he kept Marin's ass in his sights. Not that Griffin could blame the guy because the woman did have a very fine ass. Clearly, he'd been out in the hot sun too long because Griffin had a sudden vision of his hands on that ass, not to mention other parts of her ample, well-proportioned body.

The light at Constitution Avenue was green and Marin jogged across without breaking her stride. Griffin gave his head a shake to refocus his thoughts. The guy pursuing her picked up his pace as they circumvented the Ellipse headed for the White House. Which meant Griffin had to pick up his own pace if he was going to make their meeting look accidental before the other guy decided to hit on her. He cursed the bum knee he'd aggravated kicking down the kitchen door yesterday, and he practically had to sprint to overtake the other guy. The three of them reached E Street at the same time and stopped at the light. Griffin sauntered up on her right side and blew out a breath.

The chef did a double take before she recognized him. "Agent Keller. This is. . . unexpected."

So was the sound her voice, raspy with exertion. Griffin's mind wandered to the bedroom, wondering if she sounded that erotic after sex and suddenly his shorts were tight around his junk. He needed a distraction, or he'd be forced to abandon his casual questioning of her for a cold shower.

Griffin looked to her other side expecting to see the other guy, but he was long gone. Weird. It was almost as if the man had vanished into thin air. A surge of macho pride raced through him at having chased a competitor off before remembering he wasn't pursuing Marin Chevalier for anything other than information. The sooner he figured out this piece of the puzzle, the sooner he could go back to New York and his pursuit of The Artist.

"Are you coming, Agent Keller?"

The light had turned green. The chef stood in the center of E Street looking a little like a warrior princess with her long legs and determined chin. How had he thought this woman was a dough-faced cherub? There was more to

Marin Chevalier than his initial impression. He was going to make it his mission to find out what that was.

Two of the K-9 dogs stood like sentries at the southeast gate. Despite the warm afternoon temperatures, their feet were kept cool by an air-conditioned pad they stood on. The Uniformed Division officer checked their IDs before waving them through the metal detectors.

"I heard you were back, Agent Keller," the officer said.

"Just for a few days, Shorty," Griffin replied.

"That's long enough."

Marin looked at the officer, clearly appalled at his jibe.

The officer shrugged. "I'm only saying what every single guy in DC is thinking. None of us stand a chance with the ladies when Prince Charming here is around."

"Right," she said with a dismissive shake of her head before strolling onto the path leading through President's Park. Griffin wasn't sure if he should be insulted or not when he fell into step beside her.

"So, you worked at the White House once upon a time?" she asked with a cheeky grin, probably amused with her own fairy tale reference.

"Yeah. I was on President Manning's detail when he was running for office and then when he first came to the White House."

"But you're not anymore."

"Nope."

They turned onto the path parallel to the White House and continued toward the West Wing. The chef stopped in the middle of the pavement and crossed her arms over her alluring chest while she simply stood and stared at the White House.

"I don't know if I could ever leave this place," she said, her tone reverent. "It's magical. The grounds look so impressive with the spring flowers and trees in full bloom. When I think of all the famous people who have lived here, I feel privileged to come to work every day. Working here is like working in a museum surrounded by treasured artifacts and so much history." She looked at him expectantly, apparently waiting for him to wax poetic about the White House. Griffin was more interested in her fondness for the "treasured artifacts."

"It's a place to work."

With another shake of her head, she ambled on past the tennis court and the children's garden and up toward the putting green on the South Lawn. "So where do you work now?"

Griffin pondered how much to tell her. If she were part of the counterfeiting ring, she'd likely know the investigation was being spearheaded out of the New York office. He decided to keep things vague so as not to spook her. "I work out of a number of field offices." Technically, not a lie. "Wherever they need someone to troubleshoot a situation."

"Like Wes's death?"

Her question caught him off guard. "Wes?"

"Wes Randall. The curator." She looked at him quizzically. "There are rumors that he committed suicide. Then, in the Navy Mess today, I overheard one of the press say that the police think Wes might have been murdered. You don't think it could have been related to his work here in the White House, do you?"

Hell, yes. "No. And no one confirmed that the curator was murdered."

"So you are investigating it?"

Griffin's pulse raced at her line of questioning. Why was she so interested? Was Wes connected to the thefts? The curator story was as good a cover as any, so he rolled with it. "If I were, I'm not at liberty to discuss it with you."

"Hmm," she said with a flounce of her ponytail before her steps slowed again. "It's unnerving to know someone who has been murdered." She caught sight of Griffin's arched eyebrow. "*Might* have been murdered."

"You don't need to be worried. You work in one of the most secure places on earth."

"And yet, I almost died in a freak fire yesterday," she said softly.

Her blue eyes met his and something about the vulnerable way she held his gaze made his gut clench.

"I wouldn't have let you die." He reminded himself it was because she was a suspect in a counterfeiting crime, nothing more.

"Thank you for that." The chef bit her bottom lip before looking away. "Um... Diego and I are both grateful you were there." She glanced at the exercise tracker on her wrist. "And speaking of Diego, I need to grab a shower before heading back to work. The president and his family are leaving for Camp David shortly. I'm commandeering the kitchen in the residence this weekend to prepare the pastries for Monday's Easter luncheon. The main kitchen is a little crowded with dying and decorating several thousand Easter eggs."

Griffin's attention shifted immediately back to the case. *Wasn't that convenient?* Could that have been the reason for destroying the oven in the pastry kitchen? To give her unlimited access to the art in the residence? There were certainly many spectacular pieces to choose from on the House's second and third floors.

"I'll let you get back to it then." *And while you're showering, I'll be busy assigning agents and officers from the Uniformed Division to keep you company while you bake.*

She gave him a shy wave then headed into the White House via the Palm Room door. As she walked away from him, Griffin willed himself not to think of her sexy ass in the shower. He was unsuccessful.

"ARE YOU OKAY?" Marin asked Diego.

The pair had been working for several hours baking cookies that were to be distributed to the participants of the Easter egg hunt. Tomorrow, Marin would decorate the cookies with a photo of the White House made completely out of sugar. The process would likely take her hours. It was one of the tasks she enjoyed least, but Diego was much quicker at pulling sugar. She needed him to make the petals for the flowers that would decorate the centerpieces. One of the duties of the executive pastry chef was delegating tasks efficiently. Marin wasn't too proud to admit her sous chef was better at one aspect of the job than she was.

She worried Diego was still suffering from the effects of smoke inhalation, however. Twice she'd had to remind him to pull the cookies from the oven before they burnt.

"Yeah, sure, I'm okay," he said. "I'm just tired, I guess."

It was seven-thirty in the evening, long past their normal quitting time when the First Family wasn't in residence. But, following the fire yesterday, they'd been given much of the day off while the admiral sorted out the logistics. With Monday's event less than four days away, they needed to work late tonight to get everything done.

"If you need to call it a night, I'm okay here," she said. "One of the agents wandering around this floor will keep me company." There seemed to be a surplus of security within the House tonight, not that Marin minded. She was still spooked by Wes's death.

"Scouting out a date for your cousin's wedding?" he teased.

Marin was glad to see the infectious grin that had been absent all evening return to his face.

"I think I'll stick around and watch you attempt to flirt, Boss."

"I plan on working, not flirting." The blush warming her face wasn't helping her argument.

Otto's K-9 handler, Officer Stevens, strolled into the kitchen while the dog obediently sat in the doorway leading out to the West Sitting Hall. "That's because she's already been flirting today," he said, winking at Diego.

Diego's grin broadened. "Oh? Do tell."

"I beg your pardon. I was not flirting at any time today," Marin protested.

Otto whimpered as if to disagree and both men laughed. "Otto and I will spill for a cookie," Officer Stevens said.

"There's nothing to spill." Marin smacked the rolling pin onto the chilled dough.

Diego tossed Otto a cookie. The dog caught it in midair. Officer Stevens helped himself to one off the cooling rack. "Your friend here"—he smiled, gesturing at Marin— "enjoyed a nice long romp on the Mall with Agent Keller this afternoon."

"Get out!" Diego's eyebrows nearly shot off his forehead. "You go, girl."

"That's not what happened," Marin argued. "I went for a run *by myself.* Agent Keller showed up when I was about to reenter the White House grounds. End of story."

The sous chef laughed as though he didn't believe her, while Officer Stevens looked at Marin speculatively.

"Just a word of warning, Chef," the officer said. "Neither of you worked on this side of the House when President Manning and his family arrived. But you're a sweet person, and I think you should know that Agent Keller comes with a bit of a reputation."

Guys that good-looking often do. Marin had heard the "Prince Charming" reference earlier in the day, but something about the way the officer was looking at her made her uneasy.

"There's a rumor he was reassigned because he got too close to the president's daughter-in-law, if you catch my drift."

Officer Stevens's words landed like a lead weight in Marin's stomach. That explained Bita's over-the-top reaction to seeing the agent yesterday. Pressing the rolling pin into the dough, she vigorously worked it into a thin, round shape.

Who cares? The guy is too good-looking and arrogant for his own good. It wasn't like he was going to agree to take her to Ava's wedding anyway. Except, earlier on the South Lawn, she'd felt something happening between them. Just for a moment. But it was *something.* She sighed in frustration. More than likely, she'd only imagined it, and it was nothing rather than something.

Marin rolled the pin over the dough until it tore.

"I think you've been at that too long." Diego reached over and gently took the rolling pin from her hands. "Why don't you handle the baking for a while?"

Otto was still sitting patiently in the doorway next to the double ovens while his handler had wandered out to chat with one of the agents patrolling the floor. Marin took off her plastic gloves and idly buried her fingers in the thick fur on the dog's head.

"There's plenty of fish in the sea," Diego quietly tried to reassure her.

Marin opened her mouth to respond, but the ringing of her cell phone cut her off. She swore under breath when she saw Ava's number pop up on the screen.

"Don't answer it," Diego warned.

"I have to, or she'll call every ten minutes."

Marin pointed to the ovens as she pressed talk. Diego gave her a withering look, but he did as he was told and went back to watching the cookies bake.

"Hey there, Ava," she said. "I'm still at work so I can't talk. Is everything okay?"

"It's after seven on a Thursday night, Marin."

"Tell me about it. And I have a couple of hours more of baking to get done."

Her cousin scoffed. "No wonder you are still hopelessly single."

Marin ground her teeth. "Ava, can we talk tomorrow or this weekend? I really do have a lot to do here."

"The most important thing you should be *doing* is finding a date for my wedding! But that will never happen because you're too busy making strudel for the Mannings."

"For your information, Ava, I already have a date for your damn wedding!"

Diego's eyes went wide with surprise. Marin was a little stunned at the lie herself, but she just couldn't take another minute of her cousin's bullying.

"Seriously?" Ava asked. "What's his name?"

"We can play twenty questions when I'm not on the government dime, Ava. I'll talk to you next week once we've gotten through Easter. Bye." Marin shoved her phone back into the pocket of her chef's jacket.

"You know I love you, Boss, but I've already told you

I'm not taking you to that bridezilla's wedding. I'm beginning to think you shouldn't go, either."

Marin waved him off. "Yeah, yeah, I heard you. Unfortunately, she's family. I have to go. But I'd like to point out that I fill out your annual performance rating."

She chuckled at Diego's mutinous expression. "Relax. My lie bought me four more days of peace and quiet. I'll just use them to find a date. It's a holiday weekend, yet this place is still teeming with guys who all like me as a friend. Surely I can convince one of them to do me a favor and go with me to my cousin's wedding. Heck, I'm even willing to resort to using baked goods as bribery."

She smiled enthusiastically at Diego, but he didn't return it. In fact, he looked a little peaked.

"In that case, chocolate cream pie always works to bribe me."

Marin slammed her eyes shut at the sound of Agent Keller's voice. When she opened them again, Diego shrugged before reaching into the oven to pull out the cookies. Crossing her arms over her chest, she turned on her heel to face the agent. Her breath caught in her throat at the sight of him, rugged and sexy-as-hell, as he rested a shoulder against the doorjamb with his hands, shoved in his pockets. Dressed casually in chinos and a blue oxford shirt, he looked like an ad from one of those preppy men's magazines. The sleeves of his shirt were rolled up to reveal muscled forearms. A crisp white T-shirt peeked out of the V of his button-down shirt.

She must have been on the verge of hysteria because she

suddenly wondered how he got his T-shirts so white. Did he have a wife who did his laundry? God, she hoped not. He didn't wear a ring, but that didn't mean anything. If what Officer Stevens told her was true, the gorgeous man in front of her was once involved with the president's daughter-in-law. A married woman. Sweet little Arabelle's mother. Marin didn't much care for Farrah and her wild ways, but she adored Arabelle. And this man had the capacity to upset the little girl's life. Marin felt shameful for lusting over him.

I'm not lusting over him. I'm lusting over his ability to get his whites so damn white.

"Agent Keller," she bit out. "Are you checking up on us? I can assure you, Diego and I have no intention of setting *these* ovens on fire. But just in case"—she stormed over to the other side of the kitchen and picked up a fire extinguisher—"we've got not one, but two, working fire extinguishers. Not to mention a swarm of security staff roaming the halls."

"Down girl," Diego said softly enough for only Marin to hear.

"Good to know. But I just stopped by because I heard there were fresh cookies up here."

"Well, why don't we just hand all the cookies to the staff with nothing better to do than hanging out at an empty White House tonight? At this rate, we'll be baking until two in the morning to get the number we need for the Easter egg hunt. But, hey, as long as you're happy, Agent Keller."

She was babbling about nonsense, acting like a shrew, but she couldn't seem to stop herself. Perhaps the fire had affected her as much as she suspected it had Diego. Marin tore off a paper towel, pulled two of the hot cookies off the cooling racks and hastily wrapped them up. Marching over to where Agent Keller was still leaning nonchalantly in the doorway, she jabbed him in the chest with the cookies. His eyes appeared greener tonight and, this close, she could smell the soap he'd used to shower with after his run earlier. She had to physically stop herself from inhaling him.

"Here," she said with a croak, suddenly ashamed of her ridiculous behavior. "Enjoy."

Agent Keller didn't take his hands out of his pockets.

Instead, he carefully studied her face. He almost looked concerned for her. Too bad Marin knew that was impossible.

His eyes darted past her shoulder. Marin caught the look he shared with Diego. The silent exchange between the two men rekindled her anger. She hated how a man she'd known for barely a day could infuriate and excite her so much at the same time.

"Are you okay?" he asked. The soft tone of his voice made tears burn at the back of Marin's eyes.

"Just peachy. We just have a lot of work to do, and we keep getting interrupted. The pastry kitchen was a much quieter place to work," she said, jabbing the cookies against his hard chest one more time. "Take the cookies and let me get back to baking. Please."

Slowly, he pulled his hands out of his pockets. He reached for the cookies with his left hand while his right one traveled to Marin's cheek. Ever so gently, his thumb glided along her skin until it came away covered in flour. The intimate gesture was very nearly her undoing. Holding back tears she didn't understand, she stepped away from Agent Keller, headed back into the kitchen and picked up the rolling pin.

"He's gone," Diego whispered a moment later.

"Good," she said. "Let's get these done so we can go home. I need a big glass of wine."

Diego laughed. "It looks to me like you need something else."

Marin glared at him over her shoulder.

"Shutting up now, Boss."

CHAPTER FIVE

"I NEED TO get her to take me to that wedding." Griffin sighed into his bottle of beer.

It was a balmy Friday night, and tourists crowded the sidewalks of Farragut North. Griffin and his buddies, Adam and Ben, were enjoying a cold one while sitting at an outdoor cafe a few blocks north of the White House.

"And this is the guy who runs from any mention of matrimony." Adam tossed a chicken wing bone into a plastic basket in the center of the table.

"He's got to be desperate to solve this case if he's willing to venture within five miles of bridesmaids." Ben shuddered theatrically.

"He's more than desperate," Adam explained. "He wants to be a bridesmaid's plus-one."

Ben whistled. "On the other hand, maybe he's not that desperate. Bridesmaids usually put out."

The two men chuckled out loud before clinking their beer bottles together.

"I'm sitting right here, you know." Griffin wanted to flip them both off, but the place was filled with too many families. "If you two clowns are finished joking around, can we come up with a plan that will convince Marin to take me to that damn wedding?"

Adam leaned back in his chair and studied Griffin over the steeple of his joined fingers. "So it's Marin now. Since when did she graduate from 'the pastry chef'?"

Since I touched her. Which had been a stupid thing to do. *Fucking stupid.* He needed to keep her strictly in the suspect category. Last night, though, in her rumpled uniform, with that crazy hat askew on her head and a wayward streak of flour adorning her smooth cheek, Griffin had felt... need. A deep and urgent need to protect and possess her all at the same time. Which was ridiculous. *Fucking ridiculous.*

"It doesn't mean anything, Sigmund, other than Marin is quicker to pronounce," Griffin said before taking a swallow of his beer. Ben mouthed the name "Marin" and then "pastry chef" wearing that same look he'd use to solve complex calculus problems. Griffin slammed down his beer. "Damn it guys, can we cut the bullshit and work on this case!"

His two friends exchanged a look before both leaned their elbows on the table, their faces finally serious.

"Okay, dude, but first tell us what you can. What connection do the Chevaliers have to the counterfeit ring?" Ben asked.

Griffin ran a hand through his hair. "Hell if I know. But my gut is telling me not to ignore the possibility."

Adam lowered his voice as the three men leaned in closer. "You said some of the counterfeit drops were in or near several of their overseas hotels."

Griffin nodded. "But the trail goes cold from there."

Just like every other trail in this damn case.

He'd spoken with Leslie this morning. The FBI forensics lab hadn't found any evidence on the box truck or its driver. Not that Griffin was surprised. He was surprised, however, at Leslie's demeanor on the phone. The FBI agent was very assertive that he hustle back to New York, almost going so far as to suggest she missed him. A booty call with Leslie might go a long way toward slacking the sexual tension that had been building within him since touching Marin yesterday. Except, every time he thought of sinking into his colleague-with-benefits, it was Marin's face he saw. And that pissed him off.

"So, it might just be a coincidence that one of their family is working at the White House." Ben held up his hand to stop Griffin from interjecting. "But we can't ignore the fire in her kitchen. That was not a coincidence. Or an accident."

"Do we know if any artwork was switched out during the fire?" Adam asked.

"We can't know for sure, but there is so much beefed up security in the House right now that it hardly seems possible," Griffin said. "Marin was pretty anxious about all the extra staff wandering around on the residence floor, though."

Anxious was an understatement. Last night Marin was downright frazzled. Her demeanor only made him suspect her involvement that much more. He should have been excited he might have finally found a viable lead. Instead, he felt only disappointment. Griffin wasn't sure whether it was with her or with himself for being attracted to her and that, too, pissed him off.

"I spoke with the admiral this morning," Griffin continued. "It could be several weeks before he has a complete catalog of what is fake and what is real. Until then, eyes-on security is our best bet."

"And then there's the dead curator. Any leads there?" Ben asked.

Griffin shook his head. "We'll have the preliminary results on Monday sometime. If we're lucky, they'll be able to determine whether he killed himself or if someone else did the job."

The three men fell silent as they leaned back in their chairs.

"Well," Adam eventually said. "I could always do some snooping when I'm at the wedding."

Both Griffin and Ben stared at Adam in disbelief.

"They're taking the Counter Assault Team to a wedding?" Ben asked.

"POTUS and FLOTUS are going to the wedding?" Griffin said at the same time.

Adam grabbed another chicken wing off the plate. "FLOTUS is friends with the bride's aunt." He shot a steely-eyed look in Griffin's direction. "That would be Marin's mother in case you're not keeping score. Another reason not to presume her guilty without any hard evidence."

"The admiral has made me aware of the connection,"

Griffin said. "Several times, in fact. I just didn't put two and two together about the wedding."

"Yep. Problem solved. I'll keep an eye on your little pastry chef." Adam grinned wickedly before he chomped down on the chicken wing. "I could offer to help her out and pose as her date. I like... baked goods."

"That works," Ben agreed.

Like hell it did! Griffin didn't particularly like the way his friend said the words "baked goods." Nor did he like the idea that Adam would have the opportunity to man-handle Marin, because he *would* be touching her, dancing with her, and doing God-knew-what with her if she were his date. Adam enjoyed women. And Griffin didn't like the idea of his friend "enjoying" Marin. Not one bit.

"I mean, she's only a suspect," Adam went on to say. "It's not like I'm poaching on a woman you're sleeping with."

Griffin ground his back teeth. Adam was baiting him, looking for something that wasn't there and never would be. Adam was correct about one thing. Marin was a suspect. And that was all she'd ever be.

"Not gonna work," Griffin said. "You don't know the subtleties of this case. She might unwittingly give you a clue, and you'd miss it. It has to be me."

Adam shot Ben a smirk that shouted "I-told-you-so" before he tossed the chicken wing bone into the basket. "Hey, I was just trying to help a brother out."

"I guess you'll have to depend on that legendary charm of yours," Ben added.

Griffin sent his friend an unamused glare.

"Dude," Ben continued. "We all know I'm the brains of this trio." He gestured at Adam. "Adam is, and always has been, our enforcer. And you? You're the Rico Suave of the group. You'll figure something out. You always do."

"Well, I hope it happens soon. The wedding is next week." Griffin scrubbed a hand down his face, glancing at the passersby on the sidewalk as he did so.

He did a double take when he saw Marin striding toward the Metro station across the street.

"Speak of the devil," he murmured as he rose to follow her. "Metro card." He frantically patted the pockets of his jeans. "Damn it! I need a Metro card to go after her. Ben, give me your fast pass. You always have enough fare on yours."

"Seriously, dude? I need it to get home tonight."

In a few steps, Marin would be on the escalator. If Griffin didn't catch her now, he'd lose her. "Adam will drive you home. You're both going to the same damn place. Now, come on, man, this is serious."

Ben huffed as he slowly pulled the card out of his wallet. Griffin snatched it out of his hand before jumping the iron railing that surrounded the café and jogging down the sidewalk.

"Don't worry folks," Adam joked. "He likes to think he plays a cop on TV."

Ignoring the honking horn of a cab, Griffin made his way across Connecticut Avenue and ran onto the escalator, dodging tourists who didn't know well enough to stand on the right side. Once he'd reached the bottom, he spied Marin pass through the gate and head to the northbound platform. He swiped the pass and followed her to the escalator leading down that way.

"Marin," he called out from the top.

She stumbled slightly as she stepped off the escalator before turning to face him. The look on her face warned him she was still prickly. Griffin hoped the legendary charm Ben seemed to think he had wouldn't fail him.

AGENT KELLER TOOK the steps two at a time. There was no reason for him to hurry; the surprise at seeing him in the subway tunnel had rooted her feet to the floor. Marin couldn't move if she tried.

After their encounter last night, she'd gone home and downed a hefty glass—maybe it was two—of wine before soaking in a hot tub. She'd spent today hiding out in the chocolate shop, meticulously pasting the sugar image of the White House to the cookies. The task was mind-numbing, but she was at least able to hide in plain sight. Now she was looking forward to another glass—or two—of wine and a bath. Unfortunately, the reason for her being so discombobulated was bounding down the subway escalator after her.

"Agent Keller," she managed to say. "I'm starting to get the feeling that you're following me."

"Griffin." He sounded winded, as though he'd been

running.

"Griffin?"

"Griffin. It's my first name."

"Oh." Because, what else could she say?

The metro was normally busy at this time on a Friday evening. Tonight, with all the tourists in town for Easter and the Cherry Blossom Festival, the platform was shoulder to shoulder with people. Griffin stepped out of the path of the escalator and indicated that she should follow. Like a lamb to slaughter, she did.

"And I was following you tonight."

His admission startled Marin even more.

"I was hanging out with some friends when I saw you walk by the restaurant," he said. "I wanted to talk to you. To ask you something."

"To ask me something?" Anyone listening to their conversation would think that Marin didn't have the strongest handle on the English language.

"It's about the wedding you need a date for."

Marin's breath froze in her lungs. *Was he serious?* He wanted to rub it in that she didn't have a date to Ava's wedding? She didn't want to have this conversation with Agent Keller. *Griffin.* She wanted wine and a bubble bath. Marin shook her head. Then she allowed the sea of tourists to propel her in the direction of the train tracks.

"You'd be doing me a huge favor if you'd let me go with you," he called out after her.

What did he just say? She'd be doing *him* a favor?

He was beside her again, looking a bit flustered and

unsure of himself. Marin wondered what he was up to because she was sure there wasn't ever a moment when this gorgeous man was unsure of himself, not to mention flustered.

"At least hear me out. Please."

She blew out a breath. "Suit yourself. I get off at Dupont Circle. It's the next stop, so you'd better make your case quickly."

The corners of his mouth turned up in a conqueror's grin, his dimples so potent Marin saw the woman next to her clutch her chest in delight. The lights on the edge of the platform blinked to indicate an incoming train and the crowd pressed closer together. When the train arrived, and the doors opened, Marin and Griffin were lucky to get the last two spots against the doors. Just as they began to close, a young black woman leaped aboard the train. She smiled gleefully before she accidently shoved into Marin.

"Sorry," the woman said.

There was a shout from the platform, but the doors had already closed. The train lurched forward. Marin had to move in closer to Griffin to make room for the latecomer. He braced his arm above her head, holding them steady in the crowded car.

"The train ride is barely three minutes," Marin said.

"I'll have you agreeing in less than two."

She rolled her eyes at his arrogance and forced herself to look away from his compelling stare. That was when she saw the blood. Lots of blood. The young black woman's chin was tucked to her chest. She seemed to be gasping for breath. Her hands clutched the front of her white shirt that now had a dark red stain seeping out from her flat abdomen.

"Griffin!" Marin cried, but he'd already seen it.

He pushed Marin flat against the wall and edged himself over to the woman.

"I've got you," he told her. "When the doors open, you just lean on me."

He looked desperately toward the back of the car.

"Hey!" he yelled. "Someone pick up that phone and tell them we need an ambulance at Dupont Circle!"

As the train slowed, a man made his way to the emergency phone near the doors that joined the cars together.

"She's barely conscious," Griffin said. "I'm going to have to carry her out."

Marin maneuvered her arm around enough to pull her dirty chef's jacket out of her backpack. She handed it to him. "Use this to apply pressure."

The doors opened. The woman would have collapsed on the platform had it not been for Griffin's hold. Marin wadded her jacket up and thrust it between him and the woman. He lifted her in his arms and carried her to the stone bench along the back wall. Many of the passengers stampeded out behind Marin, some fearful, while others remained in the Metro car, oblivious that a stabbing had even occurred. Two Metro transit officers charged down the escalator.

"Did anyone see what happened?" one of them asked the assembled crowd.

The woman on the bench moaned. Marin crouched down next to her. "She was smiling when she got on the train." Marin swiped at the tears she hadn't realized were streaming down her face. "She has such a pretty smile," she whispered.

There was a sudden frenzy of activity when the EMTs and DC police arrived on the scene. The woman, still unconscious, was quickly whisked away to the hospital. Marin barely remembered the seven-block trip up New Hampshire Ave to the police station. Griffin hovered over her like a sentry as they both told, then retold, their account of the incident to police detectives.

"Surveillance video at the McPherson Square station shows a figure running from the train as it was pulling away. The perp could be a man or a woman. Hard to tell," one of the detectives told them. "He or she was dressed in a giant hoodie and baggy pants. Typical gangbanger garb. Of course, that only narrows our search area down to most of Southeast DC and half of Baltimore," he added sarcastically.

"Any chance I could get a look at that video?" Griffin asked.

"Any chance you'll tell me why you're so interested?" the detective responded.

"Professional curiosity," Griffin said. "Maybe seeing the video will jog something in my memory. Years on a protective detail gives you a different perspective. We're trained to spot things in the crowd."

The detective sighed. "Just as long as you promise to

share if you do see anything." He got up from his desk. "I'll download a copy to a disc for you."

"The victim is a student at Howard University," the female detective said. "But her brother is a known member of the Deuce Deuce gang. He's currently serving time for drug dealing. We're probably looking at some sort of retaliation crime here."

A young, innocent woman, brutally stabbed because of who her brother was. The thought made Marin physically ill.

"What's her name?" Marin quietly asked. "I want to pray for her."

The detective looked from Marin to Griffin. He brought his hand to the back of Marin's neck and gently rubbed. The detective cleared her throat before looking down at her notes.

"Anika," she said. "She suffered injuries to the liver and spleen. Doctors are operating now. They're optimistic." She looked at Marin and smiled kindly. "But prayers are always good, too."

Two men who seemed to know Griffin joined them. One man looked vaguely familiar to Marin.

"Our ride is here," Griffin announced.

He helped her to her feet. She was grateful for his arm, as well as his presence of mind to get them a ride home. Her legs felt too unsteady to walk farther than the elevator. Marin gathered up her backpack, but she felt as though she was forgetting something. She glanced around at the table they'd been sitting at for the past hour.

"You gave your chef's coat to me," Griffin reminded her gently. "It must have gotten left in the metro station."

Marin nodded. The entire evening felt like one of those dreams where she was supposed to know what was going on but didn't.

"Yeah," she said. "I don't know why I'm so confused about everything."

"Shock will do that to you," one of Griffin's friends said. "I'm Ben, by the way. I brought you some water and peanut butter crackers. Hydrating and getting some food in you will help." He handed her a brown bag.

"Ben's a perpetual Boy Scout," the one who looked familiar to Marin said as he pushed the button for the elevator. "Which makes me Adam, the chauffeur." He bowed deeply just as the elevator doors opened. "At your service."

"Ignore these two jokers." Griffin guided her onto the elevator. "They would have never gotten through West Point without my help."

Their humorous bantering helped to chase some of the fog in her brain away. Griffin kept his hand at the small of her back and her body relaxed into it. She took a few swallows from the water bottle, suddenly realizing how hungry she was. Lunch had been nine hours earlier.

Adam led them to a small SUV parked out front. Griffin handed her into the back seat. Adam and Ben got in front while Griffin walked around the car and slid in beside her. His warm body felt comforting next to hers as she munched on the crackers. The sense of calm that had been absent for the past couple of hours slowly returned. When they pulled up outside her apartment building, she was surprised, however.

"I didn't tell you where I lived."

She met Adam's bottle green eyes in the rearview mirror.

"It's the Secret Service's job to know where all the White House employee's live," Adam informed her.

That explained why he looked so familiar. Griffin had gotten out and was opening her door. "Well then, I'm glad you were the ones who came to pick Griffin up. Thanks so much for the ride."

"Oh, trust me," Adam replied. "If there wasn't the promise of meeting a beautiful woman, Griffin would have been taking the metro home."

Marin blushed at his words as she slid out of the car.

"I'm going to walk Marin inside," Griffin told is friends. "Just drive around the block a few times until I get back."

"Sure thing, Miss Daisy," Adam called out before Griffin shut the door.

Arnold, the weekend doorman, jumped from his seat at the concierge desk when Marin and Griffin entered.

"What's cookin' tonight, Chef?" he asked, reciting one of his frequent quips.

Marin smiled graciously, even though the doorman was always the only one who thought his line was funny.

"Easter eggs," she replied. "Thousands of them."

"My grandbabies are looking forward to it, Chef Marin." Arnold beamed as he buzzed them through the secure gate leading to the elevators. "Thanks so much for those tickets."

"It was my pleasure."

Griffin steered her toward the bank of elevators. He'd likely already taken in the opulent lobby. She wasn't sure she wanted to see his reaction when they rode up to the penthouse. It was no secret that the Chevalier family was wealthy and Marin made no apologies for how she lived. But something about giving Griffin a glimpse into this part of her life made her uncomfortable.

"You don't have to come up," she said.

His eyes assessed her from head to toe. "It's been a crazy evening. Let me be the gentleman here and make sure you get all the way home."

"I'm feeling much better. The water and the crackers helped. Ben was very thoughtful."

The elevator doors opened. "Humor me," Griffin said, gesturing for Marin to precede him in.

"Your friends are very nice." She pushed the button for the top floor.

"Mmm-hmm. I can't imagine any other two people I'd want to have my back."

His words caught her off guard after the earlier razzing among the men, but they didn't surprise her. Griffin's actions tonight had been those of a man with a good heart. She was having trouble reconciling that man with the one he was rumored to be.

The doors opened, and he followed her across the hall

to her apartment. Marin steeled herself for his reaction as she turned the key. She opened the door to reveal a panoramic view of Washington, DC in all its nighttime glory. Griffin was silent behind her. She dropped her backpack on a Louis the XV chair she and her mother had restored after Hurricane Katrina.

"Wow," he finally said, his tone slightly awestruck as he took in not only the view but the room full of antiques and rare treasures she'd collected over the years. "This place is… amazing."

"My grandfather and I share a love of art and antiquities," she explained. "He's helped me to make some great finds."

He walked deeper into the room, his keen gaze darting here and there. The critical way in which he seemed to be cataloging everything in the room told her he'd forever see her as the spoiled little rich girl who got her job through nepotism and not the accomplished chef that she was. *Just like everyone else saw her.*

"We never finished our conversation from earlier," she said, trying to divert his attention. "You were going to tell me why taking you to my cousin's wedding was doing you a favor."

He rubbed a hand over the back of his neck. "Yeah. Well… I'm thinking of getting out of the Secret Service in the next year or so. My goal is to work in private security. I know the Chevalier hotel chain has one of the best security reputations in the world. I thought if I took you to the wedding, you'd do me the favor of introducing me to someone within the organization. You know, get the ball rolling for when I do leave government service."

At least he was honest. Griffin was using her to further his career. Had that been his intent when he got involved with the president's daughter-in-law? To further his career? Was Griffin that Machiavellian? Of course, she would be using him if she took him to the wedding. Ava would be insanely jealous if Marin showed up with a man twice as handsome as the groom. It would certainly be a boon to Marin's ego.

Except...

She'd felt that *something* again tonight. When he'd looked at her on the subway platform telling her his name, she'd thought he'd meant it as something more. And Marin wanted something more. She told herself she wanted that something from any man who'd see her for who she was and not who her family was. But she realized she was lying. She wanted that *something* from Special Agent Griffin Keller. And that was the most frustrating thing of all. Because he didn't deserve her. Even if he did rescue damsels from fires or subway stabbings.

"Can I think about your proposal?"

He seemed startled by her words. *Serves him right.*

"Of course."

He stepped over to where she was standing and lifted his hands to her shoulders. Marin wanted to shove him away, but her traitorous body reveled in the warmth of his fingers.

"Anika has a fighting chance because of you. She's

lucky you were standing next to her." He leaned down and kissed her forehead. "Get some rest."

And with that, he was gone.

GRIFFIN CLIMBED INTO the backseat of Adam's Rav-4.

"You didn't tell me she was hot," Ben said as Adam maneuvered the car away from the curb. "I mean in a Marilyn Monroe kind of way."

"She's got that whole innocent wholesomeness thing going on," Adam added.

"She's not," Griffin snapped.

Ben glanced over his shoulder at him, a perplexed look on his face. "You don't think she's hot?"

"She's not fucking innocent." He pounded his fist on the seat. "Her place is full of expensive artwork. She's a freaking art connoisseur. One who'd know *exactly* what to steal from the White House."

Griffin was so close to busting this case wide open; he could taste it. Unfortunately, he could also still taste Marin's skin on his lips. Despite his suspicions of her, he couldn't seem to stop his body from craving more of her. *All of her.*

None of it made sense. This potent pull between him and Marin had to be screwing with Griffin's mind. The woman had sat and cried beside an injured girl she'd never met. She was *praying* for her. It had to all be an act because, in Griffin's experience, there was no honor among thieves.

No hearts either.

He swore violently, ignoring the look that passed between his two best friends.

CHAPTER SIX

O F ALL THE mornings Marin could have overslept, the Saturday before the Easter egg hunt was not one of them. She was already behind on the centerpieces. Today, she and Diego were supposed to arrange the marzipan figures in the chocolate nests and build the sugar flowers that would complete the arrangements. At this rate, she'd be working until midnight.

She was late because sleep had eluded her the previous evening. Marin couldn't seem to get the image of Anika, bloodied and unconscious, out of her head. She'd tried to call the hospital, but no one was able to give her any information on the young woman's condition because Marin wasn't family.

Anika wasn't the only one haunting her thoughts last night, either. Griffin Keller's sexy dimples kept appearing behind Marin's eyelids every time she tried to close them. Marin's body heated up when she recalled the feel of his hand on her lower back or his lips on her forehead. Thanks to the aggravating special agent, she'd tossed and turned until the early hours this morning.

She hurried through the northwest gate and jogged up the driveway to the North Portico steps. As she rushed past the usher's office, the admiral's voice halted her in her tracks.

"Chef Marin," he called after her.

Marin swore under her breath. She couldn't afford to waste any more time. Pasting a smile on her face, she turned to face her boss.

His expression softened at the sight of her; he took several steps to close the gap between them.

"How are you this morning, Chef?"

She was late, that was how she was. And a little bewildered at the admiral's obvious concern.

"I heard about the incident on the Metro last night," he explained.

Marin relaxed a fraction, fearful if she relaxed too much, she might lose her composure. "It was unpleasant," she said. "But I'm trying not to think about it. I've got way too much to do today."

He quietly studied her. "No one would blame you if you needed to take a day. You've had quite a week. I can call in some of the contract chefs to finish what needs to be done for Monday."

She bristled at his words. Marin would have to be bloody and unconscious herself before she'd let contractors—or anyone else, for that matter—in her pastry kitchen—in this case, the de-facto pastry kitchen in the residence. She'd worked long and hard planning the centerpieces and desserts for this event to let someone else mess them up.

"That's not necessary." She lifted her shoulders. "I'm

fine."

The admiral paused a moment before he nodded. "The offer stands for as long as you need it. If there's anything my staff can do to help out, you let me know."

"Thank you, sir. Now, if you'll excuse me, I'll get to work."

Marin had the sense he watched as she disappeared up the stairs to her third-floor office. She dumped her backpack onto her desk and reached into the closet to pull out a clean chef jacket and toque.

"The ladies in the linen room did their best to get the smoke smell out of your jackets and hats. I hope they were successful."

She turned to see her friend, Terrie Bloodworth, standing in the doorway. Terrie was the head housekeeper for the White House. Next to the chief usher, she was the person who kept the place running like clockwork. Terrie had left her job as an executive overseeing the entire housekeeping efforts within the forty-five Chevalier hotels to come to the White House when President Manning's predecessor was in office.

"I appreciate their efforts," Marin said. "I'll be sure and stop in to thank them when I get a spare minute."

The two women headed down the stairs. "You look exhausted already."

Marin sighed. "Trouble sleeping."

"I heard about last night."

"Word certainly travels quickly in this place."

"No one's gossiping about it, if that's what you think,"

Terrie explained. "As far as I know, the admiral, Director Worcester, and I are the only ones briefed on the stabbing. I think Agent Keller wanted to make sure you had some support today in case you needed it. He's very thoughtful, that one."

They passed the cosmetology room that served as both a barber shop and hair salon for the first family and headed to the center hall of the residence floor. Marin always loved to linger in the wide hallway because the large, half-moon windows at either end of the floor provided a gorgeous view of Washington. Today, she was more focused on what Terrie was saying about Griffin to take in the scenery.

"He was a hero for that poor woman, that's for sure," she said.

"Agent Keller is a very resourceful and dedicated agent. He cares for people. I got the sense this morning that he cares a lot about you, too." Terrie wore a sly grin.

"Ha!" Marin laughed sarcastically. "He's resourceful all right. Agent Keller only cares about my connections and how he can benefit from them. And as for being dedicated, I've heard how dedicated he was to certain members of the First Family."

She stomped toward the kitchen. Terrie reached out and took Marin's arm before she could get very far.

"Don't believe everything you hear, Marin," the house-keeper admonished.

Terrie guided her over to one of the sofas in the west sitting area.

"Sit," she commanded.

Feeling like a chastised schoolgirl, Marin did as she was told. Terrie joined her on the sofa and seemed to give careful thought to her next words.

"Despite our duty to not gossip about the First Family or what goes on inside this house, I'm afraid rumors still have a way of making the rounds. I'm assuming you heard something to the effect that Agent Keller was inappropriately involved with Farrah?"

Marin nodded, feeling a little guilty now that Terrie had put it in those terms.

"Well, I can unequivocally state that those rumors are only half true."

That got Marin's attention. "'Half true'?"

Terrie nodded. "Any relationship was strictly one-sided. Farrah was pursuing Agent Keller. Quite relentlessly, I might add."

The news didn't surprise Marin. She'd seen Arabelle's mother in action with any number of male visitors to the White House.

"Agent Keller endured it while remaining professional and stoically continuing to do his job protecting the president. I don't think he ever intended to say a word to anyone."

"But he's no longer on the president's protective detail?"

Terrie smiled smugly. "That's because someone else spoke up for him."

"You?"

The housekeeper nodded. "The poor man was miserable. And Farrah was unconscionable. Nothing will deter that girl from what she wants. I don't know how…" Terrie slammed her mouth shut and shook her head. "It's not our place to gossip. But I had to let the admiral and Director Worcester know the harassment that he was being exposed to." She let out a frustrated sigh. "Rumors had already started, probably because Agent Keller tried so hard to ignore what was happening. I doubt he'll ever set the record straight."

Marin closed her eyes and let her head drop back against the top of the sofa. Griffin *was* the man her heart believed him to be. A warmth seemed to settle over her body; she felt a slow grin spread over her face.

"I see I was right in sharing this information with you," Terrie said. Marin heard the smile in the housekeeper's voice.

"Oh, sure, Boss, you enjoy yourself lounging around on the president's furniture while I work my fingers to the bone assembling flowers in here."

Diego sounded genuinely miffed.

Marin leaped off the sofa. "I'm sorry, Diego. I'm coming right now." She gave Terrie a quick hug. "Thank you," she whispered.

"You're welcome," Terrie replied. "Don't be shy about asking for help today if you need it."

Terrie headed down the hall to check on the housekeeping staff while Marin made her way to the kitchen, her step a lot lighter than it had been moments before.

"Guess what, Diego?" she called out. "I have a date to

the wedding."

"You know what else you have, Boss?" the sous chef asked. "Thirty centerpieces that need building before you can put your dancing shoes on."

GRIFFIN LEANED A shoulder against the marble column supporting the Truman Balcony and gazed across the South Lawn. The sound of Marin's unbridled laughter floated through the afternoon air and settled somewhere in the vicinity of his chest. She looked so damn innocent dressed in khakis and a pink T-shirt that fit her to perfection. He watched as the big Belgian Malinois nearly toppled her over in its efforts to catch the rubber Kong toy used by the K-9 handlers to reward the dogs.

"Off, Otto." She laughed. "Or I won't be able to throw the ball."

The dog immediately sat, panting with anticipation.

"I'm glad to see her enjoying herself," the admiral said after coming to stand beside Griffin. "She seems to have recovered well after last night's events."

"It would seem so," Griffin agreed. He, on the other hand, was still struggling with what he'd seen in Marin's penthouse apartment.

"The medical examiner's results are back early."

Griffin pushed away from the column, his attention piqued. "That never happens."

"Mm-hmm. The homicide detectives are on their way

over to discuss them with me in person, which could mean one of two things. Either the news is dire. Or they just want an opportunity to check out the interior of the White House," the admiral mused.

"I'd like to sit in on that meeting."

"I figured you might. The director and I are meeting them in the Map Room in fifteen minutes. We'll expect you."

With a curt nod, the admiral made his way back inside the White House.

Marin was kissing the dog on the head when Griffin refocused his attention on her. Something about the way she smiled at Otto made his gut clench.

"I am *not* jealous of a damn dog," he mumbled.

A low whistle sounded and Otto sped off like a rocket racing across the lawn to find his handler. Marin watched him go before lifting her face to the bright April sunshine, seeming to revel in its warmth before resolutely striding toward the Palm Room entrance. Griffin stepped out from the shadows where he'd been observing her and intercepted Marin on the path.

"Agent—Griffin," she said with a start. She paused on the pathway, taking in his suit and tie. "I didn't realize you were working on a Saturday."

He didn't bother to tell her he'd spent much of the day in the forensics lab with Ben, the two of them going over the video from the metro station frame-by-frame. He'd only stopped over at the White House to check on the progress of the audit of the artwork. *And on her.* Griffin told himself it was because he didn't want his prime suspect to slip away. That was all.

"This job is twenty-four seven when I've got an open case," he said.

"Are you any closer to finding out what happened to Wes?"

She was awfully curious about the curator's death. Her keen interest rankled Griffin because he couldn't determine whether it was concern for the curator or herself. He debated whether to tell her the police were coming with the autopsy results, just to see how she'd react. In the end, he decided to stick with procedure and play things close to the vest.

"Still working on it."

Marin nodded. "I just came out for a breath of fresh air. Diego had to run a quick errand, and I was starting to feel closed in on such a beautiful day. We've still got hours' worth of work to do." She smiled and shook her head. "I'm sorry. I doubt you care about all that. I'll let you get back to whatever it is that you're doing."

"As it happens, I was looking for you. Again."

She blushed prettily. Griffin cursed his body's reaction.

"Well, if you're coming to make your case for me to take you to the wedding, you don't have to. I've decided to take you up on your offer. And I've already arranged my side of the bargain, as well. My brother, Sebastian, handles all the security issues. You have a breakfast meeting with him the day of the wedding."

Griffin had to keep from rocking back on his heels; he was so stunned by her announcement. Given the abrupt way she'd dismissed him last night, he figured his shot at gaining access to the Chevalier inner sanctum was moot.

"Thank you," he managed to say. "I agree to hold up my end of the bargain, complete with unending chivalry, dancing, and adoring glances when appropriate."

Marin's blush grew even deeper causing Griffin to scramble for another topic before he did something foolish like leaning in and kissing her.

"I have news about Anika."

Her face blanched at the abrupt change in subject. "Please tell me she's alive."

He nodded, feeling like a heel at the sound of concern in her voice. "She's stable, but not out of the woods yet."

She turned her face away, brushing at her cheek as she did so. "I'll just keep praying then."

Her tears didn't surprise Griffin, but they did conflict him even more where Marin Chevalier was concerned.

"Thank you for coming to tell me," she said when she'd composed herself. "I've got to get back to the kitchen. Diego should be back by now. When you've finished for the day, please stop by and I'll give you the itinerary for the wedding. We can discuss travel arrangements then, too. Of course, I'll pick up all the expenses."

"How about dinner tonight?" His sudden, unplanned invitation was an excuse to get more information out of her. Nothing more. At least that was what he was telling himself.

"This is likely the only break I'll get today," she said, ruefully.

"I could go out to get something and bring it back to

the House," Griffin volunteered. "You have to eat."

"I guess that would be okay." Her smile was bright again. "Thank you."

"It's a date," he said, causing her to blush once more.

Marin began walking backward away from him. "I have to get back up there. I'll see you later." She turned on her heel and briskly walked along the path until she disappeared into the Palm Room.

Griffin took a few minutes to compose his thoughts. Ben had been correct. Griffin just needed to rely on his legendary calm. The closer he got to Marin, the closer he was to breaking open this case. And if that meant leading her on, it was all just part of the job. The ends justified the means. Besides, he had to eat, too.

"YOUR CURATOR DIED of asphyxiation," one of the Virginia homicide detectives announced.

Griffin tried to hide his disappointment as the detective's partner slid the admiral a sheet of paper that likely detailed the medical examiner's succinct ruling as to cause of death. It would be hard to prove Wes hadn't committed suicide with asphyxiation to blame.

"Can we say for sure it was suicide?" Director Worcester echoed Griffin's thoughts.

"Actually," the admiral said as he perused the report, "Wes's death was asphyxiation by murder." He slid the sheet of paper over to the director.

"Damn," Director Worcester said before handing the sheet over to Griffin.

He quickly scanned the medical examiner's findings. Wes had died from a lethal dose of succinylcholine, a common drug used in anesthesia that causes muscle paralysis. The curator was asphyxiated before the rope was put around his neck. It would not have been a swift or painless death. Griffin cringed. As murders went, this one was particularly inhumane and despicable. He wondered what the poor man had done to deserve such torture.

"Without a heads-up from you guys here in the White House, the ME wouldn't have been looking for an injection site," one of the detectives explained. "Sux doesn't leave a metabolite trace in the bloodstream. Your colleague was paralyzed within seconds, unable to draw breath for several minutes before his heart stopped beating. An ugly way to die."

The men sitting around the table in the historic Map Room were solemn for a long moment.

"Forensics didn't turn up anything at the scene?" Griffin asked, still holding out hope for a lead.

Both detectives shook their heads. "We canvased neighbors, but no one saw anything. In a wealthy neighborhood like that, there are lots of home security cameras. We combed through every one where the curator's house was in the frame. Nothing jumped out but a paper boy." He pulled a photo out of a folder and passed it over to Griffin. The picture was grainy, but it showed a person on a bicycle with a large sack over his shoulder. A dark hooded rain jacket was pulled over his head, the brim of a baseball cap peeking out.

"I didn't know papers were delivered by bike any longer," Griffin commented.

"Not too many folks get a printed paper these days." The detective shrugged. "Old-school delivery for old-school people."

"Bottom line," the other detective put in, "we're coming up empty at every turn. Whoever killed your curator knew how to stage the scene and inflict ligature marks so that it looked like a routine suicide."

Griffin's adrenalin shot up another level as he exchanged a look with Director Worcester.

"We're looking for a professional assassin here," the director said.

"Yeah," the homicide detective agreed. "And I was hoping you guys might have some leads since we don't see too much of that in the suburbs of northern Virginia."

"Gentlemen, I think it might be time we check in with our friends at the FBI," the admiral announced.

ARNOLD LOVED WORKING as the doorman at the Dupont, but never more so than on spring evenings like the current one. He propped the door open and stood in his red uniform, adorned with its sharp gold braids and epaulets, watching the happy tourists parade past after a long day spent wandering the monuments. When a sleepy young girl riding on her father's shoulders dropped her stuffed rabbit, Arnold bent down to retrieve it, tipping his hat to the child as he handed it back to her.

"Thanks, mister," the girl called out.

"You have a good evening," Arnold responded.

Raised voices in the lobby drew his attention and Arnold marched inside.

"Is there a problem Mr. Harris?"

"This guy tried to jump through the security gate behind me and follow me onto the elevator."

Mr. Harris was one of the Dupont's more snobbish residents, but the rules were the rules, guests had to sign in before going upstairs. Arnold gestured to the interloper who was dressed in a delivery man's garb to meet him at the concierge desk.

"Who are you here to see?" Arnold asked. He looked up from the directory sheet when the guy didn't immediately answer. The poor man probably didn't speak English. The city was filled with immigrants trying to eke out a living working at any job they could get without having fluency in the language.

Arnold noticed the guy was carrying a box with him. "You have a package to deliver?" he asked, careful to speak slowly and annunciate the words.

The man's black ball cap nodded up and down.

"Well then, you've come to the right place," Arnold said jovially. "You didn't need to go upstairs at all. Residents pick up their packages right here at the desk. Just leave it with me. I'll get it to"—he glanced at the package—"there's no name on there. Who's it going to?"

"The chef," the guy mumbled, keeping his head dipped toward the counter. "In the penthouse."

The doorman shook his head in aggravation. There was no problem with the delivery guy's English, apparently. Arnold went to take the package from him, but the delivery man's grip on it was firm. And the dope was wearing leather gloves. In April. Not an immigrant then, just a run-of-the-mill weirdo.

"If you leave it with me, I'll make sure that Chef Chevalier gets it," Arnold said before tugging on the box again.

"Today," the delivery guy insisted, his hold on the package still strong.

"Sure thing, buddy." Arnold was finally able to take the box from the guy's grasp. "She'll get it as soon as she walks through those doors."

The other man nodded again.

"No need for you to worry about it being stolen or whatnot because those cameras behind me record every-thing." Arnold pointed over his shoulder, his chest puffed up with pride. "Between you and me, this is a safe place with an honest staff. We don't need Big Brother to keep it that way. But try telling that to management."

The delivery guy did look up then. When his icy blue eyes met Arnold's warm brown ones, the doorman felt the breath freeze in his lungs. And then the guy was gone.

"Weirdo," Arnold murmured to himself as he carefully placed Chef Marin's package on the shelf behind him.

CHAPTER SEVEN

D IEGO KEPT GLANCING at his cell phone while he and Marin put the finishing touches on the last few centerpieces.

"If you need to be somewhere, I can handle the rest of this," Marin told him. "You did beat me in by an hour this morning."

"I'm good."

His tone told Marin he wasn't good, but she let it go. The sous chef had been edgy and distracted since the fire. Of course, the frenetic pace they were working under didn't help anyone's disposition.

Marin carefully set the nest of marzipan flowers and sugar hydrangeas onto a cart. "These are the last three. Once we have finished here, you can take them down to the refrigerator room and then skedaddle. I don't want to see you back here until six a.m. on Monday."

"We still have to make the pies for the Manning's party tomorrow. I don't know why they couldn't just stay up at Camp David for Easter dinner," Diego grumbled.

"I'll take care of those," Marin said.

The First Family would arrive midmorning tomorrow to attend Easter services at St. John's. Afterward, they were hosting dinner for twenty friends and family. Marin had already volunteered to work in the main kitchen so the culinary staff with families could have the holiday off. Tonight, she would make the desserts. Unlike the stressful task of creating delicate, edible artwork, baking was relaxing. She was looking forward to a quiet night of losing herself in her craft, concocting delicious treats for the Mannings and their guests.

She was also looking forward to her "date" with Griffin. And, as much as she loved, Diego, she wasn't sure she wanted him chaperoning their dinner here in the kitchen.

Fifteen minutes later, Diego was carefully wheeling the cart to the service elevator.

"G'night, Boss," he called over his shoulder.

"See you Monday, Diego."

Marin quickly tidied up the kitchen in anticipation of Griffin's arrival. He hadn't said what time he was bringing dinner, but when she looked up from the list she was creating of ingredients she needed to bring up from the main kitchen, Griffin was casually leaning a shoulder against the wall, quietly studying her.

"You're very stealthy," she quipped. "Do they teach that in Secret Service agent school?"

"Nope. I perfected that skill in the army when I was part of special forces." He grinned slyly. "Of course, years of spying on my older sister and her boyfriends gave me a good head start."

Marin returned his smile.

"Are you ready for dinner?" he asked.

She glanced at his empty hands. "Sure, but it looks like dinner is going to be a little sparse."

He stepped away from the wall, that sly grin still firmly in place. "Oh, I guarantee you won't go hungry. I just thought you might like a change of venue after being in the kitchen all day."

"I meant it when I said I couldn't take much of a break, Griffin. I don't have time to leave the House and still finish what I need to finish tonight."

"Who said anything about leaving the House?"

He extended his hand. When Marin didn't immediately take it, he arched an eyebrow, issuing a challenge. Marin reluctantly placed her fingers in his. Griffin drew in a quick breath at the contact of their skin before tugging her forward. Was he feeling the same something she'd been feeling for days? Marin's heart sped up at the thought.

Griffin led her out into the center hallway before turning to enter the Yellow Oval Room. Marin glanced reverently at the beautiful china housed in the display cases. Like the rest of the White House, the artwork in this room was stunning. She was so busy taking it all in, she didn't realize he was guiding her out onto the Truman Balcony until she felt the cool evening air brush her cheek. A table for two was set on the patio overlooking the South Lawn and the Washington Monument.

Ernie, one of the White House butlers, pulled out a chair for Marin. "Evening, Chef Marin," he said, wearing a cat-ate-the-canary grin when Marin took her seat.

Griffin sat down across from her. He was once again

studying her closely while the flame of the candle between them danced in the breeze.

"When you said you'd get takeout, I assumed we'd be eating in the kitchen. On paper plates. Not"—Marin gestured to the plate and goblet in front of her—"White House china and crystal. I'm pretty sure this is probably illegal."

He had the nerve to chuckle. "My go-to takeout meal is pizza, but everyone I called hung up when I said I wanted it delivered to sixteen hundred Pennsylvania Avenue. So I asked Terrie to help me out. This"—he gestured to the table between them—"was all her idea."

Ernie came back out onto the balcony carrying salad dishes, setting one in front of each of them. Marin leaned back in her chair, not surprised the head housekeeper had had a hand in the dinner. Now, staff throughout the House would be gossiping about her. Marin wasn't sure how she felt about that.

"You do realize that the entire kitchen staff is working around the clock to prepare the food for Monday. I can't imagine they're very happy with me right now."

"Precisely why I ordered from Old Ebbitt Grill. Relax, Marin. No one here begrudges you a dinner break. Especially after the week you've had."

"You went across the street to get dinner?" she asked as she picked up her salad fork. The chef at Old Ebbitt Grill once worked in the Chevalier hotel in San Francisco. Marin's stomach growled, making her suddenly realize how hungry she was. "They have the best butternut squash ravioli."

"The maître d' was right then. He said it was your favorite dish, insisting that I come back with nothing else but that."

She sighed with delight in anticipation of the meal. Griffin laughed out loud. They were quiet for a few moments as both enjoyed their salad.

"So, we've established that you love butternut squash ravioli, Belgian Malinois dogs, and artwork," Griffin ticked off on his fingers. "I'll make up my mind about the ravioli. And I do agree that dogs are much better pets than cats." He made a face that had Marin smiling. "But you don't see too many twenty-somethings with such extensive art collections as yours. You must have started acquiring pieces when you were young."

Marin glanced out toward the Washington Monument, unsure why this line of questioning always bothered her. She was used to men dating her because they were interested in her money or family. Griffin had been honest about that being the reason he'd agreed to be her wedding date. Still, she felt uncomfortable having to always justify her wealth; as though it was a crime for her to like nice things.

She fiddled with her napkin. "My mother is an interior designer for the hotels. My grandfather hired her on the spot after he saw her outmaneuver a museum curator at an estate sale auction. He always said her eye for treasure is impeccable. My grandmother used to joke that my grandfather made my dad marry my mom to keep her from going to the competition. Growing up, my brothers and my cousins hated my grandfather's art history lessons, but to me, they were like fairy tales. Every piece has a story. Some happy. Some tragic. I love finding out the legend behind a particular piece of art almost as much as I love the art itself."

He was studying her intently again, causing Marin to shift in her chair, uncomfortable with his perusal.

"My mom talks about art the same way."

Griffin's quiet admission surprised her. "Your mom is into art?"

He winced. "Way into art. She's an art teacher at a high school in Boston. I'm afraid my sister and I were a lot like your siblings and cousins when we were kids. She would adore you, though," he added wistfully.

Marin felt a warm flush spread over her cheeks. Ernie arrived at that moment with their ravioli. The aroma made her mouth water. Griffin took a bite and closed his eyes. A reverent look passed over his face.

"Mmm," he said. "Okay, this deserves some serious praise."

"Doesn't it, though?" She smiled at his pleasure before digging into her own plate.

They ate in companionable silence. Serenaded by the sounds of the nation's capital at night.

"What about the rest of your family?" she asked once they had put their forks down. "You mentioned an older sister. Does she live in Boston?"

He nodded. "She's married to a guy she met while working for a software company. They're expecting their first child in August. My dad owns an insurance agency. He loves it because he gets to play golf with his clients."

"Sounds idyllic."

Griffin shrugged. "Pretty boring typical family compared to yours. I'm surprised you'd choose working in the White House over one of your family's hotels. You certainly wouldn't be slaving at the oven on a Saturday night if your name was on the door."

"You don't know my grandfather. Most of my family are the first ones in and the last ones to leave every day. If the Chevalier name is 'on the door,' it means we have to work harder than anyone else."

"Still, I don't see the White House as a place where you come to rest on your laurels."

Marin rubbed a finger over the rim of her water glass. "Especially when your oven catches fire and you have to improvise during crunch time. But when Aunt Harriett—Mrs. Manning—asked me to come work for her, I couldn't say no. I told you before, just the history of this place alone was intriguing to me. Besides, it's nice to be one among a team of chefs. No one here cares what my last name is. I'm glad I took the job."

He leaned forward in his chair. "So am I, Marin. So am I."

Dusk had faded into night. Marin was grateful for the darkness so Griffin couldn't see how brightly she was blushing. Ernie emerged from the Yellow Oval Room and began to load their dinner plates onto one of the carts.

"Just take them into the kitchen up here, Ernie," she

said. "I'll wash the dishes."

"No can do, ma'am. Ms. Bloodworth said we weren't to disturb your work so that you can leave at a decent hour. I'll take these down to the big kitchen."

Marin huffed in exasperation. "In that case, I'd better get back to work." She stood from the table and Griffin did as well. "Thank you for a lovely dinner. I'd say you shouldn't have, but it was too delicious."

"It certainly beat pizza in my hotel room," he agreed as they passed through the Yellow Oval Room.

His remark reminded Marin that he was only in Washington temporarily while he worked on a case. She wondered about his life. Where he lived. He'd been evasive when she asked before. But he'd have to tell her so she could book his airline ticket, wouldn't he?

"I'll have my grandfather's assistant make the travel arrangements to the wedding. What city will you need to fly out of?"

Griffin didn't so much as twitch. "I'll make my way to DC and we can fly out of here. It's just easier."

Well, that was a swing and a miss. His secrecy seemed a little over the top, but Marin figured his job likely required it. He put his life on the line every day, which had to be stressful not only for him, but to everyone he cared about. She wondered if that was the reason he wanted to get out of the Secret Service. Marin felt an unbidden sense of relief knowing Griffin would be safer once he changed jobs.

"Thank you again," she said when they reached the kitchen. "Enjoy the rest of your evening."

He grimaced. "I still have a few hours of work to do myself tonight." His mouth then curved up into that slow grin that had the power to make her knees buckle. "But at least I enjoyed part of my evening."

Marin hurried into the kitchen so he wouldn't see her ridiculous glow.

"PILLSBURY IS ON the move."

Griffin glanced at the text on his phone, shaking his head at the ridiculous code name Agent Todd had dubbed Marin. He'd asked his friend to give him a heads-up when Marin was leaving the kitchen so he could intercept her on her way out of the House. After last night's incident on the Metro, he didn't want her traveling home alone. He wasn't usually so chivalrous with women he suspected of grand theft, but in this case, he was playing a part. Besides, he wanted a second look around her penthouse.

Their dinner earlier had been part of the act, too; a ruse to fish for information. The fact that he had enjoyed the meal was a bonus. The food had been delicious and how many guys could say they'd had dinner with a beautiful woman on the Truman Balcony of the White House? So far, everything was going according to plan.

As long as he didn't touch her.

He swore under his breath as he pulled on his suit jacket and headed out of the Secret Service office. Griffin had always thought that whole bullshit about sparks flying when people touched someone happened in chick flicks and his mother's romance novels. But when he'd taken Marin's hand earlier, shock waves had reverberated up his arm. And yet, the last thing he'd wanted to do at that moment was let go of her.

"This case is messing with my head," he mumbled as he made his way up the stairs to the north lobby.

"Talking to yourself?"

Griffin had to brace a hand on the wall to keep from mowing Marin down. *Or from touching her.*

"Still here?" he asked, trying to appear nonchalant.

"I'm headed home now."

Dark shadows had begun to form beneath her eyes, and her body looked weary from the long day on her feet. She was making his plan way too easy to execute.

"I've got an Uber coming to take me to my hotel. It's two blocks from your place," he said. "Let me give you a lift."

She studied him thoughtfully. "You always seem to be around to rescue people. Me in particular. I'd love a ride home. Thank you."

They made their way out of the White House into the warm spring night. The Uber was waiting at the northeast gate. Marin closed her eyes as soon as she hit the seat and Griffin did his best to snuff out that feeling of tenderness she kept stirring up inside of him. Reminding himself for the hundredth damn time she was a suspect, he focused his gaze out the window as the car began to move.

"Sitting may have been a bad idea," she murmured. "I

don't know if I can make it up to my apartment."

He smiled smugly to himself. "Don't worry. I'll carry you up if I have to."

When they reached Dupont Circle, however, Marin was able to walk into her apartment building without any help. Griffin followed her into the somber lobby. Apparently, most of the residents called it a night early on Saturdays.

"Chef Marin," the guy at the concierge desk called as she blindly walked past him.

It wasn't the same boisterous doorman who'd greeted them last night. In fact, this guy wore a gray uniform of one of the maintenance staff rather than the bright doorman's uniform.

"You have a package," the guy told her.

Marin blinked twice seemingly trying to orient herself. "Oh. Hey there, Seth. What are you doing working the desk tonight? Where's Arnold?"

"You haven't heard?" The guy at the desk looked down at his lap. He struggled to swallow. "He—he, uh, he had a heart attack earlier this evening."

Griffin caught Marin just as her knees began to buckle. "Please tell me he's going to be okay," she cried.

Maintenance guy's eyes drifted away again. He shook his head. Marin let out a sob.

Griffin gathered her up in his arms, taking the package from her hands and shoving it in her backpack as he steered her to the elevator. "Come on. Let's get you upstairs."

She clung to him, silently crying, as they rode up to the

penthouse. Griffin pulled her key out of the pocket of her backpack and opened the door. Marin hurried over to a side table and grabbed a tissue while he dropped her backpack on the same chair where she had put it the night before.

"I'm sorry," she said, her back to him. "I don't know what has come over me. But this week—Wes. The fire. Anika. And now this. I'm not sure how much more I can take." She turned around and gave him a watery smile. "Thank you, *again*, for being here when I needed someone. You've been so kind to me. And dinner, it was amazing and so sweet."

Tears began streaming down her cheeks again.

Griffin's head was telling him to say "you're welcome" and get the hell out of Dodge, but his feet weren't listening. Instead, they seemed to be moving toward her as though there was an invisible tether connecting them.

She drew in another ragged breath when he stopped inches from her. "I'm usually not one of those women who dissolve into hysterics."

"Shh. Like you said, it's been a pretty shitty week." He reached up and fanned his fingers on the sides of her face, gently pulling her body closer to his.

Her hands seemed to float between them, hesitating briefly, before they landed softly on his chest. He stifled a groan at the contact.

"Arnold was going to take his grandchildren to the White House on Monday," she whispered through her tears. "It's so unfair."

"I know," he said as he bent down to brush his lips over her forehead.

This is all part of the role I'm playing, Griffin silently reminded himself. Any self-respecting guy would do the same to provide comfort to a woman he was interested in. He'd just kiss her on the head, pat her on the back, and send her off to bed.

Alone.

So why the hell had his lips found their way to the corner of her mouth? She tasted so damn good. Like sugar and lemons. He'd just take a taste of the other side of her mouth, then he could walk away.

Marin's lips parted with a breathy sigh and, just like that, Griffin was a goner. He sealed his mouth over hers, swallowing up the keening sound of need that rose in the back of her throat. A wave of reckless desire spurred him on as he explored her mouth with a tactical thoroughness. She slid her tongue against his seductively causing his control to slip a notch more. When she shifted her body closer so she was practically his second skin, he gave up the game altogether and let his libido take control.

Griffin's hands left her face to explore the voluptuous curves that had haunted his dreams—and his showers—for the past few days. Trailing his fingers down her back, he groaned into her mouth when he finally filled his hands with her sexy ass. Marin nipped at his lip in response. He slipped his hands beneath the fabric of her T-shirt, grazing his fingers along her soft, warm skin.

She tore her mouth away from his, threw her head

back, and sighed his name. The sound made him hard enough to pound diamonds. His lips took advantage of their change in position to explore the tender skin of her neck. Marin scored her fingernails along his chest, seeming to demand more.

Far be it for Griffin to disappoint her.

He wedged his thigh between hers while he unclasped her bra at the same time. Marin's eyes were wide and wild when they met his. They were still for a long moment before she oh-so-slowly ground down on his thigh, her eyes never leaving his. His breathing fractured when she sank her teeth into her bottom lip, closed her eyes, and with an erotic moan, began to rub against him.

Mesmerized, Griffin watched her pleasure herself. But only for a moment. If there was pleasure to be had, he was damn well going to provide it. Gripping her waist, he lifted her to the sofa. He yanked her T-shirt and bra over her head, tossing them across the room. Then, he laid her down, spreading her out on the cushions like a veritable feast for his out of control sex drive. Marin was breathing heavily, panting in fact, making those gorgeous breasts of hers quiver tantalizingly.

"Damn, but you're beautiful, Marin."

His fingers worshipfully skimmed the delicate skin around her nipples. At his touch, she gasped his name. Desire shot to his groin at the breathy sound. His touch became firmer. She sighed deeply as her head began drifting from side to side. Marin's hands were suddenly on his shoulders, gripping him with a determined strength. He could feel the heat of her fingers through his suit jacket as she tugged his body closer.

Griffin didn't bother resisting. Not when his lips were on a collision course with her amazing breasts. He blew gently on the aroused tip. Marin's fingers began clawing frantically at the fabric of his clothing.

"Easy, babe." He trailed his lips over her flushed skin.

She let out a frustrated cry making Griffin chuckle before he put her out of her misery.

MARIN ARCHED HER back, pleasure pooling at her core when Griffin finally—*finally*—put his lips to her skin. Another gasp escaped her throat when he blew on her nipple before trailing a row of kisses on the underside of her breast. Threading her fingers through his thick hair, she tried to guide his head to where she wanted him—*needed him*—most. She felt him smile against her skin. But then he was there, his wet mouth closing over her nipple, bringing her both pain and pleasure at the same time.

Her pulse throbbed wildly throughout her body. An agonizing tension was building between her thighs. She needed relief. But when she tried to move her hips, she couldn't; his hard body had her pinned to the sofa. She tugged on his hair, but Griffin ignored her, too busy enjoying the banquet that was her breasts.

"Please, Griffin," she cried.

This time he laughed out loud. Marin couldn't decide

between punching him or kissing him, the arrogant jerk. But then he shifted his torso upward allowing just enough room for his wicked hand to pass between their bodies.

"Is this what you want?" he whispered seductively just as his finger found her sweet spot. Slowly, he stroked her through her clothing, the silk of her panties dragging against the over-sensitized skin had her seeing stars.

"Does that feel good, Marin?" he murmured against her ear just before taking her earlobe between his lips.

"Oh, God, yes!" Marin panted.

Griffin chuckled again before sinking his teeth into her collarbone. His finger was still working its magic at her core. "What else do you want, Marin? Tell me. Tonight, I'm going to give you whatever you want. As often as you want it."

She nearly came at his words. But she needed more. Wanted more. She worked her hand between them, her fingers finding the hard ridge of his desire. Now it was her turn to torture him. She cupped him through his trousers, taking great pleasure when he hissed against her shoulder.

"I want you," she demanded. "Inside me. Now."

He pushed up on his forearms so he was looking down on her. She shivered without his body to warm her. His eyes were as dark as the ocean in a storm. And they were full of so much desire her breath caught in her throat.

Marin reached up and brushed her thumb over his kiss-swollen bottom lip. "Make love to me, Griffin. Please."

His lips slowly turned up in that devastating grin of his. "As often as you want."

"You're a little overdressed, though."

She pushed his suit jacket off his shoulders. It got stuck at his elbows, but Griffin was too intent on kissing her to slide it off himself. While he plunged his tongue deep into her mouth, she yanked at his tie and then the buttons of his shirt until she could feel bare skin beneath her fingertips. He moaned into her mouth when she dragged her fingernail over the flat pebble of his nipple.

Griffin's kisses became more frenzied further stoking the fever that was raging within Marin. She tugged his shirt free from his pants. Reaching beneath the fabric to touch his flat stomach, her hand hit something hard on his side. With a start, she realized his gun was in a holster at his waist. A second later, she realized that Griffin's body had frozen.

He pushed off of her with a jerk, his gaze moving erratically around the room as if he was seeing it for the first time.

"Shit!" He jumped off the couch. "Shit, shit, shit!"

Pulling on his clothing, he spun in a circle, one hand gripping the back of his neck.

"How could I let this happen?" He scrubbed his hands down his face. "I've got to get out of here."

Marin didn't move. She couldn't. It felt as if she'd been doused with a bucket of water. Griffin looked everywhere in the room except at her. The icy fingers of rejection began to claw at Marin's belly. He turned for the door.

"Griffin?" She managed to push the word out around the boulder in her throat.

He hesitated ever so briefly, his hand on the doorknob. Marin's breath stilled in her lungs. But then he was gone. Without looking back. She heard the chime of the elevator and then its door closing, but still, she didn't move. It wasn't until her teeth were chattering that she pulled the cashmere blanket from the back of the sofa and wrapped her body in it. Marin took some solace in the warmth it provided. Too bad the blanket didn't help alleviate the shame she felt.

CHAPTER EIGHT

THE SOUND OF the fire alarm awakened Marin from a fitful sleep. Disoriented, she glanced at her clock. Five a.m. She'd been asleep for barely forty-five minutes. She fell back down against her pillows, closing her eyes until the persistent ringing permeated the fog of her brain.

"Oh, my God!"

Marin jumped out of bed, grabbing her phone from the nightstand and her neatly piled clothes from a bench at the end of the bed. She slid her feet into her Skechers and headed for the front door, crying out when she bumped her knee on the corner of an end table in the dark living room. Snatching up her backpack from the chair in the foyer, she shoved her clothes inside. The alarm was still blaring when she reached for the door handle. Her father's voice in her head stopped her from bolting out the door, however.

She turned on her heel and dashed to her kitchen, shooting up a prayer of thanks for the paranoia of the previous owners of the penthouse. She turned the key in the dead bolt on the back door leading to a private stairwell only accessible from her apartment.

"If the fire alarm ever goes off," her father had advised her when she'd bought the place, "use this stairwell. It's constructed from concrete blocks. A fire anywhere else in the building would never be able to permeate it."

Marin placed her hand on the door, checking it for heat. Feeling nothing, she opened it cautiously.

"Bless you, Daddy," she said when she slipped from her kitchen into the cool, quiet, smoke-free stairway. "And bless the archaic ordinance that says buildings within Washington, DC can only be thirteen stories."

She trudged down the stairs, her exhaustion making her feet feel like lead.

"Shitty week is an understatement, Not-So-Special-Agent Dickweed," Marin mumbled to the quiet walls. "*Two* fires! Who gets stuck in two freaking fires in one week?" She rounded the corner leading down another flight. "And two friends dead in the same week. How does that happen?"

She was surprised by the burn of more tears behind her eyes. Marin swore she'd cried them all out last night. "And let's not forget the knife fight on the Metro where an innocent girl was injured." She swiped at her nose as she descended another floor.

"And, thanks, by the way, for leaving me hanging last night, you colossal ass!" Marin's mumble had risen to a shout, her words echoing off the cement walls as tears streamed down her face. "Because every woman enjoys being rejected in the middle of hooking-up." She stomped around another corner. "You can forget your cushy security job with my family," she yelled. "I'm calling my big brother right now to tell him what an ass you are!"

Marin sank down on one of the steps and dug her cell phone out of her pocket. "Great. With my luck, there will be a cute fireman waiting to rescue me, and I'm strutting around in my SpongeBob pajama pants." She leaned her head against the wall and sighed. "No signal. It figures." A fit of hysterical laughter bubbled up from her throat. "And to think, a few days ago, all I cared about was getting a date to Ava's stupid wedding."

She pushed to her feet. "Back to square one on that quest."

Quickly jogging down the last four floors, she pushed through the exit door into the boiler room. The fire alarm was still blaring, although its sound was partially drowned out by the loud hum of the machinery that kept the eighty-one units of the Dupont comfortable. Marin glanced down at her phone, relieved to have signal finally. She scrolled for her father's number, needing to hear his voice right now. Just as she was about to press the call button, however, she tripped and went sprawling across the floor. Marin glanced back to see what had caused her to fall.

It wasn't a what, but a who: Seth, the building's maintenance man. Lying on the floor in a pool of blood. A scream of shock caught in Marin's throat. She struggled to breathe. She glanced around the vast room while her limbs were frozen in terror. Could whoever have done this still be here hiding? Not wanting to find out, she scrambled to her feet and ran to the lobby with a speed she didn't know she possessed.

"WE HAVE TO stop meeting like this, Chef Chevalier," said the distinguished police detective who'd interviewed her and Griffin two nights ago. He set a steaming cup of tea down in front of her before he slid into the chair opposite hers. "Mayhem seems to be following you around, lately."

"Tell me something I don't know." She reached out to pick up the tea, but her hand was shaking too badly to manage it, so she shoved her fingers into her pockets instead.

Marin had been sitting in the manager of the Dupont's office for over two hours while a string of firefighters and police officers asked her the same questions, over and over again. Her head was pounding so badly; she was surprised none of the others in the room heard.

"You didn't exit your apartment at all after arriving home last evening?" the detective asked.

"No." She swallowed painfully remembering how it had taken her an hour to drag her limp body off the sofa and into the shower. After thirty minutes of sobbing under the warm spray of water, she'd staggered to her bed, wrestling with sleep for several more hours. "Not until the fire alarm went off this morning."

"And Agent Keller, what time did he leave?"

Not soon enough. Shame made Marin's cheeks flush. She imagined the detective interpreted her blush a totally different way.

"Uh, he stayed for maybe fifteen minutes, but I'm not

sure exactly. They keep a log at the front desk." She nearly choked on the last two words remembering that the last two people to man the front desk were now dead.

"And no one else came to the penthouse last night?"

Marin was surprised by the intensity of his question. "I told you, no."

He looked out the window and sighed heavily. "There was no fire here this morning, Chef," he said. "It was a false alarm. A prank, it would seem."

Her head spun when she sat up too quickly in her chair. She'd been so overwrought stumbling over Seth's dead body that she hadn't even asked about the fire. "Someone pulled the fire alarm?"

The detective eyed her carefully. "Yes. The one on the penthouse floor."

"What!" Her stomach rolled, and she had to sit on her hands to keep their trembling under control. "You have to have a key to get up to my floor. Even when using the stairs."

"So I understand."

"Well, I don't!" Marin cried. "I don't understand any of this. People around me are dying all of a sudden! And I can't make any sense of it!"

The detective left his chair and came around the table to sit next to Marin.

"You don't have to make any sense of it. That's my job," he tried to soothe her. "Like I said, I think you've just had a run of bad luck by being in the wrong place at the wrong time. We'll figure it out, though. You just need to get some rest now."

Marin glanced at the clock on the wall. *Seven thirty-five.* She needed to get to work on the Easter luncheon the First Family was expecting later that day. "I need to get to the White House." She tried to stand up, but her legs didn't seem to be getting the message.

"You just sit. Someone from the White House is on the way here now. They'll drive you."

"No!" Marin surged to her feet, grabbing onto the table for support. The last person she wanted to see was Griffin Keller riding in like a white knight. "I can get myself to the White House."

"All the same," the admiral chimed in from behind her. "I'd appreciate it if you'd ride with me. I can make that an order if I have to, Chef. Please don't force me to do so."

"I wish you had let me go upstairs and change out of my pajamas," Marin said when they arrived at the White House ten minutes later. She didn't bother apologizing for her churlish tone. Her SpongeBob pajama pants were embarrassment enough.

The admiral smiled. "They're nothing I haven't seen before. My daughter took a similar pair to college this year." He took her elbow and helped her up the steps.

"Marin!" Her aunt Harriett, the First Lady, charged out of the usher's office. "Sweetheart." She wrapped her arms around Marin, holding her tightly. It was too much. Marin dissolved into tears again.

Time seemed to be hopping because the next thing she knew, they were standing in the Queen's bedroom on the second floor. The ornate four-poster bed swam before Marin's misty eyes.

"I need to be in the kitchen," she stammered.

"Not today," Aunt Harriett insisted. "You, my girl, are going to rest."

One of the maids arrived with towels and a glass of water.

"Thank you," Aunt Harriett murmured, taking the glass from the maid. She handed it to Marin, opening her other hand to reveal a small pill. "Here, take this."

Marin blanched. "What is it?"

"Something to help you sleep. From the looks of you, sixteen hours ought to do it."

"You're drugging me?"

"I may be the First Lady, but I'm also your godmother. And I still have a license to practice medicine. Don't forget I used to treat your diaper rash, young lady."

She reluctantly took the pill from her aunt's hand and swallowed it with a gulp of water.

Her mother's best friend gently brushed the hair out of Marin's eyes. "You've had quite a week. Let me take care of you. Your mother would do the same for my family if it came down to it. There are toiletries in the bathroom. Don't be shy about asking for whatever you need. I'll just be down the hall."

When Marin emerged from the bathroom a few minutes later, Arabelle was leaning against one of the Queen Anne chairs, wearing a frilly pink dress, shiny white Mary Janes, and carrying a pile of books in her hands.

"Arabelle, don't you look beautiful in your Easter dress."

"I have a hat that goes with it, but Momma says I can't wear it until we leave for church. She said I wasn't supposed to come in here because I'll wrinkle my dress, but Grandma Harriett said it would be okay if I read you some stories. Would you like that?"

The child's expression was so earnest, Marin didn't have the heart to disappoint her despite the fact that she was already feeling woozy. "I would love that, sweetie."

Marin climbed into the big bed, pulling a blanket over her weary body. Arabelle walked to the other side and carefully spread the books out on top of the coverlet. "Which one do you want me to read first?"

"You pick."

"Oh! I almost forgot." Arabelle raced over to the chair, coming back with a worn stuffed elephant clutched to her chest. She carefully lifted the blanket off Marin and tucked the toy next to her. "This is Ellie. She always makes me feel better when I'm sick."

The supply of Marin's tears seemed to be endless because her eyes welled up again. Arabelle flipped the pages in the book, retelling from memory the story that she'd likely heard a thousand times about a moose who wanted a muffin. Marin drifted off to sleep dreaming of muffins shaped like moose, vowing to make them for Arabelle's birthday.

GRIFFIN WIPED THE steam off the bathroom mirror and, with a glance at his reflection, confirmed he looked as crappy as he felt. He swallowed two acetaminophens with a bottle of cold water hoping like hell they'd kick in soon. Not that he didn't deserve the throbbing in his head. He deserved that and more after losing control and taking things too far with Marin last night—*way too far*. Today, he needed to get his head—the one on his shoulders—back on the case. And that meant some serious rethinking of the evidence and the suspects.

He stepped out of the bathroom and abruptly halted in his tracks, astounded to find Leslie sprawled out on his unmade bed, an empty bottle from the mini-bar dangling from her fingers.

"Did you have a little party for one last night?" the FBI agent asked, arching an eyebrow at him.

Griffin glanced at the door, but given his condition the previous evening, he obviously hadn't bothered with the security lock. Adjusting the towel more snugly around his waist, he met her amused gaze.

"What are you doing in DC, Leslie? Specifically, in my hotel room?"

"Aw, come on, Griff. The last time I surprised you in your hotel room, you were a lot"—she glanced in the vicinity of his crotch—"happier to see me."

"This isn't Rome, Leslie." And Griffin wasn't sure he'd be happy to see any woman in his present condition. Not when the taste of Marin Chevalier was still haunting him.

Tilting her head to the side, she rose from the bed and

crossed the room to where he stood. She reached out a finger, presumably to trace the drop of water sliding down his pectoral muscle, but Griffin flinched before her finger made contact.

Pain flashed in her green eyes before she quickly shuttered them. Griffin felt like an even bigger ass. Apparently, disappointing women was becoming a habit.

"Huh," she said, dropping her hand to her side. "I'm here to investigate the homicide of the White House curator."

"We turned that over to the local Feebs."

"And they turned it over to me since the guy potentially died at the hands of a nasty counterfeit ring I'm investigating."

The fact that she'd used the word 'I'm' and not 'we're' wasn't lost on Griffin. Nor was the fact that, given the trail of bodies the counterfeiters were piling up, this case could become solely that of the FBI at any moment. He needed to keep the peace with Leslie before she pulled the rug out from under him. But that didn't mean he was going to have sex with her.

"It's Easter Sunday. Shouldn't you be hunting for Easter eggs with Dylan?" he asked carefully.

Her eyes shuttered again. "Dylan is with my ex this weekend."

So she was lonely and deflecting with work. And, apparently, she'd hoped with Griffin's body as well.

"I figured I could swing down here and piece through the evidence before anything gets cold," she continued. "I brought Eric with me to dig through the curator's personal computer. We might find something once we can access his email."

"Eric's one of the best at overriding a login password."

"Well, if you're not too hungover, we can take a ride over to the field office and see what he's turned up."

"I'm not quite dressed for it at the moment."

Leslie's mouth turned up at the corners. "You're wearing too much if you ask me. Sure you don't want to reconsider?"

"I'm not, um, at my best today, Leslie." *Said no red-blooded male ever.* Griffin swore silently.

She had the nerve to laugh. "Not to feed your ego, Griff, but you at only half your best is a lot better than most men."

Griffin sighed. "Thanks, I think. But I still need to get dressed."

Leslie crossed her arms beneath her breasts—breasts that used to turn him on. Not today. He was beginning to wonder if something was physically wrong with him.

"Don't let me stop you," she purred.

"Damn it, Leslie!"

She laughed again before she turned and walked to the window. "I don't know why you're acting so shy. It's not like I haven't seen your good stuff before. Or touched it," she added slyly.

Griffin shed his towel, pulled a pair of boxer-briefs from his suitcase and quickly slid them on. He grabbed his jeans off the pile of dirty clothes on the floor and stepped into them.

"So how is your search for the White House thief going?" she asked, her back still to him.

Shitty. He'd spent last night counting the numerous ways he'd screwed the investigation up, chasing each revelation with a swig from one of the bottles in the minibar. He'd almost compromised the whole damn case by sleeping with Marin. *Not that there would have been much sleeping involved.* He snatched a shirt off the hanger and shoved his arms into the sleeves.

"Are you still concentrating on Max Chevalier's granddaughter?" She looked over her shoulder at him.

If concentrating was the same as lusting over, then, hell yeah.

Griffin didn't bother sharing that little bit of intel with Leslie, though. There was no chance in hell he was going to the wedding after last night, either. He'd have to look for a link to the Chevalier family from another angle. If there even was a link between the hotelier and the counterfeit ring.

"I'm beginning to think the pastry chef is a red herring." He buttoned up his shirt. "The director has given me until the end of the day tomorrow to flush out suspects. I want to dig a little deeper into the sous chef. But, really, anyone working in the White House could have had access to the kitchen towels, so this whole thing might just be a damn wild goose chase." He pulled on his socks and sneakers. "Until we can determine whether or not any other artwork in the House is forged, I'm at a standstill."

Leslie turned from the window and walked to the bed to retrieve her purse. "Well, I wouldn't write off the pastry chef as a red herring just yet," she said casually. "She apparently literally stumbled over a dead body early this morning leaving her cushy penthouse."

Griffin's hands stilled in the act of tying his shoes. "What?"

"I know how you feel about coincidences, Griff. This one may be too big to ignore."

He shot out of the chair, grabbing his badge and his holster. "I'm gonna need to talk to her." Provided Marin didn't kick him in the balls as soon as she laid eyes on him. But a part of him just needed to know she was okay—the very same part of him that he shouldn't be listening to right now.

"Word is she was pretty shaken up. FLOTUS has her resting at the White House. Of course, if she's our thief, it was the perfect way for the fox to get into the henhouse."

Leslie's accusation angered Griffin, which was ridiculous because he'd thought the same thing of Marin after the fire in the pastry kitchen. Clearly, he was going soft on a suspect. And that path led to all kinds of trouble.

"Let's go," he said as headed out the door.

"I'll text Eric and tell him we're on our way."

"Not yet. We're stopping at the Dupont first."

CHAPTER NINE

"I WAS WONDERING when you'd show up," the police detective who had interviewed him and Marin two nights before remarked when Griffin entered the lobby of the Dupont.

Griffin extended his hand to the white-haired gentleman. "Detective Bill Gerkens, this is Special Agent Leslie Morgan of the FBI." He gestured to Leslie.

Detective Gerkens shook Leslie's hand. "I wasn't aware this was a federal case."

"I'm not here in a formal capacity. Yet," Leslie explained. "Today, I'm just tagging along with Agent Keller."

"Can you fill me in on what happened here?" An unfamiliar tension had gripped Griffin as soon as Leslie mentioned Marin tripping over a dead body. He chocked the feeling up to the hangover because he was working hard at keeping Marin strictly in the suspect category.

The detective looked at him speculatively. "I would have thought you'd already heard the whole story from your friend the pastry chef by now."

Griffin rubbed a hand over the back of his neck. "I haven't spoken to Mar—Chef Chevalier."

"Huh." Detective Gerkens scratched his head. "Watching you two the other night, I figured you'd be the first person she called. She mentioned that you were the last one to leave the penthouse late last night."

Griffin could feel Leslie's eyes on him, but he ignored her. "We shared an Uber back from the White House."

"Huh," the detective repeated before, thankfully, recounting the events of the morning.

"Any idea how long the guy was dead before the chef stumbled upon him?" Griffin asked when the detective had finished.

"The ME estimates about twenty minutes."

Jesus. Marin could have walked in on the murder. *And been killed in the process.* He sucked in a sharp breath.

"That's assuming the chef didn't kill him herself and hang out there for twenty minutes," Leslie theorized.

Both men stared at her. The detective's face was inquisitive. Based on Leslie's tight mouth, Griffin's expression was likely hard.

"Don't look at me like that. The woman is a chef. Presumably, she's skilled with a knife," she argued. "She could have raced back upstairs, pulled the alarm and then come back down again. Faking the whole thing about finding him."

"Then she's a talented actress as well as a chef," Detective Gerkens maintained.

"Why would she do that?" Griffin wondered. "What would be the motive? Why kill someone and then pull the damn fire alarm? Why not sneak out? It makes no sense. And why is everyone assuming that Marin set off the alarm?

Surely someone else had access to the penthouse." His pulse raced to keep up with his train of thought. "Like one of the maintenance workers, for instance."

Detective Gerkens's face was grim. "His keys weren't on him. We combed the boiler room and all the stairwells, but no luck."

Griffin scrubbed a hand down his face and groaned. A young man dressed in a Marvel Comics T-shirt and shorts with a police badge hanging from around his neck, strolled up to them.

"Bad news, Detective. The hard drive housing the surveillance cameras was completely erased."

"Why does that not surprise me?" Detective Gerkens murmured.

"Except there's good news," the guy added. "This security firm always backs up everything onto their cloud."

"So why aren't you downloading that video for me right now then, Kevin?" Detective Gerkens demanded to know.

"Well that's the hitch; the security firm requires permission from the property owners before they can release any video. The owners are traveling out of the country. It may take a day. Or two."

"We don't have a day—or two," Griffin said through clenched teeth.

"I'll see if I can scare up a judge who'll give us a warrant," Detective Gerkens offered. "It's a holiday, so it won't be quick. In the meantime, Kevin, you get your butt to that security firm's office and have a seat there until we hear from either the building owner or the judge."

Kevin gave the detective a sheepish nod before sprinting out of the lobby. Griffin glanced around the crowded room, finally noticing all the somber people milling about.

Detective Gerkens followed his gaze. "With two employee deaths in less than twenty-four hours, the tenants are a little spooked," he pointed out.

"Two?" Leslie looked from one man to the other.

"The weekend doorman died of a heart attack yesterday evening," the detective explained.

"And how sure are we that it was an actual heart attack?" she asked.

Griffin's pulse sped up again. *Damn it.* He'd forgotten about Arnold. Could Leslie be right that both deaths are connected? But how? And why? At least Marin had been at the White House when the doorman suffered his fatal heart attack. Leslie's theory about Marin pulling the fire alarm as a distraction while she murdered Seth seemed a little out there. Even if Griffin did like Marin as the art thief, he couldn't see her as a murderer.

Or was it that he just didn't want to believe he'd misjudged her, especially since, the night before, he'd had his mouth and hands all over her?

"Perhaps you two should stop playing games with me and tell me what's going on," Detective Gerkens demanded.

Griffin exchanged a glance with Leslie.

"This may be part of an ongoing international investigation," Leslie revealed. "Any more than that, we're not at liberty to divulge at this time. But we will need the door-man's body."

"That's going to pretty much take me all through Easter dinner to arrange," the detective grumbled.

Leslie turned on the charm. "I don't want you to miss dinner with your family. If you run into a problem, call this number." She handed the detective her business card. "Sometimes a little push from the FBI is all that's needed."

Detective Gerkens nodded grudgingly. "I'll let you know when we get access to the security video."

Griffin and Leslie turned for the door.

"Agent Keller." The detective's voice stopped them. "I've been doing this a long time. If the chef had a hand in this, I'll turn in my badge."

Leslie was quiet throughout the cab ride down Massachusetts Avenue to Fourth Street. She exited the cab, but instead of heading inside the FBI field office, she marched down F Street. Griffin fell into step beside her. They both paused for a moment in front of the National Law Enforcement Officers' Memorial. Griffin silently remembered colleagues who gave their lives for the job. Leslie was likely doing the same.

Turning abruptly, Leslie then headed into the historic red-bricked building that housed the National Building Museum. Griffin followed, figuring if she didn't want him around, she would have bitten off his head already. She sat down on one of the iron benches that dotted the perimeter of the building's ornate great hall. Griffin strolled through the café, picking up two coffees before joining her on the bench.

They watched as a toddler raced over to the giant fountain in the center of the hall only to have his father scoop him up steps before the child reached the gurgling water. The boy's happy squeal echoed throughout the fifteen-story high gallery.

"This is my favorite place in this city," Leslie said before taking a sip of coffee.

Griffin took a good look at the massive room. Eight towering Corinthian columns supported the building's vaulted roof. Small, Doric columns surrounded the atrium like soldiers standing at attention. The floor featured a stunning design of terra cotta tiles. Before today, he'd never been inside this building; but he had to agree, the light and airiness of the space was relaxing. Settling back against the bench, he took a pull from his coffee.

"They hold the most amazing inaugural balls here. Daniel took me to one six years ago. It was an incredible night."

Leslie tilted her head back and closed her eyes. Griffin wondered where this little trip down memory lane would end up. But he'd been around enough women to know not to ask.

"He proposed that same night. It was perfect." A long moment later, her eyes snapped open. "And then it wasn't. He wanted a trophy wife to help his law career along and further his political aspirations." Her laugh rang a bit hollow. "Can you imagine? Me sitting by quietly while he had a scintillating career?"

There wasn't a right answer to that one, so Griffin kept his mouth shut.

"I'm sure you're wondering what my point is, Griff."

He arched an eyebrow in response.

"Daniel saw in me what he wanted to see. It happens. Lots of people do that." She looked over at Griffin. "Perhaps you're seeing something you want to see, too. In the pastry chef."

It took everything Griffin had within him to remain seated. No doubt she'd brought him to this tranquil place so he wouldn't explode. "I'm not 'seeing' anything in the pastry chef besides the fact that she's a suspect." He practically growled the bold face lie.

She sighed heavily. "You forget I know you. Intimately. Every time someone mentions her, your face changes. You're attracted to her."

Griffin quickly schooled his features to be impassive. "You're way off base here, Agent Morgan."

"Mmm," she said. "One of us is definitely 'off base here.' And for the sake of this case, I hope it is me."

Her cell phone rang before Griffin could get another protest in. She stood up to take the call while he sat and fumed, the calm of the open-air atrium suddenly chafing at him. *Leslie's accusation is bogus.* Yeah, he'd screwed up and kissed Marin. But that wasn't happening again. He could still keep this case in perspective.

"That was Eric. He found something of interest in the curator's email cloud."

Griffin shoved to his feet and followed her out of the

building and around the corner to the FBI field office.

"From the looks of his email, the curator was a fan of the White House pastry chef," Eric announced when they arrived.

Griffin ignored Leslie's *I-told-you-so* look. "What makes you say that?" he asked, trying to keep his tone neutral.

"She must be an art enthusiast," Eric continued. "They exchanged multiple emails on the subject over the past months."

"The guy was the curator of the White House," Griffin argued. "Not surprising his emails discuss artwork."

"Yeah, much better that than them talking about kinky sex," Leslie said.

Griffin did glare at her this time. She shrugged.

Eric pulled up one of the emails. Griffin's gut clenched when he saw that the subject was about the very same Cezanne painting he discovered last week rolled up in a truck in New Jersey.

Leslie leaned in over Eric's shoulder. "Interesting."

Her word was a lot tamer than the ones ricocheting around inside Griffin's head. The email contained two paragraphs on the history of the painting, including an estimate of the piece's overall worth.

Damn it.

"Yeah, but that's not why I called you." Eric pulled up another email. "I don't think the curator is part of our counterfeit ring. It looks like he was getting suspicious about one of the pieces. He sent this to a colleague at the Smithsonian."

They both scanned the email.

"That painting doesn't look like one of the ones you found in the truck," Leslie said.

"It wasn't." Griffin shook his head in frustration. "That's a Jackson Pollack. From the Map Room. The admiral's team will have to discreetly check that one out right away. Do we know who received the email?"

"Yeah, but the recipient hasn't actually received it yet," Eric explained. "The curator sent it ten days ago. But he got back an out-of-office reply. Apparently, his friend at the Smithsonian is in Italy through the end of next week."

"Well at least that eliminates one potential suspect. The curator was concerned enough about the Pollack being a forgery to contact a colleague." Leslie paced the small conference room as she theorized. "He probably mentioned his suspicions to someone else, too. It would have to be another person knowledgeable about art. And if that person is part of the counterfeit ring, that's what likely got our curator killed. Now we just need to find out who he might have mentioned his theory to."

Eric's fingers tapped rapidly on his computer keyboard. "I'll do a keyword search through all of his sent emails."

Griffin knew where Leslie was headed with her theory. Hell, a kindergartener could follow Leslie's reasoning. She suspected Marin and she wasn't going to let it alone. True, if the curator thought enough of Marin's expertise in art, he'd likely confide in her about the Pollack. But it was circumstantial, at best. Unfortunately, Griffin's gut told him were Marin any other suspect, he wouldn't dismiss an email as evidence of her involvement.

Eric's search seemed to take hours instead of a few minutes. Leslie continued pacing while Griffin stared out the window, his conscience chastising him for lusting after a potential thief and murderer.

"There's nothing here," Eric finally declared.

Leslie raised an eyebrow at Griffin's quick exhale of breath, but she thankfully kept her opinions to himself.

"Okay," she said. "Then what about the rest of the curator's staff? He might have said something to one of the two of them. Have you questioned anyone there yet, Griff?"

Griffin shook his head. "We decided to let the police handle those interviews. We don't want to tip them off that we know about the forgeries just in case someone in that office is involved."

"I'll go over the notes from the detectives in Virginia, but you might need to start feeling them out," she said.

"I'll have a chat with the sous chef first," Griffin added, glad that the focus had shifted off Marin—for the time being, at least. He headed out to find Diego Ruiz.

CHAPTER TEN

"COME ON, CHEF Marin. We're gonna miss the Easter bunny." Arabelle tugged on Marin's arm, while the child's mother and father wandered hand-in-hand a few feet behind them.

It was Easter Monday and the South Lawn of the White House was awash with nearly five thousand people enjoying music and chasing Easter eggs under a cloudless blue sky. A line of thousands of more guests snaked around the Old Executive Office building; all of them waiting for their allotted time to enter Presidential Park. The crowd buzzed as Arabelle passed, many eager for a glimpse of the president's granddaughter and her parents. The family's Secret Service detail surrounded them closely as they all traipsed across the grass. Marin caught sight of Otto calmly sitting on the perimeter of the lawn as his handler kept his vision trained on the visitors.

An unexplained tremor ran down Marin's spine. She attributed her jumpiness to the stress of the past few days. Still, the tense faces of the Secret Service and uniformed guards reminded her of the dangers a group this large posed to the First Family. *Nothing is going to happen today..* She'd had her fair share of tragedy to last for quite some time.

Still, her anxiety left her on edge.

Marin also felt awkward mingling with the guests while dressed in her chef's uniform. She would prefer to be in the kitchen helping the staff prepare for the luncheon celebrating the sponsors of the event. The busywork would certainly help keep the thoughts of Arnold, Seth, and even Anika, at bay.

But Arabelle was insistent that Marin join her on the White House lawn. Not only that, the First Lady still had Marin under house arrest, adamant that she take it easy. The problem was, with the Secret Service out in force, Marin couldn't help but worry she might cross paths with Griffin. He was on the top of that list of people she was trying hard not to think about.

Especially after dreaming of him the entire night.

The sleeping pill had been effective, helping Marin fall asleep; she'd missed all of Easter Sunday. But the drug had done nothing to block out the powerful dreams she'd experienced. Each time her subconscious replayed the image of Seth's body, however, Griffin was there to rescue Marin. Just as he did the day of the fire. He comforted her the way he had the night of the attack on the Metro, with a firm hand at her back and a strong shoulder to lean on. In her sleep, Griffin did not abruptly abandon her, either. Instead, he slowly made love to her, cherishing her, protecting her. Marin woke up more agitated than when she'd gone to sleep, angry at how much she craved Griffin Keller's presence.

Arabelle's hand suddenly slipped from her grasp. Marin

tripped as she reached to grab the child back. A strong arm caught Marin before she face-planted in the grass.

"Whoa there, gorgeous," a familiar voice said.

Marin glanced around wildly. She blew out a relieved breath watching Arabelle scramble into the president's lap. Arabelle's grandfather kissed her on the head before continuing to read a book to a group of children seated on the grass in front of him; a crew of photographers clicking away behind them.

"Are you okay?" Griffin's friend Adam asked, his arm still loosely wrapped around her stomach to steady her.

"Um, yeah," Marin answered. "Just a little twitchy today, I guess."

Adam studied her with his devil-may-care green eyes before slowly pulling his arm away. Today, he was dressed in the uniform of the president's protective detail—a dark suit, a pin in the lapel, and an earpiece disappearing into the collar of his white shirt. And he was looking at her as if he couldn't decide if she was a ticking bomb or a plate of nachos he wanted to devour.

Marin took a giant step back, adjusting her chef's jacket as she did so. She longed to ask him if Griffin was near. Except she wasn't sure whether she wanted Adam's answer to be yes or no.

"Yeah, crowds have a way of making certain people twitchy," he drawled.

She had the funny feeling Adam meant something else with his words, but before she could contemplate them further, Simon, one of the assistant ushers was at Marin's shoulder.

"Excuse me, Chef Marin," Simon whispered. "We're setting up the tables for the luncheon. But we can't seem to find the centerpieces."

"Diego put them in the cold storage room with the flowers," Marin said.

"Ah, mystery solved." Simon nodded and turned back toward the White House.

"Wait," Marin called after him. "Diego knew where they were. Why didn't you just check with him?"

Simon shook his head. "He didn't show up for work today, Chef."

No!

There was that tremor running down her spine again. Marin dug her cell phone out of her pocket and hit Diego's number. Her call went straight to voicemail. Adam's hand was on her shoulder before she realized her whole body was shaking. There had to be a simple explanation for why Diego wasn't at work. Although it wasn't like him to just not show up. Especially on a day as busy as this one. Maybe he left a message on her office voicemail? That had to be it. She'd just go and check. And after that, she'd help out in the kitchen where she belonged.

Marin shook off Adam's grip. "Simon, wait for me."

The assistant usher glanced around anxiously. "The First Lady left instructions that you were to have the day off."

Marin's godmother was nowhere in sight. "Don't worry about her." Marin needed to keep her hands busy and her mind occupied or else she'd go crazy.

Adam reached for her arm again. "Marin, are you sure you're okay?"

"No." The word came out like a screech. "I'm not okay. People around me keep getting hurt, or"—she swallowed painfully—"or dying. Now Diego is missing. And I can't seem to breathe normally. I can't stand around doing nothing, waiting for Diego to show. Because he *has to* show up." Swallowing a sob, she turned and rushed after Simon.

HIGH ATOP THE promenade circling the White House roof, Griffin watched Marin pull away from Adam and scurry after the assistant usher. Minutes before, she'd been wandering around the South Lawn, almost as though she were in a trance. Griffin hated how much his chest ached at the sight of her, bewildered and lost among the crowd. *Damn it.* He needed to keep his objectivity in check, and his mind focused on finding The Artist. The link was somewhere in this White House, he was sure of it.

His cell phone buzzed.

"You were supposed to stick to her like glue," Griffin barked at Adam.

"Dude, I'm headed to the kitchen now," Adam snapped. "But I thought you might want to know that she's pretty rattled about her sous chef being AWOL."

"Me, too, since I need some answers from him." Griffin

had spent twelve hours trying to track down Diego Ruiz yesterday. But the guy seemed to have vanished into thin air.

Adam swore into the phone. "Griff, you're not listening—shit!"

A shrill scream pierced the air. The sound came from the west side of the lawn near one of the covered pavilions. Griffin watched as two of the K-9s darted through the throng of visitors. Secret Service agents quickly surrounded the president and his family. The snipers stationed around the perimeter of the roof trained their rifles in the direction of the scream.

"False alarm," Adam relayed from the ground. "The agents in the vicinity said a woman thought she saw a damn snake. It was actually one of the electrical cables."

Griffin blew out a sigh of relief, shrugging off the tension that seemed to have his shoulders in a permanent death grip. "Then maybe you should get back to keeping watch over Marin."

"Now that's more like it," Adam chuckled. "This is a protective detail, not a surveillance detail. I'll keep your girl safe, Griff, don't worry."

"Damn it, Adam, that's not what I meant," Griffin yelled into the phone, but Adam had already disconnected.

He stormed along the promenade around to the solarium, and into the center hall. Charging toward the stairs, he stopped dead in his tracks when he almost collided with Marin.

"Oh!" she exclaimed, nearly toppling back on her ass.

Griffin's arms were around her before he thought better of it. "Careful."

She went completely still. "Griffin."

Just the sound of his name from her lips made him hard. They stood like statues for a long moment, gazing into each other's eyes; the only noises around them were her fractured breathing and Griffin's pulse hammering in his ears. Adam suddenly rounded the corner, shattering the moment. Marin jerked out of Griffin's arms.

"Um, yeah. I'll just make myself scarce." Adam disappeared back down the stairs.

Marin pivoted on her heel and marched to her office. Since Adam had abdicated his surveillance—*and it was a damn surveillance*—Griffin had no choice but to follow her.

"Damn it, Diego, where are you?" she demanded as she slammed down the landline phone in her office.

Griffin leaned a hip against her desk. "Problem?"

The look she shot him shriveled his balls.

"You know, I do have a problem. Lots of them. And they all seemed to have begun around the time you showed up." She jabbed a finger into his chest. "As I see it, Not-So-Special-Agent Keller, the way to solve my problems is for you to get the hell out of my office. And my life."

He stared down at the finger still impaling his chest, because he couldn't look at her and say what chivalry demanded he say. "Look, Marin, I need to apolo—"

"Don't. You. Dare." She punctuated each word with a fingernail to his pectorals. "Man up. You were into me the other night. Don't lie about that. And don't give me some lame excuse for why you suddenly had performance issues." Her furious gaze fell to his crotch.

Performance issues? Griffin shot off the desk.

"Hold on a minute, Marin. I don't have any 'performance issues.' Never have. Never will."

She crossed her arms over her chest. "So, you're just a tease then? Good to know. On behalf of women everywhere, maybe you should get some help with that issue."

The roaring in Griffin's ears did nothing to drown out the loud guffaw from outside the office. He snapped his head around just in time to see Adam doubled over in laughter. Griffin slammed the door shut.

"Listen up, because I'm only going to say this once," Griffin growled.

But Marin wasn't listening. Instead, she was standing over her backpack holding a package wrapped in brown paper. The same one Griffin had shoved inside the bag two days before.

Marin's voice was quiet. "Seth gave me this the other night. I was so upset about Arnold, and later, Seth, that I forgot about it." Slowly, she turned the package over in her hands inspecting it for clues. "It's not even marked. I wonder how he knew it was for me?"

Griffin suddenly went on alert. "Were you expecting one?"

"Not that I recall."

Something about this package gave him the willies. "Let me open it," Griffin commanded.

The look she shot him said she was going to argue, but

she silently gave in, tossing the package on the desk. "Suit yourself."

Griffin grabbed a pair of scissors and slit the brown paper, peeling it back to reveal a generic white shirt box. He tore off the paper and set it aside before carefully opening the box. Marin gasped at the sight of her bloodied chef's jacket. Griffin lunged for her just as her eyes rolled back in her head and her knees gave out.

"Adam!" he yelled.

"DRINK THIS," AUNT Harriett urged.

Marin shivered. She already missed the feel of being cocooned by Griffin's warm body. When she'd come to in his arms, she'd felt safe and protected—just like in her dream. His lips had been pressed against her forehead, whispering at her to wake up. Unfortunately, waking up meant that he deposited her on the sofa in the Yellow Oval Room with the eyes of seven people trained on her like she was a high school science experiment.

"I'm fine." Marin instantly regretted her peevish tone. "But thank you, Aunt Harriett," she added.

Leaning in on Marin's other side, Terrie tried to wrap a blanket over Marin's shoulders.

"You're shaking," the housekeeper said, pointing out the obvious.

Opposite from the sofa where the First Lady and Terrie were hovering over Marin, the FBI agent with the abundance of red hair and perky breasts leaned forward in her chair.

"Chef, we are sending your jacket and the box it was returned in to forensics." She tried to reassure Marin. "Your name and the White House emblem are on the jacket. In all likelihood, this was just a good Samaritan who wanted to return it to you without getting involved."

"My address is unlisted," Marin replied curtly. Did this woman think Marin was that gullible? "And Diego is missing."

"We are looking for Mr. Ruiz," the admiral said. "I promise we'll find him."

Marin glanced over to where Griffin paced, his cell phone glued to his ear. Her traitorous body willed him to look over at her; better yet to come sit beside her, but he kept his eyes averted.

"I'm glad for the opportunity to finally speak with you, Chef," the FBI agent said. "I wanted to ask you about your relationship with Wes Randall, the curator."

Griffin stopped his pacing. His face was a stone mask as he stared down the FBI agent. The First Lady sat up a little straighter beside Marin. The rest of the room's occupants—the admiral, Director Worcester, and Adam—seemed to be on the edge of their seats.

"My relationship?" Marin asked. "What exactly do you mean?"

The FBI agent glanced down at her iPad before speaking. "When we went through Mr. Randall's emails, we found some correspondence between you and him regarding the Cezanne in the library."

Marin tried to recall the many conversations she'd had with Wes over art. "Oh, you mean the 'House on a Hill.' It's stunning, isn't it? My grandfather owns the companion piece. He was thinking of donating it to the White House Historical Society as a gift. Grandfather hates for art to be split up. I relayed the information from Wes to my grandfather's assistant. I never heard whether the other piece arrived yet or not." She looked at the First Lady expectantly.

Aunt Harriett nodded. "Max's gift is very generous. I believe he's sending it later this month."

"What about the Jackson Pollack piece in the map room?" the agent persisted. "Did you ever have occasion to discuss that piece with Mr. Randall?"

Marin's temper was fraying. "Wes and I discussed a lot of art. It's one of my passions. I don't understand what this has to do with my bloody jacket and Diego being missing!"

Terrie draped an arm over Marin's shoulder while Aunt Harriett patted Marin's leg.

"I'm putting you on notice, Agent Morgan, tread lightly here," the admiral warned.

"Tread lightly with *what*?" Marin practically shouted. "What is everyone talking about?"

"We believe Wes's death may be related to some art thefts here in the White House," Director Worcester explained.

Terrie gasped beside her, but Marin was more concerned about the eyes of the agents in the room trained on her, as if waiting for a response.

"Several pieces have been taken and replaced with very authentic looking forgeries," the director continued. "Including the Cezanne and the Jackson Pollack."

Marin flopped back against the sofa. "Wes wouldn't steal any art," she argued. "He'd spent the last twenty-five years in this house. Every piece here was like one of his children. I don't believe he could be involved."

"Me neither," Terrie interjected. "There's no way."

"We don't have any evidence linking him to the thefts," the FBI agent admitted. "In fact, we think he might have become suspicious that some of the pieces in the White House are forgeries. He was concerned about the Pollack in particular. Chef, are you sure he didn't say anything to you about that painting?"

Marin wracked her brain. "He asked me to meet him in the Map Room a few days before he died. He didn't say he wanted to discuss the Pollack, though."

"You didn't meet him?" the FBI agent asked, her interest clearly piqued.

"When I got there, he was talking to Ari, the intern from the curator's office." Marin hesitated. "It sounded like Wes was upset with Ari. I didn't want to intrude, so I left. When I came back a few minutes later, they both were gone."

The FBI agent was scanning her iPad. "Why is this the first I've heard of this Ari person?"

"He's a graduate fellow with the White House Historical Society," the admiral answered. "He only works on

Thursday and Friday."

"I'll need his contact information immediately," the FBI agent insisted.

The admiral nodded. "Of course."

"Chef, I understand you're very knowledgeable about art and antiquities," the agent went on to say. "Have you noticed anything unusual about the art work here at the White House?"

"No." Marin shook her head. "But then again, I wasn't looking. I just assumed everything here was as it should be." She pulled the blanket around her shoulders, grateful for its warmth. The revelations of the past few minutes left her cold. Clearly, nothing in the White House was as it should be.

LESLIE SLAPPED HER iPad down on the conference room table in the Secret Service director's office. "This case gets crazier by the minute."

"We're missing something obvious here." Griffin dragged his fingers through his hair.

"The only thing *obvious* is that there is a string of questionable events and dead bodies connected to that chef, whether she's tripping over them or not," Leslie said.

Griffin crossed his arms over his chest. "I've said it before and I'll say it again, she's not a murderer."

Slumping down into a chair, Leslie sighed dejectedly. "No, I don't think she's capable of killing anyone, either.

And, unlike you, I'm not saying that simply because I want to sleep with her."

"Can we cut the bullshit and discuss the case," Griffin snarled.

Leslie chuckled as she held up both hands in surrender.

The director's secretary stuck her head into the conference room. "Agent Keller, Detective Gerkens from Metro PD is on line two for you."

"Thank you." He picked up the phone and punched in line two. "Good morning, Detective, tell me you're not calling just because you missed me."

"Not particularly, but I wanted to let you and Agent Morgan know that the doorman's body has been transferred to the FBI. The family has a lot of questions and they're not happy. But after looking at the video surveillance tape, I think you and Agent Morgan might be right about his death."

"Is there something specific on the video that makes you say that?" Griffin asked as he put the call on speaker.

"There's a guy who showed up at the front desk who clearly didn't want to be IDed."

Griffin glanced over at Leslie. She arched an eyebrow in question.

"Let me guess," Griffin said. "The guy was delivering a package."

"Bingo. And it was for your favorite chef," the detective added. "Any idea what might have been in there?"

"Her chef's jacket that we used to soak up the blood in the Metro the other night," Griffin explained.

The detective whistled.

"The delivery guy," Leslie said. "Could we be lucky here and have him be a perp you already know?"

"Nah, this guy isn't a local gangbanger. Based on how he handled this crime scene, he's a professional," Detective Gerkens answered. "We've got a BOLO out for him, but since he kept his face averted, it's not likely we'll find him. This guy's slippery. You keep an eye on the chef, Agent Keller, you hear me?"

"Yeah, I hear you, Detective. She's safe here at the White House." But as the words left Griffin's mouth, a tremor of uncertainty seized his gut.

Hanging up, Griffin powered up his iPad and opened up the email from Detective Gerkens. Leslie stood at his shoulder as they both watched the surveillance video.

"Stop!" Leslie commanded when they got to the part with the package. "That's our guy."

There was something familiar about the man hiding beneath the black baseball cap. *Or maybe it was the baseball cap itself.* The back of Griffin's neck tingled when he remembered the jogger trailing Marin on the Mall. He'd been wearing a similar hat.

"Shit!" Griffin opened another file.

"What is it?" Leslie asked.

Griffin loaded the video of the stabbing on the Metro. He zoomed in on the assailant with the hoodie pulled over his head. The bill of a baseball cap was clearly visible. His hands shook when he reached into the file on the table and pulled out the picture of the paper delivery person spotted outside the curator's house. Same sweatshirt. Same damn hat peeking out.

"I missed it," Griffin murmured through the tightness in his throat. "She could have been killed."

"Earth to Griffin," Leslie said. "What are you seeing that I'm not?"

The fire. The pursuer on the Mall. The stabbing on the Metro. The deaths at the Dupont.

"Marin's not our perp. She's a target." His chest constricted painfully. "And this asshole is still out there somewhere."

CHAPTER ELEVEN

Marin scooted out of the way of the butlers who were busy shuttling food from the main kitchen to the big tent in the rose garden. She only had a few minutes before Terrie or Aunt Harriett noticed Marin hadn't come back from the bathroom. The dread she felt over Diego's absence kept rolling through her stomach, making her woozy. She had to find him. Maybe one of his former coworkers in the Navy Mess had heard from the sous chef. Or knew where he'd likely be. The admiral said they were looking for him, but Marin was too on edge to sit around and wait for news.

She cut through the Palm Room leading to the West Wing. Otto was stationed at the door. He let out an excited yip when he saw her. Marin leaned in to give the dog a hug.

"You're turning my K-9 into a lovesick puppy, Chef," Officer Stevens accused. The smile on the Emergency Response Team officer's face took away the sting of his words, however.

"I'm sorry to disturb Otto when he's working. I just needed a hug."

"He's on standby today, so hug away."

Tears welled up in Marin's eyes when the dog nuzzled her cheek. How had her life become so frightening? And why?

"Are you okay, Chef?"

Marin stood up and brushed the dog hair off her jacket. "Yeah, just having a crazy day. I need to check on something in the West Wing." She patted Otto on the head. "You be a good dog."

Otto's body suddenly tensed beneath her hand. A scream came from somewhere within the rose garden. The dog took off like a bullet.

"Not again," Officer Stevens complained. "People keep thinking the media cables are snakes." He jogged after his dog, only to quickly change course when someone called for help. Marin hurried down the path after him.

When she turned the corner, she stopped dead in her tracks. Angie, one of the temporary chefs the White House hired for big events, was on the ground holding her arm; it was oozing with blood. Two of the butlers were gingerly helping her stem the flow.

Officer Stevens crouched down beside her. "What happened?"

"Some guy jumped me," Angie cried. "He stabbed me with something."

"Did you get a look at him?" one of the other officers who'd just arrived asked.

"No. The pervert stayed behind me. He had on leather gloves, if that helps."

Marin cried out sharply before slapping her hand over

her mouth. The creepy guy she'd met on the stairs last week had worn leather gloves.

At her cry, Angie and the crowd surrounding her turned to stare at Marin.

"He thought I was you," Angie accused. "He kept calling me Chef Chevalier. Then the dog showed up, thank God."

The nausea that had been rolling in Marin's stomach for the past hour threatened to come up. She spun around, cutting through the Palm Room to the deserted courtyard between the West Wing and the residence. Gulping in deep breaths, she tried to calm herself. *Was someone trying to kill her?* None of this made any sense.

She staggered in the direction of the carpenter's shop, but she barely made it a step before two strong arms seized her from behind. Terror shot through her. Before whoever it was could get a hand over her mouth, Marin managed to scream. The sound of her own voice buoyed her and she began struggling against the hard body holding her tightly. She kicked her legs wildly and dug her elbow into her assailant's ribs.

"Marin, settle down. It's me."

She flailed her arms and legs a few seconds more before realizing it was Griffin's voice in her ear. Marin went limp in his arms. *Of course it was him.* Who else came to her rescue like a white knight whenever she was in a life or death situation? She turned in his arms and buried her face in his chest, wishing she could crawl inside his body. Griffin ran his hands up and down her back, quietly shushing her.

Footsteps sounded on the pavement.

"Anything?" Griffin asked.

"The dog lost him when he slipped into the crowd," Adam said. "This guy is getting desperate, though. That was a pretty brazen move."

"Let's get her back inside."

"Griffin," she cried. "Why is this happening?"

"We're going to figure it out." He ushered her through the Palm Room and down the center hall. "I won't let him get near you."

Griffin set her down gently on the couch in the reception area of the Secret Service office. He crouched down at her knees in front of her. "Marin, whoever this is, we're going to get him. But I need you to answer a few questions first."

Marin's head was pounding. "Questions? I don't even understand what's happening myself. How could I possibly have any answers?"

The FBI agent sat down beside her. "Chef—Marin," she said, her voice gentle. "You may know something without even realizing it. We have the video surveillance from the Dupont on Saturday. It shows the man who dropped off the package. Can you tell me if you recognize him?"

Griffin placed an iPad on Marin's lap and swiped his finger along the screen. A photo of the man she'd seen on the spiral staircase the other morning popped up. Marin flinched.

"Yes," she whispered.

The FBI agent and Griffin exchanged a look.

"When and where?" Griffin demanded.

"Here. In the White House."

Griffin muttered something beneath his breath.

"Where exactly in the House was he?" the FBI agent continued for him. "Do you remember?"

"Yes, he was coming down the back stairs that connect the main kitchen to the pastry kitchen and the family dining room."

"When was this?" the agent asked.

Marin rubbed her throbbing temple. "Um, last week. The morning of the fire. That was Wednesday, I think?" She looked at Griffin for confirmation.

He nodded. "Was anyone else with him?"

She shook her head. "I didn't see anyone."

"Was Diego with you?" Griffin asked.

Marin shivered. "No. He came in early that day also. But he went directly to the Navy Mess. He said he had to check on a friend or something."

The two agents exchanged another look.

"Oh, God. Diego is in danger, isn't he?" Marin could barely get the question past her dry mouth.

"Whoever this guy is, he didn't want to be seen," the FBI agent said. "By you or anyone else. It's quite possible he's our art thief."

Blinking back tears, Marin stared at the picture on the iPad. "My bloody jacket was in that package. Does this mean he stabbed Anika?"

"He was likely aiming for you," the FBI agent said.

Marin tried to swallow around the lump in her throat. It was all so unbelievable. Anika's brother hadn't been responsible for her stabbing. Marin had. Her chest was now throbbing along with her head. "And Seth? Do you think this man killed him?"

The FBI agent placed a hand on Marin's shoulder. "Among others. If I had to guess, I'd say this guy was trying to flush you out of your apartment. There was no way he could know about the back stairs. But you shouldn't blame yourself for the actions of a madman, Marin. None of this is your fault."

"He had leather gloves on the day he was here. When Angie mentioned them, it made me think of him."

"What the hell is going on?" the president's chief of staff bellowed from inside the director's office. "Are the president and his family safe in the House or not, Director Worcester?"

"We've secured the First Family, sir," the director responded. "My agents have also secured the perimeter of the building. All indications are that this guy slipped off the grounds before our net was in place."

"Well that's reassuring." The chief of staff huffed. "Do we have any idea who this clown is? And why he was wielding a knife at an event that was open to the public?"

Griffin stood and walked over to the open door of the director's office. "We're running his image through facial recognition software right now. The process isn't as quick as it appears in TV crime shows," he explained. "But we suspect he's our art thief."

"That doesn't really give me any more peace of mind, Agent Keller. The last time we spoke, you suspected Chef Chevalier was the damn art thief!"

It took a long second before the chief of staff's words sunk in. But when they did, a cold wave washed over Marin's body. Her breath burned as it sawed through her lungs.

"Wait a minute. You. . ." Marin had to pause a moment to stop her lips from quivering. "You thought I was. . . *a thief?*"

"Not me." The chief of staff pointed an accusing finger at Griffin. "Him."

Griffin's face was impassive and his eyes dark when he finally turned to face Marin. Suddenly it all made sense to her. She'd been right all along. Guys like Griffin Keller only paid attention to women like Marin out of duty. Their romantic dinner on the Truman Balcony and his arousing kisses later in her penthouse had all been part of the ruse. Her only consolation was that he was not a good enough actor to carry out their lovemaking to its conclusion.

If that was actually a consolation.

It was all too much. Marin jerked to her feet on unsteady legs. She would not humiliate herself by crying in front of this jerk. Vomiting on his shoes was a distinct possibility, however.

"Marin," he murmured.

"Don't!" Unfortunately, it came out of her mouth as

more of a sob. She dashed across the hall, through the Map Room, to the women's lavatory. Locking the door behind her, she lost her battle with her nausea.

She wasn't sure how long she sat on the floor of the restroom, a damp hand towel covering her tear-swollen eyes. But she was sure of one thing. Marin Chevalier was not a victim. And she would not waste another tear over Griffin Keller. Not when Diego was still missing and a murdering art thief was on the loose. One who wanted her dead.

There was a knock at the door and a shudder wracked her body.

"Marin, it's Agent Morgan." The FBI agent's voice came from the other side of the paneling. "I thought you might like some cold water."

A cool drink sounded heavenly, but Marin wasn't sure she was ready to face anyone just yet. She reached up and unlocked the door, opening it wide enough to allow her fingers to slip through.

Agent Morgan put the bottle of water in Marin's hand. "I have some animal crackers, too, if you think you're up to it."

Marin grabbed the bag and slid the door shut. She heard Agent Morgan sit down on the floor on the other side.

"I know this is all a bit overwhelming and frightening," Agent Morgan said through the door. "But believe me when I say we'll do everything in our power to find this guy. It's what we do. And I, for one, am very good at my job. I won't let anything happen to you."

Given how the past few days had been going, Marin had to take the agent's word for it. She wasn't sure Agent Morgan was expecting a response, so she chewed on an animal cracker instead.

"Agent Keller won't let anything happen to you, either," Agent Morgan added.

At the mention of Griffin's name, the animal cracker turned to dust in Marin's mouth. She washed it down with a swig of water before she choked.

"Go easy on Griff," the agent continued.

Griff.

Marin nearly gagged again. It would figure that the model-worthy FBI agent would have an intimate nickname for Griffin. He likely had one for the agent, too. The beautiful people had a tendency to stick together. She slammed her eyes shut against the images of how 'Griff' and the sexy redhead *stuck* together. Not that Marin cared about Not-So-Special-Agent Keller any longer. She was done lusting over him. Even if he did ride to her rescue as often in real life as he did in her dreams.

"When we found the original paintings at a crime scene last week, they were wrapped in a dish towel from the White House kitchen. It was only natural that we begin our investigation with the kitchen staff," Agent Morgan explained.

A kitchen dish towel?

"That's stupid," Marin said before she realized she was speaking out loud. "Anyone working in the House could pass through the kitchen and pick one of those up."

"Mmm," Agent Morgan agreed. She sounded as though she were chewing on something.

Marin pulled the door open. "That's a ridiculous way to go about investigating art theft."

Agent Morgan pulled an animal cracker out of her own bag and contemplated it before she spoke. "We have to begin somewhere. Most times, we start with much less than a dish towel." She popped the cookie into her mouth.

"Wow, that's encouraging."

"You mentioned that your sous chef, Diego, came in early that morning." Agent Morgan was suddenly scrutinizing Marin just as she had her cookie minutes before.

Marin was sorry she'd opened the door. "Yes. He wanted to work on the marzipan figures."

"And did he?"

"I told you, he stopped by the Navy Mess first. But I assume he did after that. They were finished when I came up from the chocolate shop."

Agent Moran tilted her head. She had a long, elegant neck, Marin noticed with disgust.

"But Diego may have come in early to meet with someone," the agent pointed out. "And he could have told you he was in early to make the marzipan just to cover his tracks."

Marin scrambled to her feet. "No! Diego isn't any more of a thief than I am! You said yourself that the creepy guy on the stairs is probably the one stealing the art. There's no need to blame an innocent man. Or is that how this works?

Guilty until proven innocent?"

The FBI agent stood up gracefully, brushing crumbs off her pants as she did so. "The 'creepy guy on the stairs' wasn't working alone, Marin. I'm just throwing out theories to see what sticks."

"No, you're throwing my friend under the bus!" Marin cried. "And since I seem to be the only one concerned about Diego, I'm going to find him."

"I can't let you do that," Griffin said from the doorway of the Map Room.

THE FRANTIC EXPRESSION on Marin's face made Griffin's chest seize. Or maybe it was the way her mouth seemed to turn up in disgust when she looked at him that made it so hard to breathe. He could have decked the president's chief of staff for his reckless words earlier. Marin would have found out sooner or later that she'd been a suspect, but Griffin would have preferred it happened later. *Much later.* The poor woman was reeling with fear for herself and her friends. Not only that, Marin was also likely wrecked with guilt over the injuries and deaths of innocent people. If Griffin had learned anything about her these past few days, it was that she was a caring, sensitive woman. He worried this whole situation could break her. Griffin was going to do his best not to let that happen.

She crossed her arms beneath those gorgeous breasts of hers. Defiance shined brilliantly in her blue eyes. "You are not the boss of me, Agent Keller."

"No, but I am going to do everything in my power to keep you safe."

And by safe, Griffin meant that knife-wielding bastard trying to kill her wouldn't touch a single silky hair on Marin's head.

"Why? So you can arrest me for shoplifting sugar flowers from the White House? Or maybe I'm going to be charged with embezzling marzipan? Or will counterfeiting crumpets be my crime?"

He might have laughed at her quips, but Marin was fuming. This was good. Griffin could work with anger. Her despair and fear would kill him, though. He wouldn't be able to do his job knowing that she needed comfort and he wasn't able to be the one to give it to her. No, he'd cultivate her anger instead. It would keep her from falling down a well of hopelessness. And this way Griffin would be able to hunt down art thieves and murderers worry-free.

"Guilty conscience, Marin?" he asked, unashamedly baiting her.

"You're an asshole!"

From behind Marin, Leslie shot him a look that said he was that and a whole lot more. Perfect. Mission accomplished.

"Regardless, I'm calling the shots on this case and you are going into protective custody."

"I'm not going anywhere with you," she protested.

"A safe house is a smart idea, Marin," Leslie put in. "It won't be long until this is over."

"How long?" Marin demanded. "How long do I have to stay in protective custody?"

Leslie shot Griffin a concerned look. It would likely take days to find the guy who was pursuing Marin; provided he slipped up and made a mistake. The attack on the White House grounds today showed just how desperate he'd become, though. Still, Griffin had no definitive answer to give Marin.

"We'll do everything in our power to get you to your cousin's wedding," he assured her, hoping like hell he could keep his word.

"Ha! You don't need to be worrying about Ava's wedding any longer, because you are *not* going with me."

Leslie arched an eyebrow at him. Griffin kept his expression stoic despite the fact that a large part of him wanted to take Marin to that wedding. He wanted to protect her from the slings and arrows of her cousin and her jet-set friends. Hell, he wanted to hold her in his arms on the dance floor all night. And he hated to dance.

"We need to get you out of sight," Leslie urged. "You're compromising the First Family every moment we delay."

Marin wilted slightly at Leslie's words. "You're right," she murmured. "I don't want anyone else hurt because of me."

She headed in Griffin's direction on wobbly legs. He reached out a hand to steady her, but she recoiled like a shotgun after firing. The pain of her rejection was like a sucker punch in his gut.

"Allow me." Adam stepped around Griffin and held out his elbow to Marin as if he was escorting her to a damn debutante ball.

Griffin bit his tongue. Hard. Adam taunted him with a wink over Marin's shoulder before leading her down the hall. As much as he hated Marin's preference for Adam right now, it was necessary. If he couldn't have eyes on Marin twenty-four seven, Adam or Ben would. Griffin wasn't about to trust her safety to anyone else.

CHAPTER TWELVE

TERRIE HANDED MARIN an overnight bag with clothes and toiletries the housekeeper kept in the White House for unexpected guests.

"It's going to be okay," she promised as she hugged Marin tightly. "Griffin will take care of this. You can trust him."

Griffin was the last person Marin trusted right now. But since a guy with a knife was bent on harming her, Marin figured she didn't have much choice in the matter. Clearly, Not-So-Special-Agent Keller did whatever it took to catch his man or woman—even if it meant seducing them. At least Griffin's hunger for justice was one consolation for being dictated to by the arrogant man.

They made the trip to the safe house in one of the armored SUVs the Secret Service used to transport the president incognito. Marin was ushered out of the residence so quickly, she didn't get to say good-bye to the First Family.

"The president and his family have been sequestered until we complete a sweep of the White House," Adam explained, as if reading her thoughts. "But both he and Mrs. Manning are very concerned for your safety."

Marin nodded before directing her gaze out the window. She jumped when her cell phone rang in her pocket. "Please be Diego," she murmured.

It wasn't. Ava's face popped up on the screen. Adam snatched her phone out of her hands before she could answer it.

"Sorry," he said. "But you're going to have to cut off all contact for now."

"But my family!"

"Your parents will be informed. The First Lady insisted on it. For everyone else, though, you're going to have to maintain radio silence." Adam did a double take at Ava's picture on the screen. He wiggled an eyebrow at Marin. "But you're welcome to give her a call and set me up with her when this is all over."

"Too late," Marin replied. "That's the bridezilla. Trust me, the male species dodged a bullet. She's taken."

"The good ones always are," Adam mumbled as he stuck her cell phone into his pocket.

Marin peered through the van's blacked-out windows. They were headed into Old Town Alexandria, it appeared. The van made a series of turns before finally slipping between two row houses just blocks from the water. A garage door opened and the driver pulled inside. Adam placed a hand on Marin's arm, stalling her from climbing out of the van until the garage door was completely closed behind them.

Adam shot her a smile that wasn't as encouraging as it was cheeky. "Welcome to your home away from home,

Marin."

He escorted her inside the house. The first floor was a hodgepodge of bulky furniture that looked like it had come from a government warehouse. Thick drapes covered the front windows, making the narrow room feel like a cave.

"I'm pretty sure I've seen this place in *Architectural Digest*," Marin quipped.

"Oh, but wait until you've seen the kitchen." Adam pointed toward the back of the house.

Marin really hoped the kitchen was functional. She couldn't imagine being trapped inside this place for hours on end and not being able to cook. Thankfully, the room was in stark contrast to the rest of the house. Bright and airy, the kitchen featured Scandinavian cabinets in pickled oak with white Corian countertops, and a shiny linoleum floor. The décor was dated, but the appliances looked passable. A comfortable looking banquette with a white Formica table dominated the eating space. Marin was happy to see the sun shining through an unblocked window.

A woman turned from the refrigerator where she was unloading groceries.

"Hi there," she said. "I'm Agent Christine Groesch." She gestured to the bags of food. "Griff thought you'd like to have some supplies to keep your mind off being cooped up."

'Griff' again.

Marin hated the tingly sensation that came along with Griffin understanding how she'd feel being in the safe house all day. Not only that, but he'd known what would make her happy, damn it.

"Please tell me you got pizza pockets," Adam pleaded before he began rummaging through the freezer.

"Ugh, you have a diet worse than my thirteen-year-old nephew," Agent Groesch said. "I don't know how you manage to pass your physical each year after eating all those processed foods."

Adam winked at her. "Genetics, Christine. I'm blessed."

Stepping around Adam, Marin pulled a big bag of chocolate chips out of one of the grocery bags.

Agent Groesch looked at her sheepishly. "I wasn't sure whether chocolate chip cookies were beneath a pastry chef of your reputation."

"Are you kidding?" Marin grinned at both agents. "I won my first cooking competition when I was five with none other than chocolate chip cookies. They're my go-to comfort food to bake. And after this weekend, I could use a whole bunch of them."

Adam high-fived Agent Groesch. "I have a feeling this assignment is going to be delicious." He laughed at his own pun. "I'm just going to call in and let Griffin-the-Great know the eagle has landed."

Agent Groesch chuckled as Adam left the room. "It's fortunate that those three boys are merely *brothers from another mother* because I don't think one woman could survive raising them together. Heck, there were some days when I thought the Secret Service couldn't survive having them all as rookie agents."

Marin opened the cabinet doors in search of a mixing bowl. She remembered what Griffin had said about Adam and Ben. "I doubt there isn't anything one wouldn't do for the others."

Finally finding what she was looking for, Marin turned to catch the agent smiling knowingly at her.

"I can see why Griff is so protective of you," Agent Groesch said. "Most women are resentful of a man's buddies. Especially when they are as close as those three. I'm glad he's found someone who is supportive. Believe me, being in the Secret Service takes a toll on nearly every relationship an agent has. Those three swore to remain confirmed bachelors for life. Something tells me that might not be the case anymore."

"Uh-um, I think you've misunderstood the situation," Marin stammered. She was lucky she could even get the words out; she was so dumbfounded by the agent's assumption. "The only reason Agent Keller is protective of me is because it's his job." She hated the lump that formed in her throat.

Christine's smile didn't waver. "We'll see," was all she said.

Marin opened her mouth to argue more, but the sound of a dog's nails scratching on the linoleum made her turn to the door instead.

"Otto," she cried, crouching down to wrap her arms around the dog's thick neck.

"The third member of our team has arrived," Adam

announced.

"Otto is staying with me?"

Adam's face softened. "Griffin thought you might feel better having him here."

"I rest my case," Agent Groesch declared from behind Marin.

The lump in Marin's throat became more painful. She didn't want Griffin to be kind to her. It made it difficult to hold on to her loathing of him.

TWENTY-FOUR HOURS LATER, Griffin staggered into the Secret Service headquarters, a nondescript building on H Street. He was exhausted and frustrated at not being able to locate either Diego Ruiz or the elusive art thief who was targeting Marin.

"Detective Gerkens was right," he said as he dropped into a chair in Ben's office/lab. "This guy is slippery. It's like he evaporated among the crowd on the South Lawn yesterday."

"Lucky for you, I've got a really cool program that can put a name to a face. And it came up with a hit twenty minutes ago." Ben strolled over to one of the several computers in the room and punched a few buttons on the keyboard. The suspect's picture from the Dupont's video surveillance camera popped up on the big screen. "His name is Yerik Salenko. He's a former member of the Ukraine Spetsnaz."

"He's special forces?" Griffin asked. He, Ben, and Adam had served in a similar capacity for the United States Army. The distinction meant that Salenko was as highly trained as Griffin and his friends. That explained a lot. It also made Griffin more anxious about Marin.

Ben clicked to a photo of Salenko in his military uniform. "He was for several years. After the fall of the Ukrainian government, though, most members of the Spetsnaz have become mercenaries, hiring themselves out as henchmen to the highest bidder. Your gang of counterfeiters likely needed someone skilled in warfare. And sharpshooters," Ben added. "Salenko is on the list of snipers Adam gave you the other day."

"Damn it."

"Well, on the positive side, there's always the possibility this guy's a one-man show. He's likely your shooter from New Jersey. Once he saw that you found the paintings, he came back to the White House to make sure no one else talked."

"Your theory doesn't answer the question of why a counterfeiting ring's thug for hire is stealing paintings from the White House." Griffin began rummaging through Ben's desk drawers. He sighed with relief when he pulled out a package of peanut butter crackers. Griffin couldn't remember when he'd eaten last. "It's times like these that I'm glad you live the Boy Scout motto and you're always prepared."

"We had homemade beignets at the safe house this morning." Ben handed Griffin a bottle of water. "They were outstanding."

Griffin's stomach growled. His chest seized, too, but he was ignoring that particular sensation.

"How is she?" he asked.

Ben leaned a hip on the corner of his desk. "She's tougher than she looks. Most women would be a helpless, quivering mess after going through what she's been through. Not Marin. She keeps carrying on. I like her."

"Your job isn't to 'like her,'" Griffin growled. "It's to protect her."

"Oh, don't worry. Adam has taken protecting Marin to a whole new level."

"What the hell is that supposed to mean?" Griffin snapped as he bolted from his chair. "He damn well better not be sleeping with her!" Too late, he realized Ben was baiting him.

"You are such a sucker." Ben laughed. "Never for a woman before, though. This is new. And interesting."

Griffin sat back down with a thud, pressing his palms to the arms of the chair to keep from giving his friend a well-deserved fat lip.

"The only one sleeping with Marin is the dog," Ben informed him. "But, I'd be worried about Otto if I was you. He's likely to chew your balls off if you come between him and his lady."

He shot the bird at Ben, then shoved another peanut butter cracker in his mouth. It tasted like chalk, but Griffin managed to swallow it anyway.

Ben grew solemn. "She's worried about Diego."

"Yeah," Griffin said. "He's just as slippery as our Ukrainian friend. He seems to have disappeared without a trace."

"Diego went through some pretty extensive background checks when he came to the Navy Mess." Ben pulled up the sous chef's service record on the computer screen. "He had a gang-related run-in with the police when he was a teenager. The judge gave him the option of joining the Navy or going to jail. I'd say Diego made the right choice."

"But could his past have been used against him to co-opt him into stealing art from the White House?"

Ben looked at him skeptically. "You think that's why he's gone off the grid? Diego's in on this?"

"If so, he's likely already died an agonizing death." Griffin rubbed a hand over his eyes. "The preliminary ruling from the FBI's ME indicates the poor doorman at the Dupont was injected with enough potassium to make it look like a heart attack."

"Shit," Ben said.

"Yeah, either way, I'm probably going to be delivering bad news to Marin."

Griffin's cell phone rang. "Agent Keller," he answered.

"Hey there, Keller," the voice on the other end said. "I found that sous chef you were looking for."

THAT EVENING, MARIN sat across from Ben at the Formica

table in the safe house and watched proudly as he annihilated a plate of red beans and rice along with some citrus marinated shrimp with Louis sauce.

"I'll be your fish shop errand boy any day you ask if you'll keep cooking like this for me," Ben promised with a contented smile on his boyish face.

"I like a man who isn't afraid of a seafood market," Marin teased. "Thanks for getting the shrimp for me."

"My momma taught me right." Ben scraped his fork along the empty plate. "My family owns a place on the Eastern Shore of Maryland. Fishermen sell their catches right out of our marina."

"Is there a restaurant, too?"

"Nah, it's more like a gourmet tackle shop," Ben explained. "We sell bait, wine, and fancy sandwiches. People drive their boats up as if it's an old-fashioned drive-in."

"That sounds like a fun place to grow up." She carried Ben's plate over to the sink.

"I didn't move there until I was thirteen. I grew up in New Jersey," Ben said.

"What made your parents decide to relocate?"

"We moved to live with my grandfather after my dad died." Ben's eyes dimmed briefly. "My father was a cop. He was killed in the line of duty."

"I'm sorry." The words sounded inadequate, but Marin couldn't think of anything else to say. "That had to be difficult for a teenager to go through."

He shrugged. "It was hardest on my mom. She was lost for a long time without my dad. Law enforcement isn't conducive to long, happy marriages. If you aren't getting shot during a domestic dispute, you're working crazy hours and seeing things that make it difficult to have a normal relationship."

She cut a piece of chocolate cake and slid it onto a plate. "But you went into law enforcement. Why?" Marin asked as she placed the cake in front of him.

"I come from a long line of cops. But I don't plan on making the same mistake as the rest of my family. I'd never subject a wife and kids to this lifestyle."

"Never?" she repeated. "But what if you meet someone and fall in love?"

His eyes dimmed again for a split second. "Love is for suckers."

They were both quiet while Ben took a bite of his cake and Marin gathered the ingredients for a French toast casserole she wanted to make for breakfast. She thought back to something Agent Groesch had said the day before. *Those three swore to remain confirmed bachelors for life.*

"So, you, Adam, and Griffin have all decided never to marry?" Not that she cared what Griffin Keller did with his life.

Ben's eyes twinkled as though he suspected she did care. A lot. "Yep, we've devoted our lives to the Secret Service instead."

"But Griffin's leaving the Secret Service," she argued. "He said it was too stressful for him. . ."

She realized her mistake as soon as she heard Ben's loud snort of laughter. Griffin had never meant to retire. Neither did he want a job with the Chevalier hotels. It was all part of the web of lies he'd used to reel her in. He'd been playing her the whole time. And stupid Marin had fallen for it. All of it.

Blinking back tears, she furiously chopped pecans. How could she have been so gullible? And why did she still care?

"Something smells good in here."

Marin nearly chopped off her finger at the sound of Griffin's voice.

"'Good' doesn't even begin to describe Marin's cooking," Ben raved.

Marin kept her back to both men, mincing the pecans into sawdust.

"Just don't tell my mom I said someone else makes shrimp better than she does," Ben added. "This cake is unbelievable, too."

As far as she could tell, Griffin hadn't moved from the threshold of the kitchen. She could feel his eyes on her, though. Her mouth went dry, but she refused to give him the satisfaction of seeing her so distressed.

"Did you and Adam leave anything for me?" Griffin asked.

Before Ben could answer, Marin reached into the cabinet and pulled out a can of Spam she'd found in the pantry earlier. She turned and slammed it on the counter in front of Griffin.

"Bon appetit."

She couldn't help it. Her gaze drank him in. Marin suddenly felt appalled at her behavior. Casually dressed in faded jeans and a Boston Bruins T-shirt, Griffin appeared as though he hadn't slept in days. His eyes were bloodshot, his hair wild, and dark stubble shadowed his face. He looked weary, rumpled, and amazingly, still incredibly sexy. It wasn't fair.

He shut his eyes and sighed. "I came here to give you the news about Diego, Marin. Not to fight with you."

Marin grabbed at the counter in order to steady her suddenly wobbly knees. "Diego? Is he—is he. . ." She couldn't finish the sentence.

Griffin opened his eyes. They were filled with wonder. "He's alive," he said.

She gasped in relief. "He's. . . he's alive?"

"Yeah." Griffin grabbed at the back of his neck. "And married."

"Wait. What?" Marin's head was spinning. "What do you mean *married*?"

"The reason he was AWOL is because his partner, one of the waiters in the Navy Mess, was having a difficult time coming out to his family. Once he did, the two men got married."

"That's it?" Marin cried. "He skipped out on work on one of the busiest days of the year *to elope*? And he didn't bother to tell anyone? I spent the last two days *worried sick* over that man! I could kill him myself just for that." She picked up the knife again, poured more pecans on the cutting board and began viciously chopping. "Well, isn't that just like a man for you? All he cares about is his end goal. He doesn't care about who might get hurt in the process. As long as he gets what he wants!"

"Damn it, Marin, I was doing my job!" Griffin was suddenly beside her.

The knife stilled in Marin's hand. "Your 'job'? Your *job*." She slowly turned and pointed the tip of the blade at Griffin's chest. "Was it your 'job' to kiss me senseless? Or how about when you had your hands and mouth all over my body, was that your 'job,' too, huh?" She jabbed the knife at him. "Or what about when you were making me—"

"For crying out loud, Ben, can you give us some privacy!" Griffin yelled, his eyes never leaving Marin's face.

"Just when it was getting good," Ben mumbled. "Come on, Otto, let's go check your pee mail. Maybe we'll catch up with Adam on his run while we're out."

"Put the knife down, Marin," Griffin commanded once Ben and the dog had left the kitchen.

Marin's hand holding the knife shook, but she couldn't seem to get the rest of her body to move.

"Please," he urged softly.

The knife landed on the counter with a clank. Her eyes stung and her face burned with humiliation. This man had too much power over her. And stupid woman that she was, Marin was about to give him more.

"You kissed me," she choked out. "Why did you do that? It wasn't fair."

He stepped in closer so their bodies were only separated by a distance the same width as the blade of the knife she'd just tossed on the counter. Marin breathed him in. Despite being exhausted and bedraggled, Griffin still smelled crisp and clean, like a freshly showered man. The guy was a menace to women everywhere.

"I kissed you, Marin, because I couldn't *not* kiss you." His soft voice was like a caress to her skin. "I'd be lying if I said I tried to avoid kissing you. Because I really didn't. Yeah, it was wrong, but I'm not going to apologize. From the moment I saw you standing in the pastry kitchen looking like an Amazon goddess, I knew I had to touch you. To kiss you. And when I finally did, it felt anything but wrong." He brushed a fingertip along her jawline making Marin's breath hitch in her lungs. "You enthralled me from the very beginning. Kissing you"—he leaned in closer so that his lips were hovering over hers—"kissing you, Marin Chevalier, was inevitable."

The rasp of his breath scorched the tender skin on her cheek. But Marin didn't care because seconds later he was opening her mouth with his. He kissed her slowly, reverently, as though he was reacquainting himself with her mouth. Marin wasn't as patient. Fisting her hands in his T-shirt, she tugged him closer. He made a rough sound in the back of his throat when their tongues collided. His lips on her mouth suddenly became more urgent.

Marin felt the cold hard door of the refrigerator at her back. Griffin cupped her face as he delved into her hungrily, now just as impatient as she was. She slid her fingers beneath his shirt, spreading them out over his warm skin. He shuddered when she traced the muscles on his stomach. Feeling empowered, Marin rubbed her pelvis against his. Griffin nipped at her lips before moving to her neck. He swore roughly against her skin. She arched her back to give him greater access, smacking her head against the steel door when she did so.

"I didn't want to stop the other night, Marin," he whispered near her ear. "You have to know that."

"But you did and now you owe me," she insisted.

She didn't want to think about that night. All she wanted was the here and now with this beautiful man before she woke up from what was certainly a dream. Marin wrapped her fingers around his skull pulling his mouth down to hers.

"And you can start by shutting up and kissing me."

Griffin's grin was merciless, his eyes wicked. Using his hard body to press hers more fully against the fridge, he gently pulled her hands from his face and placed her palms against the cool door. He unstrapped his holster and carefully lifted it over his head, placing the gun on top of the refrigerator. Taking her hand, he maneuvered her onto the padded bench of the banquette in the corner of the room, his own body following her down.

"I think you need to be more specific, Chef." One of his hands slid between their bodies as his lips nuzzled her jaw. "I need to know *where* you want me to kiss you."

A low moan escaped from the back of her mouth when Griffin's talented fingers slipped inside her shorts.

"Am I getting warmer?" He teased the corner of her mouth with the tip of his tongue.

Marin squirmed when his finger found her wet seam. His other hand left her chin to gently knead her breast. She tilted her face toward his and sank her teeth into his full bottom lip. Lifting her hands from the refrigerator door, she slipped them into the back pockets of his jeans where she dug her fingers into his ass.

"Kiss me, Griffin," she pleaded. "Kiss me everywhere."

He didn't disappoint. Griffin took her mouth in a demanding kiss while his hands simultaneously pleasured other parts of her body. Marin's stomach quivered at the full sensual assault. Griffin's tongue slid over hers while his finger mimicked the same motion down below. She gasped for air, her body on the verge of shattering.

The kitchen window shattered instead.

CHAPTER THIRTEEN

GRIFFIN INSTINCTIVELY JUMPED to his feet and turned to shield Marin with his body. When he reached for his service weapon at his waist, it wasn't there. He swore violently as he spied it eight feet across the room just as two big men jumped through the broken window blocking his path to his weapon. Neither of them was the Ukrainian special forces jerk with the vendetta against Marin. But both seemed bent on doing the same kind of harm.

Adam and Ben—and even the damn dog—were out of the safe house. A fact these morons probably already knew. Two against one wasn't the best odds, especially without a gun. Griffin would have to improvise.

Grabbing one of the wooden chairs from the table, he smashed it on the floor, startling the two intruders and giving him a jagged post of wood to use as a weapon at the same time. The one with a spare tire for a neck dodged out of the way of the splintered wood while the bald guy with the bulging eyes made a beeline for Griffin.

Making sure to keep Marin behind him, Griffin lunged at the bald guy, jabbing him hard in the face with the fractured tip of the stool. Caught by surprise, bald guy howled as he staggered backward. The other guy wasted no time pulling a Glock out of his jacket and aiming it at Griffin's chest. In one quick move, perfected during his hockey days, Griffin shoved Marin to the floor just as the bullet flew past his ear and landed in the oven door with a loud ping.

Marin grabbed his hand and shoved a fire extinguisher into it. Griffin could have kissed her right then and there. Instead, he pulled the pin, turned and fired a stream of pressurized nitrogen and CO_2 into the gunman's face. The second gunshot went wild as the big man screamed in agony.

Griffin jumped to his feet, using the fire extinguisher as a weapon to crack the gunman over the head. The hit knocked the guy out cold. When Griffin turned around, however, he was staring down the barrel of a Glock the bald guy had trained on him. The thug sneered.

In that instant, Griffin's heart shattered painfully. He had failed Marin. God knew what these brutes had in store for her. He met her wide eyes behind the intruder as the guy began to squeeze the trigger. "I'm sorry," Griffin mouthed to Marin while he waited for the shot that would end his life.

It never came.

The man holding the Glock began to gurgle and his eyes bugged out even further as he struggled to breathe. The gun discharged its bullet into the wall somewhere behind Griffin just as the thug slumped to the floor, both hands clutching his chest. Griffin jumped over his prone body, being careful not to dislodge the knife jabbed into his heart from behind. He grabbed Marin by the shoulders.

"Is he dead?" she whispered.

"Let's hope so." Griffin steered her toward the front of the house, grabbing his holster as they left the kitchen. "Come on, Marin. We need to get out of here."

But she was transfixed by the man on the floor with the knife in his back. "I killed a man." Her voice trembled.

They didn't have time for this. The safe house had been compromised. He needed to get Marin out of there quickly.

Griffin cupped her chin, capturing her watery blue-eyed gaze with his. "It was self-defense. He was going to kill you."

"And you, too."

"Yeah." He allowed himself a quick sigh of relief. "And I'm going to thank you properly for saving my life later. But right now, we need to move. Hopefully, we can intercept Adam and Ben."

He laced his fingers through hers, tugging her to the front of the house where he could peek out the window. The street looked clear, but years on the job had taught him that didn't mean anything. Unbolting the front door, he led the way out. Marin followed on his heels. Since Griffin had Ubered over to the safe house they had no choice but to escape on foot. There was no sign of his buddies. Griffin hoped that was because they were blocks away from the house rather than bleeding out in the alley next door.

They headed east toward the water. Just as they made it

to the middle of the block, a car engine revved behind them. Griffin looked back to see a tan sedan screaming down the street, headed right for him and Marin. He shoved Marin down an alley, covering her with his body just in case the driver was armed. The car sped past them and screeched to a halt at the corner. Griffin pulled Marin toward the chain link fence that led to the next street and began to hoist her over.

"He's coming back!" Marin cried.

Griffin turned just as the car blocked the entrance to the alley. He aimed his gun at the driver. Someone else in the car shouted something in what sounded like Greek and the car sped off.

"Come on." Griffin yanked Marin off the fence and dragged her out of the alley right when the sedan rounded the corner.

"Will you make up your mind already?" she cried in exasperation.

But she easily fell into step beside him. Their long strides allowed them to make it midway to the next block before they heard the loud shouts in Greek come from the street beside them. The idiots had fallen for Griffin's deception.

"This way." He led her into the lobby of a small boutique hotel at the corner. From there, Griffin had a bird's eye view of the Alexandria waterfront and the two side streets leading up to it. He pulled out his phone and quickly tried Adam. No answer. *Damn it.*

"Griffin," Marin whispered urgently.

She pulled him behind one of the potted trees just as the sedan cruised past the wall of glass at the front of the lobby.

Around them, it felt like a frat party was going on. "Make sure you have everything you need for the river cruise," one of the college-aged kids called out. "The boat is leaving in ten minutes."

A boat. That would work. He had to get Marin out of the area. Their location had become known somehow and Griffin didn't feel comfortable sticking around Old Town a moment longer than they had to. He led Marin over to the concierge desk.

"Do you sell tickets to the monument cruise?" he asked.

The concierge shot him a wary look. "You don't want to take the cruise tonight." He gestured to the coeds in the lobby. "It's gonna be full of a couple hundred of those jokers trying to turn it into a booze cruise. I can sell you tickets for tomorrow if you want."

Marin suddenly draped herself over Griffin's shoulder. "But I want to go tonight, sweet cheeks."

Sweet cheeks? Griffin did his best not to look surprised. Clearly, she was trying to help out. "Whatever the lady wants," he said trying to play along.

The concierge bit back a smirk before he shrugged. "Sure thing, mister."

The spring breakers were already making their way across the street to the pier when the sedan turned the corner again. The car paused to let the kids cross. Griffin jumped behind the valet stand, pulling Marin between his body and the brick wall, to avoid being seen.

"Sweet cheeks?" He asked the question while his lips grazed against her neck. The gesture was meant to calm her down. As usual, touching her had the opposite effect on him.

She shivered against him as she fisted her hands in his T-shirt. "I'm sorry. I don't seem to know who I am right now."

Griffin glanced into her eyes, still wide with panic. He brushed a gentle kiss across her trembling lips. "You're doing fine, Marin. Just hang in there a few more minutes until we're safely aboard the boat."

She nodded, slowly at first, but then with more confidence. It was all Griffin could do not to keep kissing her with more passion. He hated how this experience would forever alter her, but he couldn't help but be proud of the way she was fighting to keep her composure. Ben was right; Marin was tougher than she looked. Griffin just hoped she could hang on to that toughness for a little while longer.

"Where's our guy?" he whispered against her cheek.

It took her a few seconds longer to focus. "He's driving past now."

"Keep watching him. When he turns the corner, we're going to briskly make our way over to the pier."

She nodded slightly. "Now," she said a moment later.

Hand in hand, they headed for the gangplank of the riverboat. He was handing the purser their tickets when the sedan come at the pier from another side street. Marin flinched beside him.

"Shit," he mumbled.

There was no place for them to hide. Griffin hurried Marin up the gangplank just as the crew was untying the lines mooring the boat to the pier. The passenger of the sedan got out and argued with the purser. Almost immediately, a beat cop on a bicycle rode up and Griffin was finally able to breathe a sigh of relief. When the boat began to push away from the pier, his cell phone rang.

"Where the hell are you?" Adam asked.

"Taking a river cruise on the Cherry Blossom," he answered as he steered Marin to the bow of the boat. "We had a couple unwanted guests at the house."

"All we have here is a broken window and a shit-load of blood. It looks like they sent in a cleanup immediately."

Griffin glanced at Marin. She was silently contemplating her hands. Her skin was dotted with dried blood spatters from when she'd stabbed one of the intruders in the back.

"We had a sendoff party at the pier," Griffin said. "Two men in a tan Ford sedan. New Jersey plates. I couldn't make out the number. We were too busy trying not to get run down."

"Were any of their party the Ukrainian sharp shooter?"

"No. A whole new cast of characters today."

Adam swore. "They'll be waiting for you to disembark when the cruise ends in two hours. I'll make sure the marina is secure."

Griffin glanced around at the passengers crowded against the rails. "Negative. Too risky. This boat is filled with civilians. And I don't trust our Ukrainian friend not to be hanging out on a rooftop ready to pick people off. I have another plan."

MARIN STOOD IN the cramped bathroom on the riverboat, feverishly scrubbing her hands beneath a stream of warm water. She pushed the button on the soap dispenser again. Still empty. It was no use; the blood stains weren't coming off. Tears blurred her eyes, but they couldn't erase the vision of her hand plunging an eight-inch chef's knife into a man's back. She abhorred violence; yet she'd killed another human being without giving it a second thought.

"He was going to kill Griffin," she reminded herself. The reminder didn't help to calm her.

There was a soft knock on the door and she jumped.

"Marin, open up," Griffin commanded.

Hysterical laughter bubbled up uncontrollably from within her. She didn't want to open the door. People got hurt or died when Griffin was around. Kissing him never ended well, either. And yet, she still jumped his bones every chance she got. She was embarrassed how often that happened.

"Marin." He knocked with a little more urgency this time.

What if more men with guns or knives were on board? Marin immediately sobered. She opened the door, telling herself he had a gun and could protect her.

Griffin stepped into the small room, locking the door behind him. He pulled a dark green fanny pack out of a plastic bag and placed it on the sink.

"You went shopping in the gift shop?" she asked incredulously.

His eyes narrowed at her. "I needed something to keep my gun in." He pulled out his revolver and his cell phone and wrapped both tightly in the plastic bag the fanny pack had come in. "Can you swim?"

"Why?" Marin's hysteria was bubbling up again.

"We're making an unscheduled exit in five minutes."

"We're *swimming* to shore? It's nearly dark out there."

"Exactly. No one will see us."

Marin was beginning to get a little miffed at his tone. "I don't understand why we can't just hide here until the cruise is finished. You told Adam where we are. He can come get us."

"This boat is filled with innocent bystanders, Marin." He shoved the plastic bag inside the fanny pack. "We can't afford any more collateral injuries. Or deaths."

Her breathing seemed to stop all at once. Light-headed, Marin sat down on the closed toilet, her thoughts drifting to Anika, Arnold, and Seth. All three of them injured or dead. Because of her. She gulped for air.

Griffin swore softly before crouching down in front of her knees. "I'm sorry, Marin. But I can't sugarcoat this. None of this is your fault, though. You need to keep telling yourself that."

She nodded and swiped at her eyes. It was easy to say

she wasn't to blame; believing it was a different story, however.

"Is there room in there for my phone?" she asked as she pulled it out of her back pocket.

He went completely still. "You have your cell phone with you?" Griffin asked, his tone menacing. "Adam was supposed to lock that down."

Marin looked anywhere but at Griffin's stormy eyes. "I-I took it back when Adam was in the shower."

Griffin flinched at the word shower. Then, he let out a string of expletives that would have likely stunned the crew of sailors operating the boat they were on.

"It was before I knew Diego was safe." She shot the words back at him defensively. "I needed to keep trying to reach him."

He snatched the phone from her hands. "Unlock it," he demanded.

Doing as she was told, she punched in her passcode.

He jumped to his feet and swore violently again. "You have your damn locator on."

"Doesn't everybody?" she asked. "Oh crap," she added sheepishly, suddenly realizing how much danger she'd put herself—and Griffin—in. "I only powered up for a few minutes in the safe house and then again just now. But that was all it took, wasn't it? I'm the reason they found us."

Griffin didn't bother acknowledging her stupidity. "Can. You. Swim?" he repeated instead.

"Yes." She wasn't going to enlighten him that she had a deep-seated fear of water snakes.

And fish. Or just about anything else found in the water. Not when he looked like he could kill her with his bare hands.

He yanked her up to face him. "Listen carefully. In three minutes, we're slipping out the gangplank door into the water. We'll be on the opposite side of the river from where we need to be. But the current is pretty mild today so we should be able to cross without issue. Still, you are to stay within two feet of me at all times. Do I make myself clear?"

"Abundantly." She tugged her arm back.

Griffin jumped up on the toilet and punched out a ceiling tile. He shoved her phone up into the ceiling.

"Hey!" she cried. Marin knew she was being irrational about keeping her phone with her, but her life was unraveling by the minute. She just wanted some aspect of it that she could control.

The look he gave her was so hard and cool she had to wrap her arms around herself to keep from shivering. Griffin jumped down and unrolled the entire roll of toilet paper, shoving it all into the toilet. He then pulled the lever to flush it.

"Let's go," he ordered as he pulled the door open a crack.

Once he determined the hallway was empty, he gestured for Marin to lead the way out. He locked the door and pulled it shut. They walked to the stern of the ship. A man in uniform sat in a folding chair beside the gangplank opening. A single chain stood between the boat and the open water.

"Excuse me," Griffin said. "My wife is looking for a bathroom. There's a line of wasted coeds at the one upstairs. The one down here is locked, but no one is answering. Did you see someone go in?"

The crewman stood from his chair. "No, but that lock is tricky. Let me try it."

Water was already spilling out the door by the time they got back to the bathroom.

"Oh, man!" The crewman banged on the locked door. "One of those kids must have already been down here. Would you mind keeping an eye out so that no one goes past this point? I've got to run upstairs and get a key. And a mop."

"Sure."

They waited until the man had started up the stairs. Griffin gestured for her to head back to the gangplank opening. A second later he was beside her, sitting on the edge.

"Hold my hand. Try not to make a splash," he said.

Marin's stomach churned as rapidly as the dark water beneath them. She didn't want to leave the safety of the boat. Griffin must have sensed her trepidation.

"Marin." He took her hand in his and squeezed gently. "Trust me. Please."

She nodded. He softly counted to three. Then they were both sliding off the side of the big boat.

The water was colder than she expected. Her muscles tensed immediately and she became a little frantic. She gulped in a lungful of diesel fuel and started to gag. Griffin threw an arm around her torso and dragged her several yards away from the riverboat's wake.

"Relax," he urged. Thankfully, he didn't relinquish his hold on her. Instead, he treaded water while keeping them afloat. "You didn't lie about the swimming part, did you?"

"No." She tried not to swallow a mouthful of water. "My swimming lessons just didn't include any practice at sneaking off boats."

Griffin chuckled. "That's my girl. We're going to hang out here for a few minutes. It will be easier to cross if we don't have to swim through a wake."

Marin wasn't too keen on "hanging out" in the cold, dirty Potomac River any longer than she had too. Wisely, she kept her thoughts to herself. She kind of liked the words "that's my girl" coming from Griffin's mouth. They buoyed her spirit. A hush settled over the water as the big paddle boat continued on its way up the river.

"Where exactly are we swimming to?" she asked quietly.

He shifted their bodies in the water to the left slightly. "See those lights about a mile down the opposite bank?"

She nodded.

"That's a private marina. We'll be able to climb out of the water unseen there. First we need to swim the mile to the other side of the river."

Her teeth began to chatter. "I'll swim to Timbuktu as long as someone is waiting for us with a towel."

"How about if I sweeten the deal with a hot shower to

go along with that towel?"

Marin couldn't quite make out Griffin's eyes in the darkness. She wasn't sure if he was flirting with her or not.

"In that case, what are we waiting for?" she said.

"Stay close to me," he instructed as they began to swim into the middle of the river. "This doesn't have to be an Olympic swim. We can go as slowly as you need to."

She was so busy trying not to ingest a mouthful of dirty river water, that she didn't bother responding. Griffin had exaggerated about the current being light. Once they'd reached the center of the river, Marin struggled to maintain the course he'd indicated. Twice, Griffin had to reach around her waist and redirect her. She was beginning to worry she didn't have the strength to complete a two-mile swim when the sound of an outboard motor roared in her ears. It was dark on the river. The driver likely didn't see either of them in the water. Marin began to panic and her stroke faltered.

Griffin wrapped his arms around her again and dragged her on her back out of the path of the rapidly advancing boat.

"Hold your breath," he ordered before pulling them both down beneath the surface of the water.

Marin thrashed her arms and legs wildly. Several long seconds later they popped out into the night air. She gulped in a lungful of air only to swallow half the river with it. They bobbed along in the boat's rough wake as Marin choked and sputtered. Griffin held her against him trying to smother her noise. Voices from the boat filtered back in the wind. Marin froze. They were the two men who had been chasing them in the car.

"Lean in to me," Griffin said quickly. Clearly, he had recognized their voices as well. "We're almost there."

Once they reached the far side of the river, the current carried them toward the marina. Marin was able to swim on her own; not as quickly as either of them would like, but still they made it to their destination half an hour later. The marina was quiet. It was after eight on a week night, which meant they could climb out of the water unnoticed. Still, when Griffin put his finger to his lips, Marin complied, silently praying that Adam or Ben was on the dock waiting with a warm towel.

Griffin steered them along a row of boats, eventually coming up beside a sailboat. The words "Seas the Day" were painted across the back. He signaled for her to grab one of the rope lines holding the boat in the slip.

"Wait," he mouthed.

The next thing she knew, Griffin was hoisting himself over the swim platform onto the boat. A moment later, he lowered a metal step ladder and attached it to the hull. He reached his hand down to help her climb up. Marin heaved her waterlogged body over the side, nearly crying out when the chilly night air hit her. Her T-shirt and shorts were stuck to her like a second skin and not much protection. She wanted to ask Griffin where his friends were, but her teeth were chattering too much. Besides, he was too busy digging around for something under one of the seat cushions.

"We are n-not br-breaking into this b-boat," she managed to get out through her trembling lips.

Griffin stood up, shoving his damp hair out of his eyes. "It's not breaking in if you have the key." He dangled a key in front of her. "And the towels and hot shower I mentioned before are on the other side of this door."

"You h-had me at t-towels."

CHAPTER FOURTEEN

GRIFFIN HAD TO get her out of those wet clothes. Mostly to keep Marin from freezing to death, but also for his own sanity. Standing in the sailboat's salon shivering in that damn translucent T-shirt and clingy shorts, she was a teenage boy's wet dream. The vision was doing crazy things to his body and Griffin was long past an adolescent. Not only that, but he wasn't sure they were out of danger yet. He needed to think clearly. And he wouldn't be able to do that until they were separated by the closed bathroom door.

Digging through the closet where Ben kept the beach towels, Griffin pulled one out and wrapped it around her.

"P-please, tell me th-this is your boat."

He shook his head. "It belongs to Ben."

Her shoulders seemed to sag with relief. He almost laughed at her unflagging sense of right and wrong. She was worried about a little B&E when not more than two hours ago, she'd killed a man. Despite the fact that it was in self-defense, the act would likely haunt this sensitive woman for years to come. He hated that she'd been exposed to this nightmare just by being in the wrong place at the wrong time. But he was going to make it right. He had to.

"Sit." He guided her down to the bench seat. Kneeling down, his numb fingers struggled with the wet laces of her sneakers before he was able to pull one shoe off and then the other. He rubbed her shriveled feet with a towel.

"You need to dry off, too," she said.

Just touching her skin was helping Griffin to warm up. He decided it was better not to mention that, though. He left her on the bench so he could reach into the small lavatory and turn on the water in the shower.

"There isn't a separate stall," he explained. "The whole room serves as the shower. But there's a removable sprayer with plenty of hot water that you can use to wash yourself off and warm up. The soap and shampoo are on the shelf behind the toilet. Do you have enough strength to do it yourself?"

Please say you do, he silently pleaded. If Griffin had to get her naked, she'd never make it into the shower.

A faint blush spread from her neck to her cheeks. She nodded before standing on unsteady feet and walking into the bathroom.

"Just hand me your clothes and the towel through the door," he instructed. "I'll see if I can scare up an extra T-shirt of Ben's for you to wear."

When she closed the door, he began rummaging through the drawers in the sleeping cabin at the bow of the boat. He pulled out several pairs of board shorts, a Smashing Pumpkins concert T-shirt, and some old sweat pants of Ben's that Griffin recognized from their days at West

Point. At the sound of the bathroom door opening, he froze, imagining her body naked and pink from the cold water. The visual made him hard and hot. He heard her drop her clothes on the floor before the door closed again. The lock clicked. Griffin couldn't decide if he was disappointed or insulted. *Neither.* He had work to do.

After he toed off his sneakers, Griffin peeled off his jeans and his boxer briefs. His T-shirt was next. He dried himself off before pulling on Ben's sweat pants. Then, he scooped up Marin's wet clothes and hung them along with his on a clothes line in the aft cabin. The water was still running and, if he was not mistaken, Marin had begun to hum quietly. Griffin dug into the fanny pack he'd bought on the Cherry Blossom. He needn't have bothered; his phone was completely waterlogged. His service revolver, too.

Griffin then searched the cabinets for food. He found tea bags and immediately filled a saucepan with some water and set it on the stove to boil. In another cabinet, he found a box of Teddy Grahams, better known as Ben's crack. They'd have to do for tonight.

While the water boiled, Griffin unlocked the cabinet beneath the charting desk and pulled out a burn phone and .35mm pistol Ben always kept onboard.

He powered up the phone and immediately texted Adam. "*Great night for stargazing.*"

He was loading the gun when the water shut off.

The bathroom door opened a crack. "Did you have any luck finding clothes?" she asked.

"Here." He placed a dry towel and the T-shirt into her outstretched hand.

The burn phone chirped. "*Sounds like a fun date. Meeting friends in Old Town tonight. Will bring coffee in the morning.*"

Griffin relaxed a bit knowing his friend had the situation under control. Adam would secure the perimeter of the marina making sure he and Marin were safe on the sailboat tonight.

He responded back. "*Grab me a couple of souvenir T-shirts while you're out tonight, too.*"

Marin emerged from the bathroom just as the water began to boil in the pot. When she reached up to adjust the towel she'd wrapped around her head like a turban, the T-shirt rode way up her toned thighs. Griffin's mouth went dry. He must have made some sound because her free hand tugged the hem of the shirt down. His gaze refocused on the pink skin of her fingers still dotted with dried blood. She'd nearly scrubbed her hand raw trying to wipe off the bloodstains.

"Come here," he said as he reached above the stove and pulled down the first-aid kit.

She stood before him and Griffin marveled at how Marin could still smell so femininely delicious after bathing with Ben's obnoxious woodsy soap. He tried to ignore the painful tightening of his junk in the already snug sweat pants. Instead, he dug the petroleum jelly out of the kit.

He held his palm out. "Let me have your hand."

There was a brief hesitation before she did as he asked.

Using his thumb, Griffin gently rubbed the petroleum jelly over the bloodstains.

"Will that work?" She leaned in to inspect what he was doing and Griffin got another whiff of her musky scent.

It would work to get rid of the stains, but sadly, not her memory. "Yeah." He continued to massage her hand.

Marin sighed contentedly and Griffin felt it all the way in his groin. The chirping of the burn phone made her jump. Griffin snatched it up and looked at the message.

"*Your chaperones are in place. If you can't be good, be careful. B*"

Smart asses. Griffin snapped the phone closed as he let out a relieved sigh.

"Are your friends coming to get us?" Marin asked as she wiped off her hands.

"We're staying put here tonight. There's a team of agents just outside keeping watch. The guys in the speed boat never saw us. Adam will have the Coast Guard pick them up. We're safe where we are."

Marin nodded, but with little enthusiasm.

"I found some tea bags and some cookies." He gestured to the pot of water on the stove. "We'll have to make do with that for food."

"And you found a gun, too, I see," she added.

"It's always better to be prepared."

She wrapped her arms around her midsection. "I just want this to be over," she whispered.

He reached up and caressed her face. "You were amazing today."

Marin leaned her cheek into his palm as tears welled up in her eyes. "I killed a man today."

The ache of her words nearly broke him. "I believe I owe you a thank you for that." He leaned in and took her mouth in a gentle kiss.

She amazed him every time with how sweet she tasted.

"I need to shower before I stink up the place with the perfume of the Potomac," he murmured after reluctantly releasing her mouth.

She shot him a guilty look. "I might have used all the hot water."

That was probably a good thing. A cold shower was just what he needed right now. "I'll make do."

THE BREEZE HAD picked up outside causing the sailboat to sway gently from side to side. Marin rinsed her bra and panties out in the galley sink and hung them back on the line. While sipping on a cup of tea, she finger-dried her hair and braided it to the side. Then she explored Ben's boat. Anything to keep her mind off the sexy man in the shower who kept doing things to make her like him. Like kissing her.

There were three sleeping berths—two at the back and one up front. All three had double beds with a door that separated them from the main cabin. Griffin was already using one as a makeshift laundry room. The other aft cabin resembled a jail cell without any windows, so Marin wandered to the one at the bow of the boat. This one featured three-foot-long horizontal windows on either side of the bed and a tiny porthole at the front. Marin climbed up onto the bunk and dragged a blanket over her bare legs.

Moonlight illuminated the narrow teak ledge that surrounded the bed and Marin was drawn to the photos Ben had displayed there. Some looked like they were of his family, but one in particular caught her eye. It was a photo of Ben, Adam, and Griffin holding a swordfish. All three men sported wide, carefree grins and a great deal of sexy, tanned skin.

"I actually caught one that was bigger, but Adam let it get away."

Marin started at the sound of Griffin's voice. The picture frame slipped from her fingers, landing on the bed. She hadn't heard the shower stop or the bathroom door open. Yet there was Griffin filling the small doorway to the cabin. And sucking all the air out of it, too.

Her breath caught at the back of her throat at the sight of him. His arms were stretched above him as he gripped the doorframe, giving Marin an eyeful of his sculpted chest, complete with a happy trail of dark hair that disappeared beneath the waistband of his skintight sweat pants. Dark stubble still shadowed his jaw making him look like a pirate. The way his eyes were devouring her, she was apparently his booty.

He let out a pained sigh. "You should get some rest while you can." He brought his arms down to his sides where they hung rigidly.

"When did *you* last sleep?"

His face grew taut. "I'll sleep when you're safe."

"But you said I was safe right now?"

Griffin dropped his chin to his chest and swore quietly. "You know what I mean, Marin. I'll sleep when this is over. And it will be over shortly, I promise. Right now, I need to figure out how all the pieces fit together in this case." His expression became shuttered. "Sleep well."

With that, he pulled the double doors closed. Apparently, she was safe from her attackers, but not from her pirate bodyguard. Marin sighed heavily and tried to relax. The sound of Griffin's footsteps as he paced the salon didn't help. Returning the picture frame to the ledge, she let her fingers wander over the other few objects Ben kept by his bedside. She picked up a Rubik's Cube, intending to play with it for a while, but it wasn't a puzzle. Instead it was a hollow box; one filled with condoms.

The foil packets fell out over the bed. Marin scrambled to retrieve them all and put them back into the box.

"Well, we know what Ben uses his sailboat for." She began to giggle.

It was only a matter of seconds before she was laughing hysterically. The doors flew open and Marin shoved the condoms behind her back.

Griffin glared at her. "What the hell is so funny?"

A snort escaped her throat and Marin doubled over, falling back onto the bed as her body shook with laughter. Griffin crawled over her trying to see what she was hiding. When his hand accidently skimmed her thigh, they froze.

His body hovered over hers, its heat warming her. His breath fanning her cheek grew ragged. He wanted her as much as she wanted him; the evidence of his desire lay hard against her stomach.

Marin had entrusted Griffin with her life—several times. Trusting him with her heart was a whole different story, however. But her body wouldn't settle down. Maybe it was the trauma of the past several days. Or perhaps it was that "something" that continued to hum between them. Either way, she was restless and punchy and she wasn't going to get any sleep. Not alone, that was for sure. Tonight, she was going to take what she wanted. She lifted her chin and pressed her mouth to his.

"Marin." Her name left his mouth as a groan.

She took advantage of his parted lips to make her own desires known. Griffin lowered his body into hers, pressing them deeper into the mattress. One of his hands fisted in her braid while the other one skimmed the side of her breast.

"You shouldn't be distracting me," he murmured against her neck. "I'm supposed to be your protection detail tonight."

Marin giggled again, finally showing him the contents of her hand. "I have all the protection we need."

Griffin buried his face into the mattress beside her head. His body trembled on top of hers. When his gaze met hers again, he was struggling to keep his face serious.

"Does this mean you're not mad at me anymore?" he asked.

"Oh, no, I still am," she replied solemnly. "Very mad at you. But I may be dead tomorrow; so I might as well take advantage of you while I have the chance."

He cupped her face between both his hands. "You're not going to die tomorrow or any day after that. I won't let anything happen to you, Marin."

"Anything could happen, Griffin. All we have is right here and right now. And I want you. Right now."

His face relaxed into a resigned smile. Marin reached up to brush his hair back.

"Two rules," he stated.

Her hand stilled. "Rules? You have rules?"

"Rule one. At no point during the night may you refer to me as 'sweet cheeks.'"

She stifled the giggle that bubbled up. "And rule number two?"

"I can't do this if you're wearing Ben's T-shirt." He looked so serious. "I'll just keep imagining his ugly mug in the cabin watching us."

"I thought it was implied that I'd be naked," she teased. "But given that I'm already well acquainted with your performance issues, I'll happily comply with both your rules."

Griffin stalked off the bed and Marin worried she might have pushed him too far. But then he was stripping out of his sweat pants and she swallowed a moan at the sight of him flaunting his arousal.

"I told you this once, I don't have performance issues. But I guess you won't be happy without a demonstration, will you?" He gestured to the T-shirt. "Rule number two."

Marin quickly shimmied out of Ben's shirt and tossed it out the door. She shivered at the wicked grin on Griffin's face. He grabbed her ankles and dragged her body to the end of the bed so her feet dangled off. Spreading her knees wide, he stepped between them.

Marin's body quivered. "Griffin, I—"

"Hush," he commanded as he knelt down between her legs. "Or there will be a rule number three."

She lifted her head to argue with him, but he was studying her body with such undisguised hunger she flopped back down in embarrassment.

"I've told you this before, but I don't think you can hear it enough," he murmured. "You're beautiful, Marin Chevalier. Damn gorgeous, in fact. Do you know that?"

Marin hoped he didn't expect an answer because her throat had become choked up again. She squeezed her eyes shut to stem the tears that threatened. His lips found the inside of her thigh and she bucked off the bed when his rough beard abraded the sensitive skin there.

He chuckled softly. "You're very tense. Before we get to the demonstration of my sexual proficiency, I think I might need to let you fly solo."

With that, his mouth moved to her core. Marin moaned loudly as she fisted her hands in the sheets. She had no argument with the proficiency—she would call it artistry—of his tongue. Within minutes, she was soaring over the edge panting his name.

Griffin kissed his way up her torso all the while repositioning her on the bed. Marin's body grew warmer and more agitated with every touch of his lips. She reached for his shoulders and dug her fingernails into them.

"Please," she pleaded.

His lips sealed around her nipple and her body arched against his mouth. She twined her fingers through his hair, holding his head to her breast. Griffin's finger slid inside her and she squirmed.

"No," she whimpered. "I want you inside me."

He lifted his mouth from her breast. "For someone who doubted my abilities, you're very impatient."

But he moved further up her body so his erection was poised at her entrance. Marin couldn't make out his eyes in the moonlight, but his lips were turned up in a sly grin. The sound of the foil packet ripping filled the small berth. Marin noticed his fingers shook slightly when he sheathed himself. Then, Griffin slid slowly inside her. She sighed with each gentle push.

When he'd filled her to the hilt, his lids drifted closed as he paused to seemingly savor the moment. It was costing him to take his time. That much was evident by the tightness of his expression.

"Your equipment seems to be adequate," she remarked.

His eyes snapped open. "I haven't had any complaints yet."

Marin didn't like the feelings the thought of him being with other women brought on. She squeezed her muscles around him. "If you don't hurry up, I might complain."

"Do you like it when people rush you in the kitchen?"

he demanded.

Marin threw back her head and laughed until Griffin captured her mouth in a hot, glorious kiss that scattered her wits. He began to move inside her and the gentle rocking of the boat heightened the pleasure of his movements. Their tongues dueled; he slid in and out of her, moving in time with the current. She moaned into his mouth as the fever began to build inside her again.

Griffin's pace never wavered and Marin became frantic for more. She freed her legs from beneath his to wrap them around his waist. The change in position brought more friction where she needed it. Panting now, she scratched her fingers down his back impatiently. He nipped at her mouth, but he didn't hurry his cadence. A powerful wave of pleasure teased Marin, but she couldn't seem to reach it.

"Griffin!" she pleaded.

He brought his forehead down to hers. "Is this what you want, Marin?" He shifted his position slightly and moved within her using more energy. Marin shattered beneath a thousand points of light, her body convulsing in places she didn't know existed. She was gasping for air beneath closed eyes when she realized he'd stilled above her.

When she lifted her lids, she was met by Griffin's hot, triumphant look. She would have rolled her eyes at him had her body not been so sated. With a groan, he began to move, driving into her with such intensity that she came again. This time, Griffin followed her over the edge, sighing her name next to her ear when he collapsed on top of her.

"MMM." GRIFFIN SCRAPED his spoon against the plastic bowl. "I never knew oatmeal could taste that good."

He glanced up as Marin sashayed through the salon, Ben's T-shirt riding up her thighs slightly.

"All it takes is some doctoring up," she explained. "I found some chocolate in one of the drawers. And I chopped up the Teddy Grahams for the cinnamon topping."

"You know you should really think about becoming a chef," he teased.

She stuck her tongue out at him playfully. But then she grew quiet as she washed the pot at the sink.

"Hey." Griffin got to his feet and wrapped his arms around her waist from behind.

He inhaled the musky smell of sex that clung to her skin and the need to have her again gnawed at him. But as much as he wanted a round two, not to mention a round three, something was troubling her.

He hoped like hell it wasn't regret. "What's wrong?"

She sloshed the water around the sink. "I love being the pastry chef at the White House."

"And?"

"And I feel like I'm never going to be able to resume my normal life again."

He brushed his lips along her neck. "Nonsense. I told

you this will all be over soon."

Marin pulled out of his embrace. "But I don't even know what *this* is." Tears welled in her eyes.

Griffin took the pot from her hands and guided her over to the table. "Sit," he commanded.

When she did, he picked up the dish towel and began drying the pot. "What do you want to know?"

"You and Agent Morgan said the creepy guy I saw on the stairs was after me. But who were those guys who attacked us today?" She swallowed roughly. "The one I killed."

Sighing, Griffin put the pot away and sat down beside her. "They were speaking Greek. If I had to guess, they're part of a counterfeiting ring."

"Counterfeiting ring? How do they fit into this? I thought you were investigating art thieves?"

"I work for the Secret Service's Criminal Investigations Division. We concentrate on ferreting out counterfeit bills within the US monetary system. And the crooks who print them. Most people don't realize that was the agency's original mission when it was created. For the past couple of years, I've been working out of the New York office taking down the money makers."

"You went there after you left the President's protective detail?"

Griffin tensed at her question. He wondered how much she knew. Given her friendship with the First Lady and the head housekeeper at the House, he guessed she knew the entire sordid story. He nodded.

"And you work with Agent Morgan?"

He tried not to flinch at Leslie's name. The last thing Griffin wanted to do was to discuss his and Leslie's colleagues-with-benefits relationship with Marin. Even if it was in the past. "On this case, yes. She heads up the FBI task force. We've been trying to track down a ring of counterfeiters responsible for flooding the US with fake hundred dollar bills. They have ties to a crime family in Greece."

"But they steal art, too?"

Griffin scrubbed a hand down his face. "Apparently. This gang's claim to fame is a person known as The Artist. He makes the bills look unbelievably realistic. We had no idea The Artist was forging art until we stumbled on the originals from the White House."

"Agent Morgan said that your only clue was a White House dish towel. And that led you to me. Why?"

Was it his imagination or was she getting defensive? He decided she deserved the truth.

"Several of the money laundering drops occurred at Chevalier hotels."

Marin's mouth dropped open. "What? Does my grandfather know that? My brother Sebastian is going to freak out."

"We were never able to link anyone at the hotels to the counterfeiters, Marin. It was all circumstantial as far as we can tell."

She stood up abruptly. "Then if everything was circumstantial, why was I the prime suspect?"

Griffin didn't have a ready answer to offer her. At least one that he wanted to admit. After a few moments of charged silence, she turned for the front cabin with a huff.

"Wait." He wrapped his fingers around her wrist before she could storm past him. Sighing heavily, he tugged her onto his lap. "I told you before, I was attracted to you the moment I saw you," he admitted. "I concentrated on you as a suspect because I wanted to be near you. Plain and simple. And that's definitely not the way we're trained to conduct an investigation."

"Why did you leave me that night?" she whispered.

Jesus, she wanted her pound of flesh.

He swallowed roughly. "Because you scare the hell out of me, Marin. *This* scares the hell out of me."

Her mouth curled up into a contented smile as her body relaxed into his. "Because I'm irresistible?"

"Something like that," he replied.

"Well, you're pretty irresistible, too, you know." Her hand traced a path down his bare stomach.

Griffin's body shot to attention. "Is that so?"

"Mmm."

His chest seemed to be occupying her entire focus. When she leaned in to draw her tongue over his nipple, Griffin nearly exploded.

"Back to the bedroom. Now."

With a sensuous laugh, she straddled him instead, pressing his body into the banquette seat. "Oh, no you don't. This time, we're playing by my rules."

She reached into his pocket, presumably to grab a condom, but she lingered a minute to stroke him. Griffin hissed in frustration when she squeezed his balls.

"Once again you're overdressed, Agent Keller."

Griffin wasted no time shucking his sweat pants down to his knees and kicking them the rest of the way off. She tore open the condom and reached to put it on him.

"Rule number two," he protested.

Marin laughed again before stripping out of Ben's T-shirt.

"Better?" she asked.

He was eye level with her amazing breasts. "Hell, yeah."

As she rolled the condom on him, Griffin reached up and undid her braid, combing his fingers through her silky hair. She leaned forward and kissed him, enclosing them in a curtain of her hair. He let her have her way with the kiss for a moment before lust propelled him to take over. The heat built between them as their kisses grew more frantic. Reaching down between their slick bodies, Marin guided him to her entrance. It took every ounce of strength he had not to explode when she sank down on him. His chest constricted and his mind went fuzzy from the sheer pleasure of her body closing around him.

"This isn't scary," she said. "This is the only thing during these past few days that's felt real. And perfect."

She began to move on him and all coherent thought deserted Griffin. All but a wisp of an idea that perhaps Marin was right.

CHAPTER FIFTEEN

MARIN WOKE TO the sounds of footsteps on the boat. "Griffin," she whispered, trying to untangle her arms and legs from his. "There's someone here."

He moaned and rolled over, pinning her to the bed. When a pair of sneakered feet passed by the narrow window inches from their naked bodies, she frantically tried to remember where he'd put Ben's gun.

"Griffin!" She thumped his bare chest. "Wake up! Someone is on the boat!"

His eyelids raised to half-mast just as the sneakers went back the other way. Griffin lowered his lids again and settled back down on top of her. "Not to worry," he mumbled. "Those ugly ankles belong to Adam."

"Are you sure?" She glanced frantically out the window.

"Positive," he murmured against her shoulder, the rasp of his two-day-old beard tickling her skin.

She reached for the blanket and tugged it over their bodies just as the engine roared to life. Marin would have jumped, but she had two hundred pounds of muscled, naked man holding her captive.

"The boat is moving!" she shrieked.

"Mmm," he said, his lips nipping at her collarbone.

"We've been making it move all night."

"That's not what I meant." She smacked his butt.

His eyes snapped open. Marin sucked in a breath at the heat in them. "I didn't realize you liked to play that way. I doubt Ben has anything more than rope that we can use for sex toys. But I'm happy to go check with him."

"Will you please be serious? I've had a crazy few days and I have the right to be a little jumpy."

His face softened. He reached a finger down to brush a stray hair off her face. "I know. But you can trust Adam and Ben to protect you. They're just taking us somewhere safe. That's all."

"Shouldn't we go out there and see where we are going?"

He kissed the tip of her nose. "Not yet. I'd rather stay in here and torture you for using your hands when you should have used your words."

She squirmed beneath him impatiently. "I was using my words. You just weren't listening. You still aren't."

His hot gaze locked with hers again. "Damn it, Marin, the minute we leave this cabin things go back to the way they were. You go back to being a protectee. I go back to being who I am, a special agent, wearing a gun, doing everything I can to keep you safe. I just want a few more minutes of this, you and me. Stress-free and real."

As Griffin bent his head and brushed his lips over her breast, Marin tried to relax beneath the warmth of his body. These last hours aboard Ben's boat had been a magical time-out from her threatening reality. But she wanted to think they could continue like this, intimate and connected, long after the danger has passed. His words held a warning, however. One that was almost as frightening as the man who wanted her dead.

She leaned forward and kissed the top of his head. He tugged the blanket to form a cocoon over them. When his mouth found hers, Marin responded with a kiss as hungry as his. The boat picked up speed, but Griffin was unhurried as he made love to her reverently.

"AGENT MORGAN'S TEAM found the curator's intern," Adam said. "Or what was left of him. Looks like he died the same way as Wes. A lethal dose of Sux."

Griffin glanced toward the bow of the boat. Dressed in a white T-shirt and a pair of Daisy Duke jean shorts his idiot friends had picked out for her, Marin was out on the pulpit with Ben. The two of them were doing a stupid impersonation from the movie *Titanic*. Ben's hands were all over her body. Her laughter floated through the air. Griffin should be glad to see her so relaxed. Instead, he was miffed his supposed friend was manhandling his woman.

His woman.

Jesus. Marin wasn't his woman. She was a suspect turned protectee. Nothing more. Except for those hours they'd spent locked away belowdecks. Griffin had been more real with her than he ever had with any other woman he'd had sex with. He thought it was because he wanted to console her, to protect her. But she did something to him. And he was telling the truth when he said it scared the hell out of him.

"Shall I turn the wheel sharply so they both fall in?"

"What?" Griffin turned his head to face Adam.

His friend peered over his Ray-Bans. "You haven't heard a word I've said."

"I heard the part about the White House intern being offed. Do we think that was our Ukrainian friend or the Greek buffoons who attacked us yesterday?"

Adam scoffed. "Those Greek idiots were an embarrassment to hit men everywhere. We could have rounded them up with a damn Taser last night. It's no wonder they had to hire a Ukrainian henchman to be their muscle. By the way, I gave Agent Morgan the collar. She said they lawyered up almost immediately."

"Then the Ukrainian killed the intern. But why?"

"Leslie thinks he was the guy on the inside," Adam explained. "Apparently, Intern Ari comes from a well-connected Greek family."

"That brings us back to the million-dollar question of why steal artwork from the White House? They've got a successful counterfeiting gig going. Why branch out?"

Adam steered the boat around a buoy. "That's the question that kept Leslie and me occupied for most of the evening. Among other things."

"Hmm," Griffin responded refocusing his gaze on Marin and Ben.

"That's all I get is 'hmm'?" Adam asked. "I tell you I

spent the night with a woman you've been sleeping with and you can't be bothered. Yet Ben barely has his hands on Marin and you're ready to throw him overboard."

The waves crashed against the side of the boat. Griffin's insides felt just as choppy. "Leslie and I were never serious. She's all yours."

"And Marin?"

"She's a witness in our protection. Nothing more." *You keep telling yourself that, Griff.*

"Right. And the condom wrappers strewn about the boat are because you opened them up to make balloon animals last night."

Griffin glared at Adam. "It's complicated."

Adam laughed. "That's the call sign for any guy to run in the other direction. You'll be able to think more clearly once we drop her at the base."

Ice rushed through Griffin's veins. "I'm not leaving her there alone."

His friend eyed him warily. "The director wants you back at the White House. This case has everyone tense and he wants you to dodge the flying arrows. Marin will be surrounded by agents on the base. She'll be safe."

"Not good enough," Griffin said through clenched teeth.

"What's not good enough?" Marin asked.

Following Ben, she climbed off the bow agilely, only to slip on the last step. Griffin caught her before she fell. Marin leaned into him coyly, but he held his body away from hers. Confusion marred her pretty face. Griffin didn't blame her. He was conflicted by his need to keep her close when finding the thief should be his top priority. If he was going to find this creep, he needed to listen to Adam and put some distance between him and Marin. It wasn't like he hadn't warned her an hour earlier in the cabin. He just hoped she'd gotten the message.

Marin's stepped out of his grasp and crossed her arms in front of her. "Do I get to know where you boys are taking me?"

Ben pointed toward a marina up ahead before taking Adam's place at the wheel. "We're docking adjacent to Fort McNair. From there, Agent Groesch and some others will take you to a State Department safe house on base. I hear it has a fabulous view."

She worried her bottom lip. "I need to be in New Orleans by Friday night."

"You're booked aboard Air Force One," Adam informed her. "And you'll have a lucky Secret Service agent as your wedding date."

"You?" she asked Adam, her tone a little too hopeful for Griffin's comfort.

"Hell, no," Griffin declared. "I told you I was taking you to that damn wedding and I still am."

Marin's face was hard to read. "Try not to sound so enthused about it, Agent Keller."

She disappeared into the cabin. When Griffin went to chase after her, Adam stopped him with a hand to his arm.

"Dude, worry about the guy trying to kill her," his friend reminded him. "You can kiss and make up with

Marin afterward. And then you'll both live happily ever after."

Griffin grabbed Adam by the shirt. "I told you it's not like that."

Adam pushed Griffin's hands away. "Yeah, yeah. It's complicated. Too bad you're the only one who thinks that."

"Guys," Ben interrupted. "Can we gab about Griffin's need to get in touch with his feelings another time? I really need each of you on either side of the bow to tie the boat off."

Adam made a kissing noise before scrambling up top and heading to the left side of the bow. Griffin debated going below to check on Marin. Adam didn't know what the hell he was talking about. Except for the part about catching Marin's attacker. That needed to be Griffin's first priority.

Ben steered the boat alongside the dock. "Keller, get your ass up there to grab the lines on the starboard side."

Griffin made his way to the front of the boat.

BEN WAS RIGHT. The house they took Marin to did have stunning views of the Washington waterfront and Arlington beyond. It was also furnished more tastefully than the last house, befitting of the foreign dignitaries who used this address as a hiding place. The home would be perfect if she were enjoying a weekend getaway in Washington, DC.

Except she wasn't. She was essentially a prisoner. And even worse for her psyche, Griffin was obviously not sticking around to play the role of her bodyguard.

"There's a gorgeous tub in the master bath if you'd like a long soak after swimming in the Potomac," Agent Groesch said. "I guessed at the sizes of clothing you'd need, but you should find something upstairs that will fit you." The female agent tsked at the tight shorts Ben and Adam had brought for her that morning. "Leave it to a man," she mumbled as she walked back into the room the agents were using as an office.

Marin buried her hands into Otto's fur. She was delighted to see the big dog awaiting her when she arrived. Otto's presence almost made up for the fact that Griffin was abandoning her.

"The windows are bulletproof," Griffin told her after he'd inspected the entire house.

He was standing in the wide hallway, carefully maintaining his distance from her. Just as he had during the boat ride; determined to play the cold, detached special agent. Marin was trying desperately not to let his distance hurt. She wasn't having much success, however. She thought what they'd shared the night before—what he'd shared with her—meant something. Apparently, she was wrong. Again.

"There are two Uniformed Division officers at each exit, not to mention that you're on a military base," he added. "You'll be able to relax here."

Given how strung out she was emotionally, Marin

wasn't sure she could relax anywhere, but that was beside the point. "What time does the yoga instructor arrive?" she quipped.

He arched an eyebrow at her sarcasm, but he stayed where he was, poised to make a break for it through the steel front doors. Marin just wanted him to leave. The pretense of having a civilized conversation with him was too draining on her raw emotions. The sooner he left, the better. She opened her mouth to make another witty remark, one that would let him think she wasn't dying inside, but emotion clogged her throat.

A whispered "be safe" came out of her mouth instead.

Not waiting around for his answer, she climbed the stairs quickly, wanting to put as much distance as she could between them before she broke down. She just made it over the threshold of the master bedroom when the door slammed shut behind her. Marin whirled around to find Griffin standing in the center of the room, a thunderous look on his face.

She gaped at him for a moment before indignation took over. Was she to be further humiliated by breaking down in front of him?

"Is there something else you needed, Agent Keller?" she choked out. "Or something else you *didn't* want to say?"

"Don't."

"Don't what?" she cried. "Don't be frightened to death that a crazy man is trying to kill me? Don't be anxious because I'm trapped somewhere and can't even talk to my family? Don't be heartsick because the idiot I thought I felt something for is really a freaking robot!"

An instant later she was on her back on the king-sized bed, Griffin on top of her. She struggled to push him off, but he grabbed her wrists with one hand while the other hand gripped her chin. A tear leaked out of Marin's eye making her even angrier. She bucked against him.

"Damn it, Marin, settle down."

He bent his face to hers so his lips could catch the tears falling down her face. The air in the room seemed to still at the sheer intimacy of his gesture.

"I'm not a robot," he said, his breath caressing the sensitive skin beneath her ear. "If I was, I could have walked out of this place without doing this."

He took her mouth in a hot, demanding kiss that had her heart breaking even more. She wanted to resist him, but her body wouldn't. *Couldn't.* So she kissed him back with the same fervent desperation. Their tongues dueled and their teeth collided as they breathed the other one in. When Griffin released her wrists so his hand could join the one caressing her face, she reached beneath his T-shirt to skim her fingers along his warm skin. A groan escaped the back of his throat at the contact.

Marin gulped back a sob when his lips broke free to graze down her neck.

"The last thing I want to do is leave you here, Marin," he whispered hoarsely. "But this is who I am. This is what I do. I'm not good at compartmentalizing. I never have been." He took her earlobe between his teeth before soothing it with his tongue. "It's all or nothing with me.

And I have to be all work. I wish I could be the man you want, Marin. But I have to find this son of a bitch and make him pay for what he's doing to you. I need you to understand this."

Her heart shredded a little more at his honest confession. The pathetic part was, she did understand. Griffin was hardwired to spend his life protecting people. And he was good at it, if the men and women who worked with him were to be believed. What she didn't understand was why he couldn't acknowledge the "something" between them; something that she had was starting to feel a lot like love on her part. Why couldn't there be both in his life? She'd have to debate that subject at another time, however. That battle wouldn't be won tonight.

She shoved at his chest and Griffin pushed up on his elbows, his face hovering inches above hers. Those ocean eyes of his were turbulent and wary. Marin traced a finger along the perfect outline of his jaw.

"I do understand." She hesitated so she could pull together the words that needed to be said. The ones that would let him do his duty without worry. "You've been tracking this gang of thieves down for years. You need to go and find this guy. Last night—last night was about two people finding comfort together. That's all. I'm a big girl." She kissed the corner of his mouth. "Thank you for being there for me."

Relief washed over his face. "I want you to be able to have your life back," he said.

Too bad he didn't want to be in it.

His tongue slid past her lips and he was kissing her again. This time, he kissed her like he had all the time in the world; savoring her mouth as though he was storing it up as a memory. Tears pressed the back of her eyes once more. She was grateful when Adam's voice called out Griffin's name.

She averted her face so he wouldn't see the tears rimming her eyes. Griffin slowly got to his feet. Marin heard him walk to the door. She heard him pause briefly before opening it.

"I'm gonna get your life back for you," he said softly.

Marin nodded her head so he'd know she was listening while silently praying for him to leave before the full waterworks started. When she heard the door click, she buried her face in a pillow and sobbed for what might have been.

CHAPTER SIXTEEN

M ARIN AWOKE TO find Otto poised at the side of the big bed, his chin resting on the mattress; the sound of his tail swishing on the hardwood floor serenaded her. She reached over and gave his head a pat.

"At least one male in my life is loyal." She climbed out of the bed and stretched in the afternoon sunshine. Things always looked a little better after a warm bath and a nap. Marin pulled on a pair of jeans and a bubble gum-colored scoop-neck top that was much clingier than she preferred. But when she looked into the mirror, she liked what she saw.

She slipped on the pink espadrilles that went with the top. "Chin up, Otto. What do you say we go find the kitchen and make ourselves useful?"

The dog danced happily around Marin as she made her way downstairs. The large kitchen was a cook's dream with state-of-the-art appliances and plenty of counter space to work. The fridge and cabinets were stocked with enough ingredients to prepare a small state dinner. It was obvious the agents watching over her were hopeful Marin would continue to keep them well fed. She was happy to oblige them. It helped break up the futility of her situation.

"I'm feeling lemon bars." She picked up a fresh lemon from the fruit bowl and tossed it between her hands. "How about you, Otto?"

The dog barked his agreement before settling down in front of the back door. Marin lost herself in the act of baking. An hour later, the aroma of lemons and powdered sugar filled the room. Agent Groesch and her partner entered the kitchen just as Marin was slicing into the gooey treat.

"This protective detail is hazardous to my hips," Agent Groesch complained. She helped herself to a lemon bar anyhow.

"Are you kidding? This is one of the best perks of the job," the other agent said. "I wouldn't mind if this assignment lasted several weeks."

Marin felt faint at the thought.

"I'm pretty sure the chef would mind, Agent Todd," Director Worcester said from the doorway leading to the foyer.

Both agents started.

"Chef," the director continued, "I've come to return you to the White House."

"Griff didn't send word that Pillsbury should be moved," Agent Todd countered.

"Pillsbury?" Marin squeaked.

The young agent shrugged. "It's your code name."

"Agent Keller's instructions are being superseded here," the director interjected. "By orders from the First Lady." His gaze fell on Marin. "Little Arabelle is sick. And she's asking for you. I'm to bring you back right away. Otto, too."

Marin's glimmer of hope that her tormentor had been captured was replaced by worry for the little girl. Aunt Harriett was a trained pediatrician. She wouldn't have summoned Marin if something wasn't terribly wrong with her granddaughter.

Once again, they rode in the decoy vehicle, Marin and Otto in the back and the director up front with the driver. Agent Groesch stayed behind at the safe house which meant she was likely to be returned there. While Marin was troubled that Arabelle was ill, she was relieved to be returning to the familiarity of the White House. Perhaps she could convince the director to let her stay.

The admiral greeted them at the North Portico. "Good to see you, Chef," he said. "The child is distraught and demanding to see you."

They took the elevator up to the third floor where the president's son and his family lived. The First Lady intercepted them in the hallway. Otto darted past them into the little girl's room.

"How is she?" Marin asked her godmother.

"Physically, I can't find anything wrong with her." Aunt Harriett was visibly frazzled. "But she's been weepy and clingy all afternoon. She was fine this morning. Bita took her to breakfast before school. Of course, Farrah is in Santa Barbara at some charity polo event and Clark is in surgery. Neither one of them should have ever become parents," she mumbled. "Arabelle just keeps crying and asking for you. She says you're the only one who can make her better." She threw her hands up in the air. "Eight years of medical training and I didn't know what else to do."

"I'm happy to help," Marin said. "And even happier to be back in the White House."

Her aunt hugged her. "They are going to find this guy, Marin."

"Mrs. Manning," the First Lady's chief of staff prompted.

"Crap," Aunt Harriett said. "I have a speaking engagement at the Girls and Boys Club this afternoon." She glanced at Arabelle's bedroom. "I should cancel and stay with her. Bita was supposed to, but she's picked up some kind of bug. Which leads me to believe Arabelle is coming down with something, too."

"I'm here now. I'll stay with her until you get back," Marin volunteered.

"Thank you." The First Lady hugged her again. "If she starts to develop any symptoms, have the agent on duty alert me."

Arabelle's room was decorated like a castle, complete with vine-covered floor-to-ceiling turrets framing the low bed draped in crinoline. Otto was already snoring on the mattress, his big body curled around the small child.

"Marin!" Arabelle cried, jumping off the bed, startling the dog. "You're here."

"Hey, sweetie." Marin wrapped her arms around the girl, inhaling the sweet smell of baby shampoo and cinnamon candy the head butler had likely snuck to her. "Your grandma Harriet says you aren't feeling well."

"I'm not sick," Arabelle insisted with a shake of her head. "I just needed to tell you something 'portant."

"Well, perhaps we should sit down for such a serious discussion." Marin eased into the upholstered glider, careful not to dislodge Arabelle from around her waist. "Is this about that boy, Charlie, in your class?" she teased.

"I don't love Charlie anymore," Arabelle replied solemnly. "I love Peter. But this isn't about them. It's about Grandma Bita. And you."

A sense of unease crawled up Marin's spine. "What about your Grandma Bita?"

"She gave me a very 'portant job to do. But it's a secret. Just for you." Arabelle placed her chubby hands on Marin's cheeks. "You have to listen to me and do just as I say."

The unease was fast becoming a full-blown panic attack. Marin did her best to remain calm in front of Arabelle, however. She didn't want to frighten the child any further. Bita had been in the pastry kitchen the morning Marin had seen the supposed art thief. Was Arabelle's grandmother involved with the thefts somehow? Good Lord, why would the woman involve her granddaughter in any of this? Marin wrapped her arms more firmly around the child.

"I'm listening," Marin said.

"The mean man who always makes Grandma Bita whisper in Farsi to him made her go somewhere with him. He said the only way she can come back is if you go and get her. She made me promise to tell you. Grandma Bita gave me a note to give you."

Arabelle scrambled off Marin's lap and ran over to her bed. She pulled a folded piece of paper from behind one of the pillows.

"Grandma Bita said she'll take me to Build-A-Bear if I kept the secret," Arabelle said proudly as she handed Marin the paper. "I kept it good, didn't I?"

Marin could barely find the words her body had become so numb with anger. "You did awesome." Marin looked at the paper. It contained only an address—1250 Potomac Street, Northwest—and a time—eight-thirty p.m.

The child crawled back into Marin's lap. "You'll go get Grandma Bita, won't you? I want her to come home." Arabelle's thumb circled her lips as she tried not to suck on it.

Ice ran through Marin's veins. She'd seen him briefly and the man was bent on killing her. Arabelle had obviously seen him, too.

"Sweetie, have you met Grandma Bita's friend often?"

"He's not her friend," Arabelle protested. "She always gets shaky when he calls her. I only saw him one time. He was in the pastry kitchen before school. I went in there looking for you. Grandma Bita was with me. She gave him a present." The girl glanced at Marin, her eyes serious. "I asked him if it was his birthday. He didn't answer. Grandma Bita said it was a 'just because present.'" Arabelle's bottom lip trembled. "Today he was at the donut shop. Grandma Bita was mad that he was there. She took me to the potty and told me the secret. I didn't want her to leave with the mean man. I almost told Agent Joe, but Grandma Bita made me promise not to. She said I had to get you instead."

Marin kissed the girl on the top of her head. She blew out a breath to steady her nerves. "You did a great job keeping the secret," she said. "And now it doesn't have to be a secret anymore." She picked up Ellie, the same stuffed animal Arabelle had given Marin the other day, and handed it to Arabelle. "I'll be right back."

She slipped out of Arabelle's bedroom into the hallway where the two members of the child's protective detail stood guard.

"I need to see the director, right away," she told the agents. "And call the First Lady back. It's an emergency."

GRIFFIN PROWLED THROUGH the curator's office. Ben's forensics team had already picked the place clean. But waiting around for leads on the Ukrainian art thief targeting Marin was making Griffin stir-crazy. If he could figure out the connection between the White House intern and the Ukrainian, he'd be one step closer to finding the son of a bitch.

"So far, the admiral's auditors have only identified four other pieces in the House as forgeries," Leslie informed him. "Including the Jackson Pollack. They still have the third floor to go, but that would bring our total to only eight. And four of them you recovered at the warehouse in

New Jersey."

"We need to get the information about the others out to Interpol," Griffin said. "I'd like to recover them all if we can."

"I sent it out this morning. But I wouldn't get your hopes up. A lot of times these pieces end up in the home of private collectors who don't care where they came from."

"Yeah, like someone who wants to stick it to the President of the United States," Griffin added with disgust. "They'll boast about it eventually, though, and I'll nail them. Do we know how an intern was able to get his hands on valuable paintings without anyone in this place catching on?"

Leslie grimaced. "From what I can gather from the White House Historical Society, Ari's specialty was art restoration. His grant entailed examining each canvas to look for some sort of chemical breakdown."

Griffin laughed at the absurdity of the scenario. "When actually he wasn't interested in restoring anything. Just reappropriating fine art for his clients. And they say crooks are stupid. The White House just got majorly duped."

"His security clearance checked out," Leslie said. "And he came highly recommended, according to the society. The White House curator liked having fellows in the office. The society is always scrambling to fill the position. It's likely they saw a need and filled it with whomever applied first."

Griffin picked up a framed photo off the desk. The picture was of the deceased curator posing with the Queen of

England. "And Wes's enthusiasm to give back got him killed."

"I checked Ari's bank records. He's made some staggering deposits over the past several months," Leslie told him. "The deposits began about the time he started his fellowship here. His yearly stipend is paid monthly, but it's barely enough to live on in DC."

"Please tell me Ari was paid by check for his moonlighting?"

Leslie shook her head. "The deposits were all money orders issued from a Greek bank. Tracing them is going to be extremely difficult."

Griffin swore.

"Before coming to the White House, Ari was in Athens studying at the Acropolis Museum," Leslie said. "I spoke with their director this morning. He didn't want to admit it, but it sounded like they might have a case of switched art there, as well. My Interpol liaison is going to investigate whether Ari had access to any of those pieces."

"We're still missing the vital link to the counterfeiters." Griffin sat down at one of the desks, scrubbing his hand down his freshly shaven face. He'd showered and changed in the Secret Service lounge after leaving Marin at the safe house. Then, he'd spent the next several hours sifting through what little clues they had. The task had only marginally preoccupied him from thinking about Marin.

Twice he'd reached for his phone to call and check with the agents at the safe house. Despite all of his attempts—even his honest declaration when he left—he was still distracted by thoughts of her. He was sure Marin had lied when she told him she hadn't read anything more into their hookup last night. But she'd given him the out he needed this morning. And her gesture made Griffin even more enthralled with her.

Marin was brave and quick thinking. With everything they'd endured yesterday, she'd never once complained. He couldn't even blame her about the stupid cell phone fiasco. That was Adam's fault.

"Griff, are you listening to me?"

Leslie's question pulled him back into the here and now. Which was exactly where his head needed to be.

"Sorry," he apologized. "I haven't had much sleep in the past couple of days. What did you say?"

She shot him a knowing grin that clearly conveyed she didn't believe his excuse. "I've been doing some digging into Yerik Salenko, our Ukrainian mercenary," Leslie said. "He's been off the radar for over ten years since leaving the Ukrainian Army. Intelligence reports put him in Iran during that time, but that's a country that's hit or miss with regard to information. Adam is correct that Salenko is known as an expert marksman, but Interpol believes he's equally lethal with chemicals. Given what he's done here, I'd have to agree."

"Yeah, but none of that intel explains how Salenko got involved with Greek counterfeiters doubling as art thieves."

"That's because I haven't finished," Leslie said. "Would you believe he has a daughter who lives in Athens? One who also worked at the Acropolis Museum for a brief period."

Griffin bolted upright in his chair. "Definitely not a coincidence."

"Mmm," Leslie agreed. "She left the museum well before Ari arrived, but they could have met somehow. Maybe that's how Salenko became acquainted with him."

"We need to talk to her."

"I've got Interpol tracking her down."

Leslie's IT agent, Eric, looked up from the computer he was working on at the other side of the room. "I've got something here, Agent Morgan."

They crowded around one of the empty desks. Eric set the laptop down in front of them.

"Our friend Ari either didn't trust his crime-loving colleagues and wanted to keep some evidence on them," Eric explained, "or he was just cocky. He kept these files on his work computer. A middle schooler could have hacked into them."

He moved the curser to a file marked *Contracted* and clicked. Photos of the Cezanne, the Monet, the Pollack, and thirteen other paintings came up on the screen. Next to each one were two sets of numbers—the appraised value and a percentage of that figure.

"He came to the White House with a damn shopping list," Griffin said.

Leslie pointed to the second column of numbers. "I'll have to pull up the bank records, but these figures look like the amounts of the deposits made into Ari's account. Although, I don't remember there being this many."

"That's because the originals of some of these pieces are still here," Griffin explained. "You said the auditors had already checked everything on the public floor, correct?"

Leslie nodded.

"The Waddell painting is hanging in the East Room," Griffin said. "Which means Ari hadn't gotten to it yet."

Leslie eyed him curiously.

"It's one of my favorite pieces," Griffin admitted tersely.

"Seriously, you and the pastry chef were made for each other," Leslie said.

"Can we concentrate on the case here?" he grumbled.

"Hey, I'm not the one getting all moon-eyed in the middle of a conversation."

Griffin shot her a quelling look. "We've explained how Ari got his hands on the paintings. But how did he get the forged pieces in and the real ones out of the House without anyone noticing?"

"He had an accomplice," Adam announced from the doorway. "One none of us suspected. The director wants you both in his office, pronto."

The Secret Service office was in chaos when Griffin and Leslie stepped across the hall.

"Agent Morgan," the director bellowed through the crowd. "I want a log of all of Bita Ranjbar's phone records for the last six months. I want her bank statements, her credit card charges, and a record of every time she used her damn library card. Anything the FBI can get me. And I want it ten minutes ago!"

Leslie had her phone to her ear before the director finished yelling.

Griffin followed the director into his office. "What's going on?"

"This is why the woman declined a protective detail," the director ranted, ignoring Griffin's questions. "Because she wanted to rob the White House blind."

Adam entered the office. Griffin noticed his friend was dressed in his counter assault team battle gear. "We've got live feed from cameras within a four-block radius around the meeting place. The cameras are streaming to the command center at headquarters. Once Salenko shows himself to make the grab, we can nab him."

"What meeting place? What grab? Will someone tell me what the hell is going on?" Griffin demanded.

The director sighed heavily. "Bita Ranjbar has been coming and going from this house under the guise of caring for her granddaughter. She's also been working as Yerik Salenko's mule, carrying the forged artwork in and the real paintings back out of the White House."

Griffin was dumbfounded. "And we know this how?"

"Because a preschooler broke open your case." Adam jovially slapped him on the back.

The director shot Adam a withering look. "Mrs. Ranjbar confided in her granddaughter."

"That makes no sense," Griffin said. "How do we know the kid isn't making this up?"

Director Worchester picked up a plastic baggie that contained a piece of paper. "She gave Arabelle this note this morning. She told the child that Salenko was holding her hostage."

Griffin carefully took the baggy and smoothed it out on the desk so that he could read the note inside. "This is just an address and a time. How do we even know this is from Bita?"

"It's her handwriting," the director said. "The First Lady confirmed it."

Confused, Griffin glanced between Adam and the director. He was missing a vital piece of the puzzle. And he had the sneaking suspicion they were withholding it from him for some reason. "What aren't you telling me?"

A pained expression settled in the director's eyes. "Arabelle was instructed to deliver Bita's message directly to Chef Marin. Apparently, Salenko wants to exchange one woman for the other."

Griffin's chest constricted painfully and he felt like his head might explode. "Like hell!"

CHAPTER SEVENTEEN

GRIFFIN TOOK THE stairs two at a time. He could hear the director and Adam calling after him, but he ignored them. By the time he reached the residence two floors up, his fear for Marin had stoked itself into a fury. As much as he wanted to bust open this counterfeit ring and take down The Artist, there was no way he'd allow anyone to use Marin as bait.

She was too precious.

His heart nearly stopped at the sight that greeted him in the center hall. Marin's back was to him while one of the tech agents fitted her with surveillance equipment. Her blonde hair was pulled into a ponytail that stuck out of the back of a baseball hat, likely concealing the listening device. When the tech slipped his fingers inside the waistband of her jeans to insert the tracking apparatus, a million shades of red danced before Griffin's eyes. He launched himself at the agent, taking him down to the floor just as a flurry of shouting reached his ears.

"Don't you touch her again," Griffin yelled, heedless of his surroundings. "She's not leaving this house!"

"Agent Keller!" the director admonished. "You're out of line!"

"Get a grip, you dumbass," Adam said as he yanked Griffin up by the arm. "The guy's just doing his job. It's not what you think."

Adam propelled him around to face Marin. But it wasn't her pretty blue eyes staring back at him. Instead, he was looking into the bewildered brown ones belonging to Agent Jessica Pannell. Her mouth slowly turned up into a satisfied smile.

"Well, at least we know I'll pass for the pastry chef at the meeting point," she said.

"A decoy," Griffin said through ragged breaths. "You're not sending Marin into this guy's clutches."

"Of course not, you idiot," Director Worcester huffed. "We'd never put a civilian in harm's way."

A wave of relief coursed through Griffin, so powerful, he was forced to take a seat on the sofa. "Sorry about that, man." He reached a hand out to the tech specialist Adam had already helped off the ground. "I'm obviously not thinking clearly."

"Not thinking with your head, you mean," Adam mumbled loud enough for only Griffin to hear.

The tech specialist shook Griffin's hand while massaging his shoulder with his other one. "Now I know why the director hated to lose you to the New York regional office's hockey team."

"Mr. President," the director said suddenly.

Griffin jumped to his feet at the director's words as the president, flanked by his chief of staff and the admiral, strode from one of the sitting areas at the end of the hall.

"Director Worcester, Harriett and I would like for Marin to remain here with us," President Manning said.

"Marin *is* here?" The words slipped past Griffin's lips before he could stop them.

President Manning turned to study him. Griffin had always liked working for the man. The popular president was demanding, but fair. And he never took advantage of his position to demean those in service to him. But Griffin hadn't seen the president since the incident with his daughter-in-law. He had no doubt the president had been briefed on the situation. Griffin just didn't know whose side the man would take.

The president's face softened slightly and he jerked his chin to indicate the Queen's Sitting Room where he'd just come from. "She's with my wife."

"I'm sorry, Mr. President," the director said. "But protocol demands we return the chef to the safe house. If our suspect figures out we sent Agent Pannell instead of the chef, he could return here to look for her."

"Yes, but you've got this place locked down like a fortress," the president argued. "Surely he wouldn't risk coming back again."

"He's penetrated our security at least three times that we know of," the director countered. "That's three more times than he should have. We're working every scenario trying to figure out how he's getting in and I know we're close to answering that question, but until then, we have to stick to the protocol. I can allow the chef to accompany you to Camp David, however, if you'd like to take your family there." The director looked as though he wanted to beg the president to choose that option.

"The president can't leave Washington tonight," his chief of staff interjected. "Not while Congress is voting on his new jobs initiative. It will look as if we're not supporting those members who are sponsoring it."

"What good is being the damn President of the United States if I can't ever do things my way?"

His chief of staff chuckled. "You wouldn't be the first commander in chief to ask that question."

"Fine," the president said. "But I want this guy caught. This ends tonight."

"We'll do our best, sir," the director replied.

The president turned to head back to the sitting room. "Now I have to go break it to my wife and her goddaughter that we have to send her back."

"I'll do it," Griffin said.

Adam's hand was on Griffin's arm before he took a step. "Easy, buddy," his friend whispered. "We're closing in on the guy that could break your case wide open. Keep your eye on the prize. Let FLOTUS console her. Marin will be kept safe."

The president looked at Griffin curiously. Griffin shook off Adam's hand. He needed to know for himself that Marin was okay. Then he would go catch her tormentor. "I want to be at the meeting place," he told the director. "I need Salenko alive and talking so I can ferret out the rest of this counterfeiting ring."

The director nodded. Adam sighed loudly.

"I just have one thing to take care of first," Griffin said.

"Get your gear on and meet me in my office in twenty minutes," the director ordered.

The president gestured for Griffin to walk with him to the sitting room.

"Marin wants to speak with her family," Griffin mentioned. "It would go a long way toward making her feel better about this whole situation."

"I agree," the president replied. "Admiral, can you arrange a secure line for Marin to call home?"

The chief usher nodded.

"Marin's well-being is our first priority, Agent Keller. Even after this issue is resolved."

Griffin let President Manning's warning sink in as they entered the area of the White House known as the Queen's Sitting Room. Part of him was relieved that Marin had a champion aside from him to keep her safe. But the other part of him wanted to tell the President of the United States to mind his own damn business.

The late day sunlight was streaming through the window, casting a patchwork of shadows across the floor. Marin sat on a wide sofa that doubled as a daybed. She was reading a book aloud to the president's granddaughter who was listening intently while lounging against Otto. The First Lady sat across from them sipping white wine. She glanced up at her husband expectantly. He shook his head.

Clearly agitated, Mrs. Manning sprung up from her chair. "I trusted that woman, Cal. With our precious granddaughter. And this is what she does?" she whispered furiously once she'd reached her husband. "Stealing from our country and threatening Marin? The worst thing that ever happened to us was Clark bringing Farrah home. I don't know what he ever saw in that woman. I wish he'd never married her."

The president glanced past his wife, fixing his gaze on the dark-haired little girl sitting with Marin. "I'm hopeful our son saw something in Farrah other than her long legs and good looks. But wishing that he'd never married her would be wishing away Arabelle."

The First Lady wiped at her eyes. "I know. I'm sorry. Arabelle is the only good thing that's come out of this situation. She'll be devastated when she finds out her grandmother is an art thief." She turned to Griffin. "But she'll be even more upset if something happens to Bita. You have to bring her back, Agent Keller. Despite what she is, I know Bita adores Arabelle. There has to be some explanation for this. And I for one want to hear it."

Griffin never liked to make promises with regard to an op. Anything could go wrong, even when one was well planned out. Promises only jinxed things. "I'll do my best, ma'am," he said.

Mrs. Manning looked as though she was going to say more, but her husband stepped in.

"Agent Keller and his team will do what they have to do," the president interjected. "Including protecting Marin."

"My apologies, Agent Keller," the First Lady said. "I'm not myself today. You've proven yourself dedicated to our family on more than one occasion. I don't believe I ever got the chance to thank you. Or to apologize for Farrah's behavior."

Griffin was uncomfortable with the woman's words. "No need, ma'am. It's part of the job."

The First Lady's face relaxed. "Well, not all of it. But I'm glad you're such a good sport. I'm also very grateful that Marin has you to watch over her." She patted him on the shoulder.

"Mr. President," the president's chief of staff interrupted them. "We're ready to brief you on how we'd like to spin the story of the art thefts once the details reach the media."

Both the Mannings sighed. The First Lady gave her husband a smile that clearly conveyed a silent message because he nodded briefly before leaning in to kiss her on the cheek. He followed his chief of staff into the center hall.

"Arabelle," the First Lady called to her granddaughter. "Let's get you into the bathtub. Your daddy will be home from the hospital soon."

The little girl jumped up off the sofa. "Good. We have to tell him about Grandma Bita." Arabelle stopped in front of Griffin, looking up at him with her big, earnest eyes. "Maybe Daddy can go with you and Marin to get her?"

Marin stood behind the child, clutching the book she'd been reading to her chest. She wore a stricken look on her face. Griffin crouched down on his haunches so he was eye level with Arabelle. "Your daddy would be a big help tonight, that's true. But he gets to be a hero every day at the hospital. How about if tonight he stays home and keeps you company? Then us other guys will get a chance at being a hero. Okay?"

Arabelle's bottom lip trembled. "Only if you promise that Grandma Bita and Marin will be here tomorrow."

The First Lady bent down and wrapped an arm around her granddaughter. "Sweetheart, we need to let Agent Keller go now."

"But he hasn't promised yet," the child said mulishly.

Damn. It was one thing to be evasive with the First Lady. Dodging a preschooler was a hell of a lot trickier. No way Arabelle was going to let him get away with an "I'll do my best." Griffin crossed his fingers behind his back. "I promise," he said, hoping he hadn't just coopted the whole stinking op.

Arabelle threw her arms around his neck and buried her face in his shoulder.

"Thank you," the First Lady mouthed before she pulled her granddaughter away.

MARIN BLINKED BACK the tears in her eyes watching the exchange between Griffin and Arabelle. Griffin was a man who didn't make promises. Especially about the future. She knew that point only too well. But he'd told the child what she needed to hear, and for that, she loved him just a little bit more.

"Jesus, I hope my sister has a boy." Griffin dragged his

fingers through his hair as he got to his feet. "Little girls have some scary powers."

"And then they turn into big girls," Marin said softly.

The air in the room seemed to evaporate when Griffin's smoldering gaze collided with hers. His eyes were dark and his body tense. Still, he kept his distance. Marin was grateful for his self-control because she would likely shatter if he touched her.

"Yes," he murmured, "yes, they do."

Five feet separated them as they stood staring at one another in the charged silence for a long moment.

"How are you?" he finally asked.

"I'm not sure," she admitted. "Numb probably best describes it. I feel as though I'm living in an alternate universe where nothing is as it seems. Every day, this whole thing just gets more and more unbelievable." She placed Arabelle's book on the table before wrapping her arms around her midsection. "This man wants to kill me because I saw his face. But Arabelle has seen him too. What will happen to her?"

She began to tremble. Griffin quickly closed the distance between them, but Marin took a step back when he would have taken her in his arms. He swore.

"Nothing is going to happen to Arabelle, because this ends tonight."

"And Bita? What will happen to her?"

Griffin arched an eyebrow. "She's a thief. One who, as you just pointed out, put her innocent granddaughter in danger. Not to mention you, too."

Marin turned toward the window. "I know. Like I said, none of this makes any sense. Except I understand now how you thought I might be the thief. Because I never would have suspected Bita. I still can't believe it."

She felt the warmth of his body at her back as he came to stand behind her. Thankfully, he kept his hands to himself. They stood like that for a few minutes watching as dusk turned to darkness.

"The admiral has arranged for you to call and talk to your parents before you have to go back to the safe house."

His breath fanning her neck made her shiver. Or perhaps it was the knowledge she had to return to the safe house that was making her unsteady. Marin wasn't exactly sure. She was, however, grateful he'd made this small gesture to ease her anxiety.

"Thank you," she whispered.

"Marin, I promise—"

"Don't!" She spun around to face him. "I'm not a five-year-old who needs you to make promises. Go do your job without worrying about me. Or Arabelle. Promises will only trip you up when you need to be on guard."

He opened his mouth to say something before quickly closing it. His eyes were filled with wonder. Marin's hands ached to touch him, so she did, gliding her palms along his suit jacket.

"Try not to mess up this suit or your beautiful dimples while you're out tonight, though, okay?"

His chest tightened under her hands and suddenly his arms were around her, pressing her into his hard body while his mouth took hers in a searing kiss. One that was inevitable. Marin arched into him, savoring his scent, his taste, and the feel of his body. Griffin kissed her as if he possessed her, plundering her mouth like the rogue pirate she'd imagined him to be aboard the sailboat the night before. And Marin let him, succumbing to his invasion with an answering passion.

The sound of someone clearing their throat alerted them to the fact that they were not alone. Both were breathing hard when they stepped apart. Marin avoided looking at Griffin so he wouldn't see the longing that was surely in her eyes. The last thing she wanted to do was distract him from his duties tonight.

"Excuse me, Chef," Assistant Usher Peters said. "Your parents are on line three for you."

Relief surged through her at the thought of talking to her mom and dad. Surely, she would feel more grounded once she did. She turned to say something to Griffin as she reached for the phone on the side table, but he had already slipped out of the room. Marin sank down on the daybed, embarrassed at the tears that began as soon as she heard her mother's voice.

THIRTY MINUTES LATER, Marin stepped into the kitchen of the residence expecting to see Lillie preparing the First Family's dinner. Her aunt Harriett was there instead. She was mixing up a pot of macaroni and cheese from a box.

"Don't judge." She held up a hand sheepishly at Marin. "I'm a pediatrician. I ought to know better than to feed this crap to my granddaughter, but it's been a very trying day."

"There's nothing wrong with comfort food. It's actually one of my favorite food groups."

Her godmother smiled at Marin's attempt at humor. "I'm sorry that you got dragged into this, Marin. I hate that this is happening. There are days I wish we were all just back in New Orleans. Life was a lot easier then."

"But not as rewarding." Marin took the spoon from the First Lady and began preparing the macaroni and cheese for her. "You and the president are doing a lot of good for this country."

"Yeah, like letting my son's mother-in-law steal priceless artwork that belongs to the taxpayers." Aunt Harriett sank down into one of the chairs at the kitchen table. "And she brought a crazy killer with her, to boot." She hesitated a moment. "Cal said you stabbed a man yesterday. That must have been horrible."

Marin's hand stilled mid-stir as the vision of her plunging the knife into the man's back replayed in her mind. She shuddered violently. Aunt Harriett sprung up from her chair and wrapped her arms around Marin.

"It's something I'm trying to forget," Marin whispered. "But I'm not sure I ever will."

"You did what you had to do to survive. And, no, you won't ever forget because you have one of these." Her aunt tapped Marin's chest. "Not to mention a conscience. But I don't want you ever blaming yourself for what happened."

"He was going to shoot Griffin—Agent Keller."

Aunt Harriett brushed back a piece of Marin's hair. "That would have been a travesty for women everywhere. He's just too beautiful a man not to be walking this earth."

Marin resumed stirring the pasta while trying to hide the blush that was creeping up her neck. Griffin was a gorgeous man. She'd spent the better part of last night confirming that fact.

"He's a good man, too," her godmother continued. "He'll make things right. You'll see."

She wasn't sure if her aunt was talking about the return of Bita or something else, but since thinking about Griffin only led Marin's heart in circles, she kept quiet. They worked in companionable silence, her aunt handing her the ingredients while Marin prepared Arabelle's dinner. It was soothing to be doing something that was so natural. She felt loved and protected with her godmother by her side. After the week she'd had, Marin would never take moments like this one for granted again. She was glad for the opportunity to relax and regroup.

The tranquility was interrupted when one of the Secret Service agents stepped into the kitchen. "Chef, your ride is ready to take you back to the safe house."

The First Lady slammed her palm onto the counter. "This is all so ridiculous," she said through clenched teeth. "Tell me again why she can't stay here?"

The agent flinched at the First Lady's stern demand. "Director's orders, ma'am."

Marin diffused the situation by leaning in to kiss her

godmother on the cheek. "It's better this way. Everyone is safer. Give Arabelle a hug for me. I'll see you in the morning."

Her aunt hugged her tightly. "Agent Keller promised Arabelle that you'd be back here tomorrow. I'm trusting him to keep his word. Or I'll shoot him myself. I don't care how adorable those damn dimples of his are."

"I never realized you were that ruthless, Aunt Harriett," Marin said with a surprised grin.

"Not ruthless; just protective of those people I love. Sleep well, honey."

Marin doubted she would sleep at all tonight, but she didn't bother worrying her godmother with that information. Otto fell into step beside her as they made their way to the elevator.

"The media are camped on the North Lawn awaiting an announcement about the president's jobs bill, so you'll be exiting via the south entrance," the Secret Service agent explained as they exited the elevator on the ground floor.

Heavily armed officers from the Uniformed Division seemed to be around every corner. There was a frenzy of activity within the Secret Service office, as well. As they passed by, Marin risked a glance to see if she could spot Griffin, but he was nowhere in sight. Most of her was glad to not have distracted him while he was preparing to take on the murderous art thief in the next few minutes; but a small part of her—the part that always seemed to want to jump his bones—was bereft at not seeing him again.

They passed through the Diplomatic Reception Room

with its striking wallpaper featuring panoramic views of early North American life. A lump formed in Marin's throat as she thought of Wes, the curator. He'd confided to Marin that he worried about the preservation of wallpaper, first installed in 1961. Wes's passion about the artifacts within the White House most probably got him killed. Marin said a silent prayer that no one else would die at the hands of this mad man.

The agent led her out onto the driveway. The night air was balmier than it had been the night before. Otto scurried toward the Kennedy garden and the bushes beyond it. The agent glanced down the driveway toward where the armored vehicle was parked.

"Agent Todd must be inside the house," he said. "I'll go get him and we can be on our way."

"That's fine," she told him. "I think Otto needs to take care of some business before we leave. I'll meet you at the car."

Marin meandered toward the decoy vehicle while Otto relieved himself on three of the four trees lining the drive. When she and the dog reached the black SUV, the door to the back was already open for them. Otto jumped in and made himself at home on the bench seat.

"Save some room for me," Marin said as she climbed in behind the dog.

A moment later, her door was closed from the outside and the agent took his place in the driver's seat. Marin closed her eyes and rested her head against the seatback as the car pulled away from the White House. She willed herself not to think about the danger Griffin and his team would be jumping into shortly. It was easier said than done, however. Reaching over, Marin went to bury her fingers in the comfort of Otto's soft fur. The dog growled menacingly, startling Marin. Her eyes snapped open. Otto was sitting at attention, his focus on the driver. A chill ran up her spine as Marin realized there was only one agent in the car. Her breath froze when she met the driver's eyes in the rearview mirror. They were the same eerie ones she'd encountered on the spiral staircase the week before.

CHAPTER EIGHTEEN

"PILLSBURY HAS LEFT the building."

Griffin breathed a huge sigh of relief after glancing at the incoming text message from Agent Slade. The team had barely thirty minutes until the meeting time and he needed to concentrate on the scene around him. Now that Marin was out of the White House and would soon be safe at Fort McNair for the evening, he could focus on nabbing Salenko and finally having his link to The Artist.

The president's residence was heavily guarded with a double contingent of Uniformed Division staff surveilling the grounds and Sam's Counter Assault Team on duty inside the White House, so it was unlikely that even a rogue squirrel could enter the estate uninvited. But Salenko was a skilled mercenary with deadly intent. Griffin believed there could never be too many safeguards where the Ukrainian was concerned. And this whole evening had him on edge.

The FBI was assigned the lead in tonight's op, making Griffin feel a bit superfluous. He was once again second in command to Leslie. They were both overseeing the operation from a remote command post inside a van parked in Georgetown, two blocks from the designated meeting place. A light rain had just begun to fall, stirring up an eerie cloud of fog that was floating up to their location from the Potomac River a block away.

"This doesn't make sense to me," Griffin said. "Why here? There are restaurants and bars all up and down the street. Salenko has to know we'll be staking the place out. He also has to know we won't just give him Marin. What's his game?"

"He's getting desperate?" Leslie proposed with a shrug. She took a sip from her coffee. "This is the same guy who seriously blundered his attempt at Marin earlier this week. If Salenko is anything like those buffoons who tried to kill you both the other night, he's not very clever. He knows we're on to him and he's scared, so he's taking crazy risks."

"No." Griffin shook his head as the sense of unease began to swell through his body. "This guy is too well trained to take risks. And everything he's done thus far has been highly calculated." He slammed his fist into the side of the van. "We're missing something here. I feel it."

Leslie eyed him cautiously. "Okay. Talk to me. You have the best gut instincts of anyone in this business. What's yours telling you right now?"

"That we are being set up." He jumped from his chair and opened the back door. "I'm headed back to the White House. You stay here and see this through just in case I'm wrong."

Except Griffin didn't feel wrong at all.

He commandeered one of the SUVs and raced back down K Street, through Foggy Bottom and along Pennsylvania Avenue. Unfortunately, there was a logjam of people celebrating the passage of the president's jobs bill blocking the northeast gate. Griffin swore. *Of all the nights to have extra civilians camped out around the White House.* He weaved around the crowds and drove around the block, coming up Seventeenth Street to the West Wing staff entrance.

"You're not authorized to park in this lot," the Uniformed Division officer manning the southeast gate shouted at Griffin.

"Take it up with the director," Griffin said as he drove into the parking area.

Unfortunately, it seemed as if every employee of the West Wing was working late. He ended up ditching the car in the communications director's vacant spot. Entering the West Wing, Griffin chucked the keys to the guard just in case the communications director returned. Then, he sprinted down the hall to the Secret Service overflow area and lounge. He checked the electronic status board to see that the president was currently in the residence, which meant Adam would be there, too.

Griffin stormed up the stairs, coming to a halt at the crowd assembled outside the cabinet room. An impromptu party was happening among the staff and they were blocking Griffin's progress. He huffed in frustration, trying to circumvent the people lining up for glasses of champagne, while not bringing attention to himself. Unfortunately, he was unsuccessful.

"Agent Keller!" the president's chief of staff called out

just as Griffin was rounding the corner to the west colonnade that would take him to the residence.

"Damn." Griffin swore under his breath as he stopped in his tracks to wait for the chief of staff to catch up.

"What are you doing back here?" the man demanded of Griffin. "Has the situation been resolved?"

"Not yet, sir," Griffin said. "I just need to follow up on something here in the residence."

And he couldn't afford to have the chief of staff hold him up. He needed to find Adam. Griffin was being insubordinate, but he took a step anyway. The other man kept pace with him.

"Tell me the president and his family aren't in danger, Agent Keller."

"I can't tell you that, sir, because I still don't know what this guy has up his sleeve." They crossed through the Palm Room. Griffin was glad to see the two marine guards at their posts.

"You don't believe we'll be able to rescue Mrs. Ranjbar?"

They stopped outside of Director Worcester's office.

"I don't believe that's this guy's intent, no," Griffin said.

"What is his damn intent, Agent Keller?" the chief of staff demanded.

"If I knew that I wouldn't be standing here, sir."

Director Worcester and Adam rushed to the center hall at the sounds of their raised voices. Adam took one look at Griffin's face and began rapidly firing orders via the communication device he wore on his arm, demanding each of the members of his team check-in.

"What's going on, Agent Keller?" Director Worcester asked.

"I think Salenko is setting us up."

The president's chief of staff swore violently.

The Secret Service director remained stoic. "For what purpose?"

"I haven't figured that out yet."

Griffin's cell phone rang. He glanced at the screen and saw Ben's name.

"Tell me something good, Ben," Griffin said into his phone. "Has anything shown up on the net of video cameras around the meeting place?"

"Nothing yet, but I've uncovered something else and you're not going to like it," Ben answered.

"Let me go into the director's office and I'll put you on speaker."

The men gathered around the table. The president's chief of staff paced the room while the others listened intently.

"I've been investigating how Salenko is accessing the White House undetected," Ben explained. "I entered several variables in order to come up with an initial stand-ard deviation, allowing for some volatility within my sample mean—"

"In English, Ben!" Adam interjected.

"Right, right," Ben said. "Basically, I ended up with the hypothesis that Salenko is entering through the front door."

"What?" both the director and chief of staff shouted.

"Hear me out," Ben added. "My premise is that he's posing as someone else who has regular access to the mansion. So, I ran facial recognition comparisons with every employee, contractor, and subcontractor who has clearance to be in the White House. After several hours, I came up with a hit. Salenko is a dead ringer for the subcontractor who maintains the pool and the solar panels on the cabana."

Adam exchanged a look with Griffin.

"There's an underground passage that runs from the cabana to the ground floor of the residence. The First Family uses it to access the pool area," Adam whispered before stepping out into the lobby, presumably to check on the area around the pool and the passage.

"The guy's name is Willem Dunst," Ben went on to say. "I made a few calls. The real Willem Dunst broke his back three months ago and has been on disability ever since, yet his credentials have been swiped granting him access to the White House at least six times since then. He was here on the morning Marin saw Salenko on the back stairs and again later that afternoon. The credentials were also used on Monday when the other chef was attacked. And guys, here's the part you're not gonna like… Dunst's credentials were swiped again forty minutes ago."

All three men moved at once. Director Worcester pressed the silent alarm on his desk that would lock down the building. The president's chief of staff headed upstairs to move the president and his family to the secure room located in the sub-basement of the building. Griffin swiftly moved through the center hallway, commanding the other agents and Uniformed Division officers on guard to fan out and check the rooms on the ground floor. He pulled his service revolver and slowly climbed the spiral staircase to the mezzanine level.

The pastry kitchen was filled with several ozone machines meant to rid the room of its heavy smoke smell. The oven had been removed and the space remained empty awaiting its replacement. Ben said that Salenko had returned to the White House after Marin had spotted him on the stairs that day. There was only one reason the Ukrainian had come back. Griffin thought of Salenko deliberately setting the combustible materials into the oven in an effort to kill Marin and his pulse began to throb violently.

She's safe.

He pulled up the text Agent Slade had sent him earlier letting him know Marin had left the building. The time stamp was twenty-seven minutes ago. Ben said Salenko entered the White House some forty minutes ago. Griffin's chest seized as he jumped down the spiral staircase to the pantry. He dialed Agent Groesch at the safe house.

She answered on the second ring. "Hey there, Griff," she said. "How'd it go? Did you get him?"

"Let me talk to Marin," Griffin demanded.

"Marin? Todd's not back with her yet. I assume she's still at the White House."

"Fuck!" A cold knot of fear tightened around Griffin's heart as he raced down the center hall. "Slade!" he yelled at the top of his lungs.

A moment later the agent appeared out the East Room. "Right here, Agent Keller. What—"

He didn't wait for the agent to finish, instead slamming him up against the wall outside the Green Room. "You texted me that she'd left the damn house!"

"She did," Agent Slade said beneath the forearm Griffin had pinned to his neck. "I-I mean when I went back out there, she and the dog were already in the car and Todd was driving away with them."

"Did you see Todd in the car?"

The agent gulped against Griffin's arm. "N-no. But he's not here."

A crowd of agents and Uniformed Division officers gathered around them.

"Cut it out, Griffin." Adam grabbed him by the lapels and shook him. "What the hell's going on?"

The words burned in the back of Griffin's numb throat. "Salenko's got Marin."

MARIN NOW UNDERSTOOD what it meant to be paralyzed with fear. The SUV continued on its path to God-only-knew-where and she couldn't seem to move a muscle to stop it. The mad man driving hadn't uttered a word. Next to her, Otto kept up his low, rumbling growl while Marin tried to push air through lungs that threatened to strangle her.

The SUV picked up speed when they merged onto a highway. They crossed the river and panic squeezed Marin more tightly. He was taking her further away from the White House. From the Secret Service. *From Griffin.* The rain began to fall in earnest, the drops cascading down the windows like the tears Marin was too frozen to cry.

Ten minutes later, they exited the highway onto a road with more stoplights. Her captor had to decrease his speed to merge with the flow of traffic. If Marin was going to escape, she needed to do it now. A few broken bones jumping from a moving car was surely preferable to what awaited her at the other end of this wild ride.

She forced her fingers to move, quietly unclasping the seat belt. Slowly, she slid toward the door. Marin was relieved when Otto instinctively moved with her. Waiting for a red light, she prayed that someone in another car would stop and help her after she landed. The SUV began to slow and Marin couldn't wait any longer. She tried the door, but it was locked. Gulping in a breath, she attempted to turn the lock, but it wouldn't budge. Her captor smiled grimly in the rearview mirror.

His expression angered her and that fury propelled her to keep trying. She turned to hurl herself over the backseat and out the rear door, but she was stopped short by the body staring back at her. Agent Todd, his eyes bulging out and his mouth fixed wide-open in terror, lay crumpled in the back. He wasn't breathing. Marin's shriek of fear was swallowed up by the bile rising up the back of her throat. Otto crowded onto her lap pinning her to the leather seat.

The tears that she'd been unable to cry before were now streaming down Marin's cheeks. She thought of her family—she wouldn't be able to say goodbye to her parents, her brothers, or grandparents. Or even Ava whom she loved like a sister in spite of her cousin's demanding personality.

And Griffin.

He would be devastated by her death. Not because he loved her the way she loved him. But because it was his job to protect people. He was passionate about his career. And he was good at it. Griffin would take her death as a personal failure. She ached for him. Her family would have each other for comfort once she was gone. But who would Griffin have? The image of Agent Morgan comforting Griffin had Marin gulping down an agonized sob.

The car made a sharp left turn. Marin glanced out the window, but the darkness made it difficult for her to determine where they were going. They'd left the more populated area and headed into a ratty looking industrial park. There was no evidence of another human being in sight which meant screaming for help would be futile. She wrapped her arms around Otto's tense body.

"You will not die."

The unexpected sound of the mad man's husky voice made Marin jump. She met his icy stare in the rearview mirror. Otto's growl became more menacing.

Marin didn't believe a word out of his mouth. "Then

take me back."

"That, I cannot do."

"How does Bita fit into all of this?" Marin demanded.

"You will see."

Marin shivered. Despite the other woman's duplicity, Marin hoped for Arabelle's sake the little girl's grandmother would not look like Agent Todd when she did come face-to-face with the woman.

He pulled the SUV up to a deserted loading dock. There were several white vans parked in the lot, but they all were unoccupied. After turning off the engine, Marin's captor opened his door. Marin quickly tried her door again, but to no avail. She swallowed another sob.

"You will come quietly. Or I will kill the dog," the man said matter-of-factly.

He exited the driver's seat and Marin noticed he was favoring his left arm. Her pulse sped up. Could she overpower him when he opened her door? Since it was likely she didn't have anything else to lose, she decided to try it. Marin was stronger than she looked and people often misjudged her athleticism. She was hoping this guy did, as well.

Keeping Otto from making the first move would be tricky. She tried to remember the Dutch commands she'd overheard the K-9 officers use with their dogs.

"Blijf," she ordered in a trembling voice, adding a whispered "wait" for good measure. She prayed Otto listened because Marin was already carrying around the weight of too many deaths at the hands of this mad man.

The door opened and her captor was careful to block any escape route. He was as wiry as she remembered, but he carried himself in a way that screamed lethal. Marin shivered and ducked her head. She wasn't sure if she could carry out her plan if she got a look at his cold eyes. Slowly, she climbed out of the car. Otto growled in protest, but, thankfully the dog didn't move. When her feet touched the asphalt, Marin leaned forward, snapping her head up swiftly so that her scalp connected sharply with her captor's chin. The move had the desired effect, startling him so he lost his balance.

Otto sprung from the backseat like a leopard, pouncing on him just as Marin tried to slip between the man and the SUV. In her worry over the dog, she hesitated. It was long enough for the man to trip her. She landed hard on the asphalt to the sound of Otto's painful whimper.

"No!" she cried.

She winced in pain as he yanked her up off the ground by her ponytail and jerked her against his body. He flashed a bloody knife in front of her face.

"I told you what would happen to the dog if you misbehaved," he hissed against her ear.

Marin's hands and knees stung from the road rash she'd gotten landing on the pavement. Her stomach lurched as he dragged her up the steps to the warehouse. When they got to the top, she hazarded a look back for Otto, hoping his death was at least swift. But she couldn't see anything through her watery eyes. He inserted a key into the dead bolt and opened the door. The room was dimly lit and it smelled of chlorine.

"I told you not to hurt her!" Bita cried as she raced over to where he'd tossed Marin onto the concrete floor.

Marin recoiled from the older woman's hand. "Don't you dare touch me!" she choked out as she scrambled to a seated position.

Bita had the audacity to look offended. "Chef Marin," Bita pleaded. "Please, this is not my fault."

A hysterical laugh escaped Marin's mouth. "Oh, really? This wouldn't be happening if you hadn't used your granddaughter to lure me here. Or if you hadn't stolen valuable art from the White House. Tell me again how this isn't your fault?"

The older woman knelt down beside Marin. "I didn't know what was in the packages," she whispered.

Marin's mouth gaped incredulously.

"I didn't!" Bita insisted.

"They know it was you," Marin said. "The Secret Service. The FBI. The president."

"Arabelle?" Bita's eyes glistened.

"When I don't come back tomorrow, Arabelle will be devastated. And that's on you."

Bita reared back and slapped Marin across the mouth. Hard. Marin gasped, tasting blood.

"Leave her!" their captor yelled from across the room where he'd been typing out a text. "She is the only thing that is keeping me from killing you, Bita. Don't tempt me to change my plans."

"You will tell the conglomerate to give me what I

want," Bita demanded regally after getting to her feet. She launched into rapid-fire Farsi as she stormed across the room. Creepy Guy didn't flinch. He simply leveled his frozen gaze at Bita.

"No," he said.

Bita twirled around angrily, but Marin was ready for her this time. She leaped to her feet so that she towered over the other woman. Before Bita could react, however, the door was flung open and several heavily armed men swarmed into the room. Her captor acted as though he expected them.

"What have we here, Yerik?" one of the men asked.

He was heavy-set with sagging jowls and protruding eyebrows. Ironically, he was also dressed smartly in a finely tailored suit, as if they were all attending an evening dinner party and not staring one another down in a dirty warehouse. The other four men seemed to take their cues from him.

"Are we to be entertained by women fighting tonight? Or are we to enjoy the pleasure of your White House mole?"

CHAPTER NINETEEN

"**A**GENT TODD ISN'T answering his cell," Adam said into the speakerphone in the White House Secret Service office. "Ben, can we get a ping from the GPS device in the decoy vehicle?"

"I'm checking," Ben answered.

Griffin had never felt so numb in all his life. He sat in Director Worcester's office staring blankly at the agents scurrying around him.

He'd lost her.

After all he'd done, it hadn't been enough. Griffin had lost colleagues before—both military and civilian—but never someone under his protection. And for it to be Marin was doubly devastating. They had a connection. One that scared the hell out of him, but not knowing her whereabouts was even more frightening. His mind whirred and his stomach lurched just thinking about the heinous murders Salenko had already committed. He slammed his eyes shut and banged his head against the wall at the thought of that monster touching Marin.

"Agent Keller."

Snapping his lids open, he met the fierce gaze of the president. He was standing in front of Griffin holding a glass with amber liquid swirling around in it.

"Take this and drink it," the president commanded. "That's an order."

Griffin was embarrassed at the way his hand shook, but he took the tumbler and downed its contents in one gulp. The bourbon burned his throat, but at this point Griffin didn't care.

"No one holds you responsible, Agent Keller," the president said. "We'll find her."

He shot to his feet. "She's still alive," Griffin croaked out. "I'd know if she—wasn't." He didn't bother explaining to President Manning how he knew. Griffin got the feeling the man understood.

The president clapped him on the shoulder. "We'll find her," he repeated.

"Damn it," Ben's voice came over the speakerphone. "It looks like the GPS in the decoy vehicle has been disabled."

The fervor in the room seemed to dim.

Griffin ran his fingers through his hair and squeezed his skull. "There has to be some other way to trace it, Ben," he groaned.

"Wait," Ben said. "Did you say she took Otto with her?"

"That's it!" Adam shouted. "The K-9s all have a GPS microchip implanted in them. Can you track them that way?"

"It's gonna take me a few minutes. I have to find Otto's specific serial number, but, yes, I'm sure that I can."

The movement in the room stilled as everyone waited

for Ben's response. Griffin's heart pounded so hard he thought it would crack a rib.

"I've got him!" Ben announced.

"Where?" Adam asked as he and Griffin headed for the door.

"Marbury Point. I'm texting you the address."

"Text it to Agent Morgan, too," Griffin called over his shoulder.

Officer Stevens, Otto's K-9 handler, fell into step with them. Griffin acknowledged him with a nod as the three men jogged back through the West Wing and out the side entrance to where the Counter Assault Team's combat vehicle was already running. Adam jumped in the front passenger seat while Griffin and Officer Stevens scrambled to get in back. The agent driving had the Humvee moving before Griffin closed his door.

"Talk to me, Ben," Griffin demanded into his cell phone.

"Otto's signal is coming from a warehouse near the water treatment plant," Ben said. "The address checks out as belonging to the pool servicing company. I'm checking for live video in the area, but so far nothing is coming up."

"Thirteen minutes out," the driver announced.

Thirteen minutes. Griffin's gut clenched. Salenko could administer any amount of torture in thirteen minutes.

"Otto seems to be pacing back and forth, but when I overlay his location with Google Images, it looks like he's outside the warehouse," Ben said.

"He's been separated from Chef Marin," Officer Stevens explained. "He's been trained to stay close just in case he can find a way to get back to her."

Griffin forced himself to take a deep breath. The fact that Salenko had somehow isolated Otto from Marin was not a good sign. They needed to get there quickly.

"The FBI has arrived," Adam said alluding to the sirens behind them. A second Secret Service vehicle filled with members of Adam's Counter Assault Team was also following them.

It took them only nine minutes to make it to their destination. They'd killed the sirens several miles back so as not to tip Salenko off.

"We'll walk in the last half mile," Adam relayed to Leslie and her team in the FBI vehicle.

Quietly, they climbed out of the Humvee. The pungent smell from the water treatment plant immediately assaulted Griffin's nose. The drizzle had stopped, leaving behind a residue of moisture that made everything around him shine in the darkness. They'd need to be careful not to give themselves away with anything shiny on their person.

Griffin checked the weapons strapped to his body. Leslie was by his side instantly. She gave his arm a gentle squeeze.

"We'll find her," she whispered.

Office Stevens pulled a dog whistle out of his pocket and blew into it; its silent call only registering with a canine's ears. A long moment later, Otto limped out of the woods behind the warehouse. Blood streamed from the dog's hind leg, but he obediently sat beside his handler.

"Good boy," Officer Stevens patted the dog.

He crouched down to examine Otto's injury. "It looks like a puncture wound from a knife." The officer's voice broke slightly. "He's lost a lot of blood. I need to get him treated before he goes into shock."

Adam nodded and indicated that one of the FBI vehicles should take the K-9 officer and Otto back. When Officer Stevens bent to lift him into the Humvee, the dog whimpered in protest at being forced to leave. Griffin rubbed a hand over the dog's ears.

"We'll bring her back to you," he whispered. He left the words 'I promise' unspoken. The promise he'd already made to Arabelle still haunted him.

The group fanned out as Adam gestured for half the team to circle around the warehouse from one side while he, Griffin, Leslie, and the others surrounded the building from the opposite end. They crouched in the damp gravel five yards from the entrance. The president's decoy vehicle sat in the parking lot in front of the warehouse along with several white vans apparently used by the pool company. A Ford Expedition was parked there, too. The tire tracks on the wet pavement indicated it had only recently arrived.

Leslie took her cell phone out of her vest and pulled up a blank screen. Eric crept to the side of the warehouse and carefully pressed his handheld radar to the wall. The image from the radar gun was immediately displayed on Leslie's phone. Adam glanced over Leslie's shoulder.

"Shit," Adam whispered. "And here I thought our odds were going to be twelve to one."

"By my count, there are eight people inside." She looked up at Griffin. "All of them breathing."

Her words didn't go very far to soothe Griffin. He was operating under the theory that Salenko had kidnapped Marin because she'd seen him exiting the White House. If that were the case, why hadn't he killed her like the others? While he was relieved that Marin was still breathing, something felt off. It was a feeling Griffin hated.

"WHO ARE THESE women, Yerik?" the big guy who appeared to be the leader asked. "You were told to bring me your White House spy."

Marin pretended to study the exchange between her captor, Yerik, and the other man. Her eyes darted from one occupant of the wide room to another while her fingers felt around on the floor beside her, scavenging for any type of weapon she could use to defend herself. Her palms burned and blood from her lip dribbled down her chin, but Marin refused to wait around and see what these men had in store for her. Slowly, she inched back toward the large drums of pool cleaner lining the back wall.

Bita stormed up to the bulky man, her cashmere wrap billowing behind her. Like the man in the suit, she was overdressed for this party.

"Do you not think a woman capable of being a spy?" she asked.

The men accompanying him drew their assault rifles

when Bita got close. Marin stilled, holding her breath. But, try as she might, she couldn't rip her eyes away from what was surely to be Bita's death. To her surprise, the big man laughed.

"Agapi mu," he said. "You are quite a handful, yes?"

Bita's face blanched. "Greek?" she shrieked. "They're Greek!" She turned to Yerik and began speaking frantically in Farsi again.

Marin took advantage of all the screaming to scoot further back into the shadows. She'd made it six or seven inches when her hand came in contact with something smooth—something smooth that kicked her in the hip. She looked over at the boot attached to the leg of one of the men holding an assault rifle. When her eyes glanced up, the man sneered at her before kicking her again. Marin added another bruise to her abused body as she slid back to the place where Yerik had dumped her.

"Enough!" the Greek man shouted. "What is the meaning of this, Yerik? And who is this shrew?"

Bita bristled at the Greek man's choice of words. She turned from Yerik abruptly and stalked back over to her tormentor. "I am no shrew! I am Persian royalty. Niece of the late Shah of Iran."

This got the big man's attention. He grinned ruthlessly.

"Well done, Yerik, bringing me the mother of the whore the president's son is married to," he said.

If Bita was angry before, his words made her positively quake. Her hand made contact with the man's face more forcibly than when she'd hit Marin earlier. Marin sucked in a breath as her body froze in fear. The Greek man's fingers latched around Bita's wrist faster than a cobra struck its victim. He yanked Bita's body in close to his.

"I am done playing with you," he snapped. "You will do as I say now."

Bita wrestled her hand free. "I can't take any more of the art from the White House," she said with a huff.

Marin snorted. "You did know what you were doing!"

"Hush." The boot connected sharply with her hip again and Marin stifled a gasp.

"Your friend, Yerik, killed Ari," Bita said. "He was the one who knew how to take the paintings from their frames and replace them so no one would notice. I refuse to do that."

Ari was dead, too? Marin glanced over to Yerik, the man who would likely kill her, as well. The expression on his face hadn't altered one bit. His cold eyes seemed to be taking in the exchange between Bita and the other man in the detached way a spectator watched a play.

"I have no need for art," the man told Bita. "That was just Yerik's ruse to entertain Elena."

"Elena?" Bita looked from the Greek man to Yerik. "Who is this, Elena?"

"Elena is not important," the man interrupted. "Neither is the art."

But Bita seemed to think whoever this Elena was, she was very important. Her face grew contorted with anger. "What have you done?" she demanded of Yerik. "Have you double-crossed me?" She rattled something off again in

Farsi, but Yerik remained stone-faced.

Bita turned back to the Greek man. "Those paintings—those paintings." She gasped. "They were to be exchanged for paintings lost in the revolution." She spun back to Yerik. "You promised! You said you would help me. Help us! You bastard! You know where those paintings are! You will tell me!"

She flung herself at Yerik. The mad man held himself still until one of the Greek man's entourage quickly interceded, pulling her away and tossing her down at Marin's feet. Bita let out a sharp cry as her body made contact with the hard, concrete floor. Marin almost felt sorry for her.

Almost.

With Bita softly sobbing, the Greek man focused his attention on Marin. She tried not to get creeped out by the intense scrutiny of his obsidian eyes.

"Who is this?" he demanded of Yerik.

Yerik stepped into the center of the room. "She is my payment for Elena," he said proudly.

Marin nearly choked on her own breath. *Payment?* And who the heck was this Elena person they were all so obsessed with anyway?

"Payment?" The Greek man echoed her thoughts.

"I will give you the chef and you will give me Elena," Yerik explained. "The conglomerate no longer needs her to create the counterfeit bills. She has given them the template."

The Greek man's booming laugh echoed throughout

the warehouse. "You fool! The conglomerate doesn't want to trade Elena for a *chef*."

Yerik's face hardened, if that were even possible. "She is not just a *chef*," he said quietly. "She is Max Chevalier's granddaughter."

An eerie quiet suddenly settled over the occupants of the room at the mention of her grandfather's name. The Greek man's eye's widened beneath his bushy brows. Marin's tormentor with the boot took a step back from her.

"You *are* a fool, Yerik!" the Greek man yelled. "What have you done?" He swore violently in his native tongue.

Yerik didn't flinch. "The conglomerate can ransom her off. Her family will pay a fortune for her release."

Marin shivered on the cold cement. It was true. Her grandfather would go to the ends of the earth to get her back. Somehow, though, she didn't think her captivity would be anything similar to what she'd experienced in the safe houses this week.

"No!" the Greek man argued. "Max Chevalier will not pay a drachma for her release."

Marin wanted to protest, but she decided these men were all fools anyway, so why bother. She raised her chin belligerently instead.

Yerik continued to press home his point. "You would be surprised what a man would do to get back one of his own."

"The conglomerate will never return Elena, Yerik. Never!" the Greek man hissed. "Not even for Max Chevalier's granddaughter. He is a formidable man. A very powerful one. You will have us all killed just for bringing her here tonight." He gestured with his chin to one of his men. "Take her and set her free."

Marin gasped sharply. Was he serious? She was to be set free? Bita also drew in a quick breath. She slid closer to Marin and grabbed onto her shoe. Marin yanked her foot away. She'd had enough of that woman touching her.

Yerik stepped between the women and the Greek's entourage. "You will give me Elena," he demanded. "In exchange for the chef."

"No." The Greek man shook his head. "But the conglomerate will let Elena live. You have done well to bring us the Iranian princess. She will serve us nicely."

Bita shot to her feet. "I beg your pardon, but I decide who I work for and I'm not sure I like you."

Marin was becoming slap happy because she almost laughed at Bita's righteous indignation. Too bad for Bita, none of the men in the room paid her protests any attention.

"You, my agapi mu, will have a new role," the Greek man told Bita. "You will assist us in manipulating the President of the United States."

ADAM SIGNALED TO the members of his team on the other side of the warehouse. Griffin fidgeted with his helmet. He was getting antsy to get to Marin. Leslie slipped her phone back into her vest and nodded to Adam that she and her team were ready to move in.

Just as Adam raised his hand to give the go-ahead, the rear doors of one of the white cargo vans in the parking lot burst open. A swarm of armed bodies stormed out and raced into the warehouse.

"Federal agents!" they yelled.

"Federal agents?" Adam screamed. "What the fuck?"

Griffin didn't wait for the chaos to be sorted out. He drew his weapon and followed the crowd into the melee. Gun fire erupted from inside the building.

"Damn it, Griffin, stand down," Leslie ordered as she followed him into the fray. "FBI!"

The clash lasted less than a minute and when the smoke cleared, there were three bodies on the floor and three others held at gunpoint. Griffin wasn't exactly sure who was who, but he was sure he didn't see Marin anywhere in the room. Salenko either.

"Where the hell is she?" he shouted as he spun around the center of the vast warehouse.

"And who the hell are you guys?" Adam demanded, his assault rifle fixed at the intruders.

"Homeland security, counter intelligence," one of them fessed up. "I'm Reynolds, the agent in charge."

"Oooh." A woman moaned from the floor. "I think I've been shot."

Blood was oozing out of Bita Ranjbar's shoulder. One of the other Homeland agents called for the first-aid kit as he knelt beside her. "Help is on the way, Mrs. Ranjbar. You were very brave."

The older woman snorted. "After all that, the double-crosser still didn't tell us where the art is hidden."

"Wait, she's working for you?" Leslie asked.

The agent in charge nodded. "Anything more than that, I'm not at liberty to say."

"Don't give me that bullshit. We all work for the same government," Griffin said through clenched teeth. "Where is Salenko? And how did he get away with Marin?"

"The guy's a regular Houdini," Agent Reynolds said. "We've been trying to pin him down for weeks. I have two guys out there set up to track him from this position. He can't go too far on foot."

Griffin wasn't going to wait around for someone else to find Marin. He charged toward the door and nearly collided with one of the homeland agents coming inside.

"We lost him," the agent announced.

"Damn it," Griffin shouted.

"Agent Keller," Bita called from where she was sprawled out on the floor. "I know how you can find her."

"How?" Griffin, Adam, and Leslie asked at the same time.

"I slipped the tracking device Agent Reynolds gave me into her shoe. If the stubborn girl keeps it there, you should be able to find her."

Griffin could have kissed the pain-in-the-ass woman, but Adam was shoving him out the door toward the Homeland Security van. Agent Reynolds followed in their wake.

"Tony," Agent Reynolds called. "Pull up Mrs.

Ranjbar's GPS."

The agent inside the van powered up a laptop. A flashing light appeared on a grid on the screen. It was moving slowly.

"They're moving through the water processing plant," the agent said. "And they're on foot."

Griffin grabbed the laptop. "Let's go," he said to Adam.

"Hold on," Agent Reynolds demanded. "We'd do better to coordinate this. I want Salenko alive. He's not going to kill the chef."

"How the hell do you know that?" Griffin argued.

"Mrs. Ranjbur was wearing a wire. Salenko is using the chef as leverage against the counterfeiters. His plan is to ransom her to her grandfather. He needs her alive to do that. Take a minute to think this through and we'll find her."

Leslie joined them at the van. "The sharp dressed man in there is our link to the counterfeiters, Griffin. We got them."

He didn't care about that right now. Not while Marin was in danger. And he really didn't feel like standing around and making nice with more federal agents. He glanced back down at the laptop. The light had stopped flashing. And then the screen went blank.

CHAPTER TWENTY

T HE SULFUR SMELL hung thick in the night air. Marin's captor had his hand pressed against her mouth, making it impossible for her to avoid breathing in the disgusting odor. She gagged as he hauled her through the darkened water treatment park. He released his hand briefly, but when Marin started to scream, he slapped his palm over her mouth once again.

"Keep quiet," the man they called Yerik ordered.

Marin struggled against him. She'd recognized Agent Morgan's voice shouting out among the gunfire. But Yerik was already dragging her through the warehouse and out into the dark woods behind it when the agents were entering the building. Still, Griffin was close by; Marin could feel him. If she could only yell, she was sure he'd hear her.

Yerik pushed open a door and slipped into another warehouse, roughly carrying Marin with him. When they had reached the center of the building, he yanked her hard against him. He pulled something out of his pocket and waved it in front of Marin's face. It was a syringe. Marin's heart skipped several beats.

"Listen carefully, Chef." His breath fanned against her

cheek making Marin gag again. "I told you before you will not die. I must exchange you for Elena. Those crazy Greeks are afraid of your grandfather. He will be the one to free Elena if he wants to ever see you again. But if you scream or call out to your friends, I will be forced to end your life."

He said the words with no emotion. As though taking a life was as routine as brushing his teeth. Marin stilled against him. Griffin was near. He would find her. All she had to do was be patient and not aggravate her captor. If it meant seeing her family again—seeing Griffin again—she would do anything. Marin nodded.

Slowly, Yerik removed his hand from her mouth. Marin took a gulp of fresh air. She kept her expression contrite as he relaxed his hold on her body.

"You are a smart woman."

He kept his long fingers tightly shackled around her wrist while he replaced the syringe inside the pocket of his jacket. Marin's mind raced as she tried to figure out her options.

"What happens now?" she asked softly.

Yerik's icy gaze slid over Marin. "We keep moving." He yanked on her arm, pulling her along the row of plastic barrels lining the wall of the warehouse. As they reached the end of the row, Yerik punctured one of the containers with his knife—a weapon that looked more like a miniature sword. Marin's nose immediately burned from the intense odor of chlorine. Shoving Marin through the door, he turned and tossed a lit match onto the spilled liquid.

His knife pressed into Marin's side. "Run!" he commanded.

Marin knew enough about chemicals and fire to follow orders. They were fifty yards away when the warehouse exploded, lighting up the night air. She heard the sound of a siren going off and vehicles moving in the direction of the warehouse and it seemed he was leading them toward those sounds. Marin gladly kept up the pace, hoping they'd confront someone who would rescue her.

The sulfur smell was now mixed with the nauseating smell of burning chlorine and Marin's breath burned when it sawed through her lungs as she tried to keep up with Yerik. Twice, she stumbled on the dirt road. Both times, he nearly dislocated her shoulder as he jerked her back to his side. The noises from the fire faded as the hum of the giant generators processing the dirty water became louder. A truck sped by them and Marin's heart leaped. But the driver hurried on, seemingly on the way to the blazing warehouse.

Yerik steered them onto another dirt road. This one weaved between the giant water treatment tanks. The humming became louder, vibrating against their feet as they ran. He was careful to keep their bodies in the shadows, dodging the spotlights wherever he could. They stopped in front of a ladder attached to one of the tanks and Marin quickly glanced around. She saw the unmistakable red beam of a security camera across the path from them. Her grandfather's hotels had similar models on their exteriors. The ones used by the Chevalier hotel chain were also motion sensitive. Marin prayed these cameras were the same. While Yerik pulled down the ladder, presumably so they could climb to the top of the water treatment tanks, Marin pretended to slip. She kicked her heel along the dirt, creating a mini-dust cloud.

"Sorry," she said in response to Yerik's angry glare. "I tripped."

She winced painfully when he jabbed the knife into her side.

"Up," he commanded.

Marin slowly made her way up the first two rungs of the wide metal ladder. After the incident in the parking lot earlier, Yerik was clearly no longer underestimating Marin's physical capabilities because he barely ceded her an inch as they climbed in tandem. Once at the top, Marin was hit with another wave of intense nausea at the heavy chemical smell rising off the water as the turbines stirred the contents of the tank. She dropped to her knees on the concrete, trying to catch her breath.

Yerik wrenched her up by the ponytail again and it was all Marin could do to keep from falling off the ledge as he led her around to the other side of the tank. The fire was blazing out of control in the distance, creating an eerie glow in the night sky, but the noise from the purifiers drowned out any accompanying sound from the flames. A blast of fresh air blew off the Potomac when they reached the other side and Marin gulped in a lungful.

He gestured to a metal platform that looked like a fire escape. In the dark, it was difficult for Marin to see down to the ground. She took the steps carefully, the two of them zigzagging their way down to the bottom of the tank. When Marin's eyes adjusted to the blackness, she realized they were in some sort of courtyard created by the positioning of the four round water tanks. Yerik led them over to a shed directly in the center. He took his knife and jimmied the lock. Inside the small room was a row of blue jumpsuits, hard hats, and safety glasses.

"Get in," Yerik ordered as he shoved her inside. "Put on a jumpsuit."

He followed her into the shed, releasing her hand as he pulled the door closed behind them. An interior light came on just as the door shut. Marin sat down gingerly on the bench; the scrapes on her knees burned when she bent her legs. Yerik tossed a blue jumpsuit at her.

"Hurry."

Marin's fingers shook as she unzipped the garment. She paused for a breath trying to calm down. Yerik had said repeatedly that he'd keep her alive, but the syringe in his pocket—not to mention the nasty knife he held constantly—wasn't very pacifying to Marin's shaky nerves. She decided to try something she'd learned in high school psychology—become friends with her captor.

"Who is Elena?"

Yerik was visibly startled by her question. He paused in the act of pulling on his jumpsuit. Marin wasn't sure, but she thought his icy expression might have softened a bit at the sound of the woman's name.

"Get dressed," he commanded once his stoic composure had returned.

She pulled one of the pant legs over her shoe before giving her tactic another shot. "She must be important to you to go to all this trouble," Marin murmured.

He was at Marin's throat in an instant. "She is very important! She is my life!"

Marin's heart thundered in her chest as she stared into Yerik's icy eyes. But the glimmer of dampness in the corners of them buoyed her to continue.

"You love her?" she whispered.

Yerik's fingers twitched on her neck. He didn't speak for a long moment. Suddenly, he released her, moving back across the shed to continue pulling on his jumpsuit.

"Your grandfather had better love you as much," he said menacingly.

Sliding her arms into her jumpsuit, Marin continued with her questioning. Perhaps her captor would say something—anything—that would help her escape. "My grandfather loves me a lot. He'll trade me for Elena. But why is your wife with the counterfeiters in the first place?"

He grabbed two hard hats off the shelf. "Elena is not my wife. She is my daughter."

His words surprised Marin. She wondered how old Elena was. Her mind raced back to the earlier conversation with the Greeks in the warehouse. From what Marin could gather, Elena was the artist creating the counterfeit money. The same one Griffin was hunting for. Had the counterfeiters kidnapped her somehow?

"And she's an artist?" Marin asked.

He nodded as he handed her one of the hard hats.

"Very talented."

"If she painted the forgeries in the White House, then, yes, she is." Marin figured buttering him up couldn't hurt. "I'd love to see some of her original work."

Yerik faced her wearing a grim smile. "I know what you are doing, Chef. But you are not my friend. You are simply a means to an end." He grabbed her wrist tightly. "We go back the way we came. Don't try anything foolish."

GRIFFIN WAS STILL tapping the computer keyboard when an explosion nearly knocked him to his knees.

"Clear the area!" Agent Reynolds yelled. "That's chlorine gas coming from the warehouse."

The team from Homeland hustled the Greek prisoners into one of the vans. Adam and Leslie jogged to their vehicles with their teams to suit up in additional protective gear. Griffin followed reluctantly, panic gripping him as he imagined Marin inside the burning building.

"He's creating a diversion," Adam reassured him. He handed Griffin a rebreathing device. "He's taken Marin somewhere else. It's what I would do. Create a crowd and then disappear into it."

After attaching his mask, Griffin checked the computer again. Still blank.

"Ben," Griffin spoke into the communication headset in his helmet that allowed him to receive radio contact from the team and headquarters via the bones in his face rather than his ear canal. The team would be able to communicate without having to inhale the chemicals. "Tell me you've hacked into Homeland's system and you can track Marin's signal?"

"Almost there, brother," Ben told him. "I'm also tracking all of the video surveillance at the treatment center. I'm replaying something now, but I'm not sure whether it's an animal or Salenko."

"Where?" Adam demanded.

"About five hundred yards from your current location," Ben replied. "Near the water treatment tank quad."

"Damn, it," Adam said. "We won't be able to get there from here because of the fire. We're going to have to go around the long way."

Griffin was already in the driver's seat of the Humvee. Adam and Leslie jumped in as he was pulling away.

"It wasn't an animal kicking up that sand," Ben said as Griffin sped toward the decontamination tanks. "When I zoom in, it looks like a person, possibly two people. Whoever it is, they're in an area that wouldn't normally have personnel there this time of night."

Adam was relaying information to the rest of their unit. He had Agent Reynolds surveilling the area around the fire, still believing Salenko intended to disappear into the crowd fighting the blaze.

The Humvee took the corner near the tank farm sharply.

"We're of no use to Marin if we're dead, Griffin," Leslie said.

Griffin's gut clenched at the word "dead." He hoped like hell that Agent Reynolds was right when he said Marin was worth more to Salenko alive. It was the only thing keeping Griffin sane right now. He pulled up to the water tanks, threw the car into park, and jumped out.

"Where Ben?" he asked as he circled the area.

"I've got you on my feed," Ben said. "Take about ten stops to your left."

He did as Ben instructed.

"There. Something large kicked up some dust right in that spot," Ben said.

Leslie knelt down to inspect the pattern in the dirt while Griffin searched around the area.

"Up here," he called to Adam and Leslie as he began climbing the ladder up the side of the tank.

Griffin scrambled to the top of the concrete tank and paused to suck down a few pulls of oxygen from his rebreathing apparatus. Behind him, Leslie pulled herself up, followed by Adam. The three of them stood silently looking around, pivoting slowly so that they could scour their surroundings. Griffin swore violently. Marin and Salenko where nowhere in sight.

"THAT'S WHY YOU stole the artwork," Marin said as she trudged alongside her captor. They were walking parallel to a giant dirt field. Unfortunately, their direction took them away from the fire. She'd been puzzling out Yerik's story for the past ten minutes. "You said the counterfeiters didn't need her to print the money any longer. So, you stole art from the White House to keep her busy."

"To keep her alive," Yerik snapped.

They continued on in silence, leaving Marin alone with her thoughts. Yerik was a father, doing what he could to protect and rescue his daughter. Hollywood made blockbuster movies about the very same subject. Somehow, the fathers in those movies seemed a lot more endearing than the cold-blooded killer walking beside her.

An SUV rounded the corner quickly, its headlights temporarily blinding Marin. The blade of Yerik's knife tore through the jumpsuit, poking into the skin at her side. She struggled to keep her body from lurching in front of the oncoming vehicle.

"Careful," he hissed.

The SUV blazed past them, apparently in route to the fire.

"Don't you want to call my grandfather?" Marin asked once the road was empty again. "I can give you his number."

"Be quiet."

"But the sooner you contact him, the sooner he can arrange to get Elena back to you," Marin insisted.

She was getting punchy. Her body ached and the wounds on her hands and knees stung fiercely. But she couldn't give up. The farther he took her away from the fire, the farther he was taking her away from Griffin. And rescue.

The blade sliced along her skin causing Marin to stumble.

"I said you'd stay alive, but I can make you wish you were dead," he threatened.

Marin held her hand to her side, wisely shutting her mouth. Tears burned behind her eyes, but she kept them at bay, not wanting to give this creep the satisfaction of seeing them. A cool breeze blew onto her face. They were walking toward the Potomac, it appeared. Marin prayed she wasn't going to have to swim in the river again. A jet plane flew low overhead. Marin could see the lights of Reagan Airport across the expanse of the river. Before they reached the shoreline, however, her captor turned them north. He guided her beneath a grove of trees lining the shore.

"Now, we wait," he said. He sat down on the damp ground, wrenching Marin down beside him.

Marin said a silent prayer that they would wait long enough for Griffin to find her.

"I'VE GOT SOMETHING on another camera." Ben's voice permeated the fog of Griffin's despair. "Two waterworks employees walking toward the river."

"A lover's tryst during the night shift?" Leslie asked.

"Maybe, but one of them is wearing pink shoes," Ben said. "I'm not sure any woman would want to wear pink shoes around this place."

Griffin exchanged a look with Adam. They both

charged toward the ladder at the same time. Adam was over the side first, skipping every rung as he slid down.

"Hey!" Leslie called as she followed them both down. "Don't you dare leave me!"

"Tell me where, Ben," Adam said as he got behind the wheel of the Humvee.

Griffin jumped in the passenger seat, leaving the back door open for Leslie. She climbed in seconds later.

"About a mile on the other side of the facility," Ben said. "They walked past the facilities workshop about four minutes ago. I've downloaded the location to your GPS."

Adam put the car in gear and whipped it around in the opposite direction.

"I need that Homeland GPS up and running, Ben," Griffin said. "This would be a hell of a lot easier if you could make that happen."

"Their computer is not being all that cooperative, but I'm working on it."

"Work harder!"

"Relax, Griffin," Leslie admonished him. "Salenko hasn't gotten far. We'll find him. And then we'll get Marin back."

Adam's driving was making Griffin queasy. Or maybe it was the fact that he hadn't found Marin yet that was making him sick.

"I've successfully hacked into Homeland's system," Ben said. "I've got Marin's signal! Keep headed in the direction I gave you." They heard him swear. "They're on the move again. And it looks like the cowboys from Homeland are trying to back them into the northwest corner of the plant."

"What's up there?" Griffin asked.

"There's a fence adjacent to the Naval Research Lab," Ben replied. "It's either that or the Potomac River."

Griffin pulled off the mask to his rebreather and tossed it in the back seat. Marin wasn't as strong a swimmer as she let on. If Salenko planned to toss her into the water, Griffin was going in after her.

"My team is coming at them from the Navy side of the fence," Leslie said. She'd dumped her mask, as well. "They won't let them pass."

Adam steered the Humvee through a field of sand used to filter the water. They went airborne when they came off the other side of the dunes.

"Reynolds isn't trained in tactical maneuvers," Adam complained. "He wants Salenko alive, but I don't think Homeland really knows what the Ukrainian is capable of."

"Hey, I don't care about a pissing match between you and some asshat at Homeland," Griffin argued. "Let's just focus on rescuing Marin."

But when the Humvee turned the corner, Griffin's breath stilled at the scene before him. Beneath the spot-lights of the big filtration tanks, there was a standoff between Agent Reynolds from Homeland and Salenko. And in the middle of it stood Marin with what appeared to be a syringe aimed at her neck.

CHAPTER TWENTY-ONE

MARIN GULPED BACK a sob before exhaling a long sigh of relief. *He'd found her.* Minutes earlier, Yerik had bolted to his feet, dragging her along with him as he ran beneath the trees. Just as quickly, they'd been confronted by a man ordering them to halt. She had no idea who the idiot was with the assault rifle trained on her, but her body relaxed at the sight of Griffin striding cautiously across the grass. Her captor's hold tightened around her, however, reminding Marin of the syringe primed near her throat.

"Stand down, Agent Reynolds," Griffin called to the man holding the rifle.

The idiot didn't listen.

"No one's going to get hurt here," Agent Reynolds said. "Let her go, Salenko. We'll go someplace and talk. You've got a lot of information that's very valuable to the United States. I'm willing to make you a sweet deal."

"He wants his daughter," Marin shouted. "Elena. She's The Artist."

The tip of the needle grazed her skin. Marin's body quaked in fear.

"Shut up," her captor said.

Griffin stepped in front of Agent Reynolds's rifle. "Is

that what this is all about?" he asked, amazing Marin at how calm he was. "Your daughter? I'm sure we can work something out, Salenko. Just put down the syringe and let's talk about it."

Marin's trembling eased in the face of Griffin's quiet, cool demeanor. The darkness and his helmet made it difficult for her to read his expression, but Marin could sense his determined gaze.

"Agent Reynolds is going to lower his weapon," Griffin said. "Why don't you do the same and we can work this out without anyone else getting hurt."

There was rapid exchange of words between Agent Reynolds and Griffin, too quiet for Marin to hear, but the other agent reluctantly dropped his rifle to his hip.

"Talk to me, Salenko," Griffin said. "What can we do to make this right?"

"You can't make this right!" her captor shouted. "Only I can get Elena back." He jerked Marin against his body as he took a step backward toward the fence. "And I will use your lover to barter with. You think I don't know what she means to you, Agent Keller? But she means more to her wealthy grandfather. He is a very powerful man. The conglomerate fears him. He will pay for Elena's release. Or the chef here will pay with her life."

A wave of terror rolled through her stomach. Griffin stood still as Marin was propelled backward several steps. Her lips began to quiver. Why wasn't he moving with them? Surely, he would rescue her.

"Talk to him," Marin urged, her words laced with panic. "He's a good man. He'll understand about Elena. He'll help you."

"She is a little magpie, your lover," Yerik shouted at Griffin. "She says I should trust you."

"She's right," Griffin said, his feet still frozen to the ground. "I want to help you get your daughter back."

They were still moving in reverse. Marin couldn't seem to stop her body from trembling.

"You think you are so powerful. These men in the conglomerate have been laughing in your face for months now," her captor bragged. "They enjoyed it every time I brought them a painting stolen from right in front of the Secret Service's nose. It was a game to them. *You* are a game to them."

He'd taken them another fifty feet from Griffin and Agent Reynolds. The Potomac River lapped against the metal storm wall to their right. Branches from another grove of trees formed a canopy over their heads. And the syringe was still millimeters from Marin's throat. She was going to die.

IT TOOK EVERYTHING Griffin had in him to keep still while Salenko retreated with Marin in his grasp. One look at her battered face and he wanted to pummel the Ukrainian to death. His heart raced and his fingers twitched just thinking about the bastard laying a finger on her.

But Griffin let his training take control of his reflexes.

He needed to keep Marin's tormentor occupied so Adam and Leslie could get into position. As far as Griffin could tell, the only weapon Salenko was using to hold Marin captive was the syringe. They'd have to overpower the Ukrainian. A sniper shot was too risky. It could trigger Salenko's reflexes to plunge the syringe into Marin's neck. Griffin's stomach rolled knowing what was likely in the barrel behind the needle. He willed himself not to think about that; to keep Salenko talking instead.

"This isn't a game to me," he said, trying to keep his voice even and calm. "It's very real. And I'm sure it's very real for Elena, too. You leave now and I won't be able to help you. Stay and let's fix this. You have my word I will see that Elena is released safely."

Salenko backed into the fence. His face grew taut when he heard the sound of multiple footsteps on the pavement behind the railing. This was where things got dicey. They had the son of a bitch cornered. But Salenko was a wild card and it would only take him a second to inject Marin, condemning her to an agonizing death. Sweat broke on the back of Griffin's neck. All he had to do was to keep the Ukrainian engaged for another minute. He didn't dare redirect his gaze off of Salenko to check on Adam or Leslie's progress. The other man was too perceptive.

Marin must have sensed the futility of Salenko's situation because tears were now flowing freely from her bright blue eyes.

"Griffin," she croaked out.

Her plea nearly wrecked him. Her face had gone pale

and Griffin ached to kiss away the panic she was surely battling. But he couldn't move. Not yet.

"He's going to kill me."

"No," Griffin said firmly. "He's going to trade you for Elena."

But Salenko was suddenly very still as if contemplating his limited options.

"Before I die, I need you to know something," Marin cried.

Griffin couldn't seem to draw a breath. "Hush." He had to push the word out around the bolder in his throat. "How many times have I told you you're not going to die?"

"I love you."

Her words hit him like a gunshot, shattering his chest and every organ inside of it. He couldn't breathe; he couldn't think. He blinked his eyes rapidly to refocus.

All of a sudden, everything seemed to be happening in slow motion around him. Agent Reynolds must have twitched beside Griffin, unintentionally tipping Salenko off that Adam was behind him because Salenko began shouting something in his native tongue. Griffin lunged forward at a run as Adam jumped from the fence. A woman screamed and Griffin felt as if his legs were immersed in wet cement, he seemed to be moving so slowly.

"Marin!" he yelled.

She was on the ground unmoving when Griffin finally reached her. Adam was wrestling Salenko. Leslie was clutching her wrist and breathing deeply. Agent Reynolds went to help Adam as Griffin knelt beside Marin. His heart pounded against his chest.

She can't be dead.

He brushed his fingers against her neck looking for a puncture wound. Her pulse was strong against his fingertips.

"Marin," he whispered.

Her eyes snapped open. A slow grin spread over her bruised lips.

"I knew you'd save me," she said between shallow breaths.

Griffin didn't bother sharing with her that he'd had his doubts moments earlier. He swept his hands all along her body. "Are you hurt? Did that bastard harm you in any way?" Marin winced at the contact in several places. "I'll kill him!"

"You're a little late for that," Adam said behind them.

When Griffin looked over his shoulder, Salenko was convulsing on the ground several yards away, gasping for breath. He quickly turned his head back and used his body to shield Marin from having to witness the gruesome scene.

"He injected himself?" Marin asked, her eyes wide.

Adam nodded. "A true martyr."

"I needed him alive!" Agent Reynolds protested, throwing a tantrum that rivaled a two-year-old's.

"Yeah, well, apparently, he preferred death to life in Guantanamo Bay," Adam shot back. "And he wasn't letting go of that syringe. The guy broke Leslie's wrist when she went for the needle."

Marin sat up and glanced around at Leslie. "Thank

God he didn't stab her. He had an ugly knife." She gulped back a sob. "He killed Otto with it."

Griffin shook his head as he brushed a tear off her cheek with his thumb. "Otto's injured, but not dead. We used his microchip to track you. Even with a deep stab wound, he wanted to jump into the warehouse and save you."

The watery smile she gave him made his heart skip a beat. Griffin ached to gather her up in his arms and kiss her senseless. Not here, though. That would have to wait for some place more private.

"An ambulance is on the way," Ben communicated through Griffin's headset. "The president is asking about Marin. He wants to know her condition."

Marin scooted over to where Leslie sat on the ground cradling her wrist. Griffin looked on in amazement as Marin gently rubbed the other woman's back. His throat grew tight with emotion thinking how easily he could have lost her.

"Tell President Manning she's fine," Griffin told him.

She was better than fine. Marin's resilience astounded him once again. The woman seemed to take everything in stride. She'd make a brilliant agent. Hell, she'd be the perfect partner.

Where the hell had that crazy thought come from?

Griffin jumped to his feet. He needed to get his emotions in check and his head back into the op.

"Ben, you can let the president and Mrs. Manning know I'll have Marin back in the White House shortly."

"ALL THIS TIME, you knew about Bita?" The First Lady shot a chilly look at her husband who was seated next to her on a sofa in the west sitting hall outside their master bedroom.

The admiral, the president's chief of staff, Director Worcester, and the Director of Homeland Security were also seated in various chairs around the room. It was nearly eleven o'clock at night, but both the Mannings were still dressed in the clothes they'd had on earlier in the day. The First Lady was clearly shaken by the events of the past several hours. "The woman was a double agent and yet you let her near our granddaughter."

Griffin was equally as furious as the president's wife. He was ready to jump out of his skin at the commander-in-chief for withholding such vital information. Especially since Bita had put Marin's life in so much danger. Director Worcester shot him a quelling look from across the room when Griffin went to open his mouth to interject his two cents.

Clearly, he'd matured a bit because Griffin kept his thoughts to himself. But he couldn't keep still. He continued to prowl behind the chair where Marin sat wrapped in a soft blanket, sipping a cup of tea the head housekeeper had provided her with earlier. Marin had been quiet and contemplative since the rescue, but he figured that was understandable after all she'd been through. The two of them hadn't had an opportunity to be alone yet, either. She was putting on a brave front for the Mannings. The trauma would hit her soon, though. And he wanted to be the one to comfort her when it did. To do that, he'd need to get her away from her overprotective godmother. Unfortunately, neither of the Mannings seemed in a hurry to retire for the night.

"I would never put Arabelle in harm's way." President Manning patted his wife's leg. His touch did nothing to erase the frosty expression on her face. The president sighed. "Bita was instructed in the security protocols. She followed them to the letter this morning. Other than that, Harriett, all I can say is that the issue is one of national security."

"How is stealing artwork a national security issue?" the First Lady demanded.

With a beleaguered sigh, the president glanced over at his Secretary of Homeland Security. "George, tell her what you can. Please."

The secretary clearly would rather do no such thing. But, after a long moment of uncomfortable silence, he sat forward in his chair, cleared his throat, and began speaking. "Mrs. Ranjbar is involved with a group of Iranian Nationalists who were deposed when the Shah was overthrown in the 1970s," he explained. "Many of these individuals were among the wealthy elite. At the time of the revolution, they were forced to flee their homeland without any of their possessions. Some of those possessions are, understandably, quite valuable; not to mention, of great significance as family heirlooms."

"But many of those items were eventually returned, weren't they?" the First Lady asked.

"Not as many as you'd think. A lot of these items were traded on a very lucrative black market with the backers to the radical government keeping the proceeds of their sale," the secretary continued. "Mrs. Ranjbar and her friends have been unofficially hunting for their lost items for decades. It's believed that Yerik Salenko, the same man who kidnapped Chef Marin, worked for the group operating the black market at some point during the last decade. He claimed to know the whereabouts of many of the items Mrs. Ranjbar and her friends are seeking."

Mrs. Manning looked at her husband incredulously. "And Bita was just going to track these hooligans down and demand her heirlooms?"

The president shrugged, smiling at his wife. "What can I say? I'm surrounded by formidable women."

"I still don't understand how Bita's search is a threat to our country's national security," the First Lady grumbled.

"It was not so much Mrs. Ranjbar's search, but her connection with Salenko. Mr. Salenko had close ties with many nefarious groups aside from the counterfeiters Agent Keller is investigating, and the operators of the black market. He worked for anyone who would pay. Most of his employers would just as soon see our country in turmoil. Unfortunately, his death puts us at a dead end with regard to locating these terror cells." The secretary glared at Griffin.

Griffin met the man's hard stare over the back of Marin's head. "With all due respect, sir, if the choice between saving Marin or saving a cold-blooded killer came up again, I'd run the op the exact same way every time."

"And we are all very grateful for your quick thinking, Agent Keller," the president interjected. He shook his head at the secretary, essentially shutting down any additional conversation on the subject.

"Well, I don't understand how you all could just let that man steal such beautiful artwork," Marin finally spoke up. "Those pieces are just as priceless and irreplaceable as Bita's friends' heirlooms."

The secretary smiled at Marin. "Then it will please you to know that the buyers of the stolen pieces all work in my agency."

His words halted Griffin's pacing. "That would have been nice to know days ago," he said through his clenched jaw.

"I agree," the president's chief of staff said. "We're lucky something didn't go horribly wrong tonight because of lack of coordination."

Their discussion was curtailed when Clark Manning escorted his mother-in-law, Bita, into the room. The woman's shoulder was dressed with a heavy bandage. Only Bita could pull off looking regal wearing it. The men in the room stood at her arrival. The First Lady was clearly conflicted on how to greet the other woman. She finally stood as well, holding her arms open to embrace her son's mother-in-law.

"Bita, you're back. How are you feeling?" the First Lady

asked.

"She's lucky it was only a flesh wound," Clark answered brusquely for his mother-in-law. "The bullet grazed her shoulder deep enough to require stitches and a round of antibiotics." He gave the woman a stern look. "It could have been a lot worse. From now on, you'll leave the espionage to those who are trained to do it. Agreed?"

Bita nodded dutifully, but not before Griffin saw her give the Secretary of Homeland Security a sly smile.

"Agent Morgan was released also," Clark reported to the room. "Her wrist is fractured, but it fortunately won't require any surgery."

Griffin shamefully realized he'd been so focused on Marin, he hadn't given Leslie's condition a second thought since leaving the crime scene. He was pretty sure Adam had the situation covered, but he made a mental note to text his friend anyway.

"Chef Marin!" Bita cried, covering her mouth with both her hands when she spied Marin.

Marin stiffened as Bita advanced on her. Griffin quickly stepped in front of the older woman. Bita's face was crestfallen when she realized he would not let her near Marin.

"I didn't mean to hit her," Bita said. "It was all part of an act. I had to make that crazy man think I was working with him."

A sudden, blinding burst of rage surged through Griffin. *This woman was responsible for the bruises on Marin's face?* It seemed he'd wrongly blamed Salenko for all of the injuries to Marin. With that man already dead, Griffin was looking for another punching bag to take his frustrations out on. He didn't realize his hands were already clenched in fists until Marin covered his fingers with hers. Rising from her chair to stand beside him, she gave his hand a gentle squeeze.

"It's okay, Bita," Marin said quietly. "We were all doing what we had to."

"But your mouth." Bita's brown eyes swam with tears. "I hate myself for doing that to you. We must get some ice. Clark, can you look at Chef Marin's wounds and make sure she's okay?"

Marin flinched again. Griffin wrapped a protective arm around her shoulder.

"No need, Clark," the First Lady interceded. "I'll take care of Marin's cuts and bruises. She'll be our guest tonight so I can keep an eye on her."

Mrs. Manning gently took Marin's arm, presumably to lead her away. At the same time, Griffin's own arm tightened over Marin's shoulders. He didn't want to let her go. Not when he needed to talk to her. Privately. He needed to tell her... *something*. Griffin just wasn't sure what he would say. Or even if he could say what needed to be said.

Her eyes held a silent question when they met his.

"Agent Keller," the director called from across the room. "You have a seven o'clock flight to Greece tomorrow morning. The Secretary of Homeland and I would like to go over some things with you before you leave."

Marin's expression seemed to dim. She stepped out

from beneath his arm.

"Thank you for rescuing me, Agent Keller. Again," she called over her shoulder as she followed the First Lady in the direction of the Queen's bedroom.

The loss of contact with her body made Griffin uneasy. He would only be gone to Greece for a couple of days. Griffin would make sure his return flight brought him back here to Washington so he could see Marin again. They would talk then. So why did it feel that with every step she took down that long hall, he was losing her forever?

"I'm afraid I owe you an apology." Bita's voice interrupted Griffin's troubling thoughts.

"She's the one you need to apologize to," he snapped. "I only heard excuses coming out of your mouth a minute ago."

Bita nodded deferentially. "You are correct. I will apologize to Chef Marin properly. But I think she will be more forgiving than you, Agent Keller."

"You got that right."

"Still, I must apologize for the wrongs I have committed against you."

The hairs on the back of Griffin's neck stood up. "Against me?"

She nodded again.

"Go on."

Bita sighed dramatically. "It's about Farrah. She is aware of my association with the committee trying to locate our country's stolen possessions. On occasion, she assists me in my pursuit of justice."

Griffin didn't like where this was going. Not one bit.

"She assists you how?"

"My daughter is beautiful, yes? Some men, their tongues are looser around a gorgeous woman. Farrah flirts. These men, they say things perhaps they shouldn't." Bita's smile was sanguine.

"I have never, ever, flirted with your daughter," he replied hotly.

The woman's face blanched. "Oh, no, that was the problem. You were too inscrutable. No matter what Farrah did, you wouldn't leave your post."

His jaw dropped and he couldn't seem to close it. "That was all a setup?"

Bita nodded again. "Once the Mannings arrived in the White House, I began baiting Yerik with the artwork here. But you were very knowledgeable of art. Too knowledgeable. You had to go." She actually had the nerve to shrug.

"*You* came up with the idea to steal from the US government?"

"As Chef Marin said, we do what we have to." Bita's tone was so smug it was condescending.

"You're right," he finally choked out. "I'm not as forgiving. The only reason you are still standing here is because I made a damn promise to your granddaughter that I'd bring both you and Marin back. Don't you dare put that child or anyone else in my orbit in danger again. Or else you'll answer to me."

Griffin stormed off without giving her the opportunity to reply. It was either that or strangle the damn woman.

316

CHAPTER TWENTY-TWO

"NO HEADACHE?" AUNT Harriet asked as she shined a penlight into Marin's eyes.

"No," Marin replied.

The rest of her body felt like it had been through a meat grinder, but, thankfully, her head felt fine. Her heart on the other hand, well, that was as battered and bruised as the rest of her.

"No concussion, then. That's good," her godmother said. "I'll bring you something to help you sleep when I go get the salve for your scrapes. Your lip will probably take twenty-four hours for the swelling to go down, but then you'll be able to cover the bruise with makeup." Her aunt shook her head in disgust. "I can't believe Bita actually hit you. For that matter, I can't believe Bita was a spy."

Marin pressed an ice pack to her tender mouth. "After the week I've had, nothing will ever shock me ever again."

Aunt Harriet gave Marin's shoulder a squeeze. "It's over now. You're safe."

There was a soft knock at the door. Marin's heart raced, the stupid organ hoping it was Griffin.

Aunt Harriet looked at her speculatively. "If that's Bita, I'm sending her away."

Marin grinned before forgetting about her sore mouth. More than likely that was who was waiting behind the door. She returned the ice pack to her lip. Griffin was still firmly in special agent mode, especially now that he was so close to breaking his case wide open. He had to go to Greece. His career came first. It always would. Nothing had changed. Marin's tender heart would do well to remember that.

But it wasn't Bita at the door. Instead, Diego's tall frame filled the doorway.

"I'll be back in a minute with those meds," Aunt Harriet said as she slipped out behind him.

Her friend looked a little sheepish holding a vase of bright tulips in his hands.

"Diego!" Marin cried. "What are you doing here so late at night?"

The sous chef ventured further into the Queen's bedroom, placing the vase on the coffee table in front of the fireplace. "Everyone is still here. The entire kitchen staff, all the under butlers, and assistant ushers," he said. "No one wanted to leave until they knew you were safe. Fran sent these from the florist shop."

Blinking back tears, Marin fingered one of the soft tulip petals. "That is so sweet."

He stared at her face before closing his eyes and shaking his head solemnly.

With a deep breath, Diego opened his eyes again. "I couldn't leave without seeing you. Not until I apologized," he explained. "If I hadn't gone to talk to Walter in the

Navy Mess that morning, I would have been on the stairs with you." Diego's face became fierce. "He wouldn't have gotten past me."

Marin took her friend by the arm and led him to the sofa. They both sat down. "None of this is anyone's fault," she insisted. *Except maybe Bita's.* But Marin knew enough not to mention the woman's involvement. "I was just in the right place at the wrong time."

"But if I had been here on Monday like I was supposed to. . ." Diego's voice trailed off.

"Now that I am a little peeved at," she said. "People were dying all around me. I thought the worst when you didn't show up for work."

Diego glanced down at his hands. "I know. The admiral told me when he was reaming me out."

"I'm glad he didn't fire you."

"Oh, I'm pretty sure he wanted to. But he said the final decision would be up to you."

He gave her a contrite smile.

Marin patted his arm. "The way you pull sugar? No way will I ever fire you," she teased before laying her head on his shoulder.

They sat in companionable silence for a moment.

"I didn't even know you were considering marriage," Marin finally said.

Diego chuckled. "Neither did I. Love kind of snuck up on me."

"But deserting work?"

"Not my finest moment," he replied. "Sometimes love

makes you do stupid things."

Marin thought of the embarrassing declaration of love she'd made earlier. Her stomach dropped as she tried not to cringe. "Yeah, I guess it does."

"Fortunately, Walter is not as impetuous as I am. I won't leave you stranded again, Boss."

"I'm eager to meet this paragon."

"Coffee tomorrow?" Diego asked.

"It's a date."

The First Lady entered the bedroom carrying a tray with some sandwiches and fruit. Marin followed Diego as he stood up from the sofa.

"Lillie made you cucumber sandwiches," he said. "I know how much you like them."

She kissed him on the cheek. "Please tell everyone downstairs I said thank you."

"See you in the morning," Diego said. He nodded to Aunt Harriet. "Good night, ma'am."

"Shower first and then eat," Aunt Harriet instructed after the bedroom door closed. "You'll feel more like yourself once you get into something clean. The agents brought over the clothes from the safe house." Her aunt kissed her on the forehead. "Just let one of the agents on duty know if you need me. Anytime, ya hear?"

Marin nodded dutifully as her aunt left the room.

She kicked off her shoes and carefully removed her clothes, trying not to jar her battered body too much. Her aunt was right, a hot shower would feel good. She headed for the bathroom.

GRIFFIN LEANED A shoulder against the arched corridor just outside the Queen's bedroom. One of the agents on the First Lady's detail stood beside the door waiting patiently for her to come out. Griffin was having a hard time remaining as patient.

The door finally opened and the First Lady exited. She stopped abruptly when she spied Griffin, still dressed in his battle dress uniform, hanging out in area of the White House where he shouldn't be late at night. Her face was hard to read when she closed the distance between them.

"It seems we owe you another debt of gratitude, Agent Keller," she stated, quietly. "Her grandfather will likely give you a hotel, if you want it."

"I'm happy with my current position, thank you."

"That's a shame. That job is likely a lot safer." The First Lady glanced back at the closed door. "She needs a shower and sleep. Looking at you, I'd prescribe the same remedy."

"Not until I know she's okay."

She let out a resigned sigh. "Not all of her wounds are visible, Agent Keller. Please be careful with her heart."

He didn't bother telling Marin's godmother that he wasn't quite sure what to do with her heart now that she'd given it to him. Griffin was using his figure-it-out-as-I-go-along strategy to deal with that dilemma. The First Lady moved past him through the archway, her agent trailing discreetly behind her. Griffin waited for their footsteps to fade before crossing the hall and entering the Queen's bedroom.

The shower was running and steam wafted out the bathroom door. Griffin should be a gentleman and sit and wait for her to finish. But his feet were moving independently of his brain. He hesitated at the threshold to the bathroom, trying to figure out a way to announce his presence without terrifying an already shaky Marin.

He needn't have bothered. She carefully peeked around the shower curtain, almost as though she had sensed his arrival. Her cheeks were rosy from the warm water and her eyes radiated pleasure when they landed on him.

"As usual, Special Agent Keller, you're overdressed," she said before disappearing back behind the curtain.

Not needing to be told twice, Griffin stripped out of his uniform, furiously yanking at the laces of his boots in order to pull them off. A moment later, he stalked across the room and joined Marin in the shower. The vision of her wet, naked body stole his breath while making him painfully hard at the same time. She was everything he dreamed about. He wrapped his arms around her.

"Marin," he murmured against her wet hair.

His hands roamed her slick body, tracing her luscious curves. She pulled his head down for a lusty, demanding kiss, only to have to break away seconds later. Her fingers went to her bruised lip.

Griffin swore. "If I never see that woman again, it will be too soon."

"Shhh," she commanded. "Turn around."

Griffin didn't want to turn around. The scenery was just fine the way he was facing. But she had a testy look in her eyes, so he did as she asked. He was instantly glad he'd listened when her teeth scored his back, and her hands reached around his waist to grip his erection. Griffin struggled for a handhold against the wet tile as she stroked him.

"Mmm." She sighed against his skin.

Her hands didn't linger there for long, however. She trailed her fingers up along his chest before reaching up to drag them through his wet hair. The next thing he knew, she was massaging shampoo into his scalp. He was amazed at how good it felt.

"Rinse," she said before sliding past him.

Again, Griffin did as he was told. When he opened his eyes, he he glanced down and saw her ravaged knees. Swearing under his breath, he slammed the water off with one hand gently lifting a shivering Marin into his arms. He grabbed a fluffy towel off the rack and draped it around her body. Stepping out of the tub, he sat her down on the counter beside the sink, wrapping the towel more snuggly around her before grabbing one for himself and vigorously drying off.

Marin sat quietly while Griffin cataloged the injuries to her body. He kissed the scraped skin on her palms before crouching down and brushing his lips over her battered kneecaps, all the while cursing the dead Ukrainian.

"Marin." He rested the side of his head against her thigh. "If I could kill Salenko again I would."

"Don't." She threaded her fingers through his wet hair forcing his eyes to meet her watery ones. "I don't want to think about him or any other part of it. And I definitely don't want to talk about it. I just want to be with you. I need to live in this moment, Griffin. Not the past. Can we do that tonight?" she pleaded.

That, he could do. His eyes never leaving hers, Griffin turned his head slightly so that his lips brushed along the tender skin of her inner thigh. Marin shivered beneath his touch. Gripping her ass, he slid her to the edge of the counter. Her lips curved up in a satisfied smile as she wrapped her legs around his neck.

Griffin would have liked to take his time and draw the pleasure out for her, but her body hummed with a sense of urgency. She needed this release to help her relax; to help her escape the ugly memories of the past week. Delving his tongue into her sweetness, her excitement built. Marin came in a rush, her body convulsing wildly against his mouth.

When he got to his feet, she was leaning against the mirror, her eyes closed, a look of bliss fixed on her face. A delicate flush had spread all over her body. Opening her eyes, she reached for him, but he backed away.

"No, we're going to do this right. In a bed," he said.

Her body was warm against his skin when he lifted her up to his chest. She draped her arms around his neck, nuzzling his jaw as he carried her over to the canopied bed that had once belonged to Andrew Jackson. Griffin laid her in the center of the mattress while he went to retrieve a condom. There was an effervescent smile on her face when he returned to the bed. It stirred up something inside Griffin so powerful he had to look away.

"Thank you," she whispered.

He crawled onto the bed beside her, resting his hand across her taut midriff. "Save your thanks for later, I'm not done with you yet, wench." He winked at her, trying to lighten the mood.

Smiling serenely, Marin cupped his jaw with her hand. "And in doing so, you will have rescued me once again."

Griffin studied her beautiful face, ignoring the niggling feeling shimmying down his spine that, perhaps, Marin was rescuing him from something. Instead, he moved over her, sliding inside her warm, welcoming body. Gently, he brushed his lips against her wounded ones. She responded by squeezing around him. Griffin's restraint slipped its leash and moments later they were a sweaty, tangled mess of limbs in the heat of passion. Marin arched against him, throwing her head back with a silent scream when she climaxed. Griffin was right behind her, following her into ecstasy with a blinding release that had him gasping out her name like a prayer.

MARIN AWOKE TO the feeling she was being watched. She fluttered her eyelids open and glanced around the bedroom. Griffin sat at the edge of the antique bed, one shoulder propped against the canopy post. He was dressed in the combat gear he'd worn the night before. She glanced over at the clock. It was five in the morning.

"I didn't want to wake you," he said softly. "But I have to go downstairs and change to catch my flight. I couldn't leave without saying goodbye."

Moving was still painful with all her cuts and bruises, but she needed to face him from an upright position. Marin armored herself by pulling the floral sheet tightly around her naked body before she sat up.

"I'm glad you woke me," she lied. A big part of her— the cowardly part—had hoped he'd be less of a gentleman and slip out into the dawn. Then there was that small part who adored Griffin for who he was.

She glanced around the room, anything to avoid having to meet his perceptive eyes. The tray of food was empty. They'd inhaled the sandwiches and fruit hours ago between bouts of lovemaking. When they weren't communicating with their bodies, they'd made easy small talk, both of them managing to tiptoe around the elephant in the room—her brash declaration of love. *The one he hadn't reciprocated.*

"You understand why I have to go?" Griffin sounded as anxious as she felt.

"Of course, I understand. You need to finish what you started. To wrap up this case. And you have to go get Elena." She forced her lips into as much of a grin as they could tolerate. "I'm done needing to be constantly rescued. Elena needs you now. Rescuing women in distress is what you do."

Those ocean eyes of him seemed to bore through her as she rambled on senselessly.

"I'll do whatever it takes to make it back for the wedding."

Marin waved him off. "Don't worry about that."

His eyes narrowed even more. "I do worry about it because it's important to you."

"Really, Griffin, after everything I've been through these last few days, I'm confident I can brazen it out and stand up to my cousin. I don't need a date to her wedding anymore."

Standing up to Ava would be a piece of cake after this conversation.

He rose slowly from the bed and began to pace around the room, rubbing the back of his neck with one of his hands while he walked. Marin swallowed uneasily. This was much harder than she thought it would be.

Griffin blew out a heavy breath and turned back to face her. "Okay. When will you be back in DC?"

Now they had arrived at the most difficult part of the conversation. Marin buried her hands in the sheets so that he wouldn't see them shaking.

"I'm not sure." Her tongue darted out to lick her throbbing lip. "But it really doesn't matter because I don't think we should see one another any longer."

His body jerked to attention. "Why not?" The two words seemed to crackle from his mouth like lightning strikes.

She sighed resolutely and pushed on through. "This"—

she waved her hand over the bed—"has been wonderful. You have been wonderful. I couldn't have gotten through any of this week's drama without you. And I'm so grateful that you were the one here to protect me. But it's over now. It has to be."

"What the hell do you mean 'it has to be'?" he demanded. "What about what you said last night? In the field. With Salenko."

Marin wasn't sure whether to laugh or cry that he couldn't seem to get out the word "love."

"You mean when I told you that I love you?" she asked.

His face looked stricken. Surely, she was imagining it. No man would want a woman gushing about love if he didn't feel the same way.

"You didn't mean it?" he asked.

She swallowed roughly, trying to get her voice to remain firm and composed.

"Of course, I meant it, Griffin. I do you love you," she said softly. "And I'm okay with you not loving me back. It's better than you saying something you don't mean. I'll survive. I promise." She paused to take a steadying breath. "I know the only commitment you ever plan on making is to your career. I get that. I've understood it from the beginning. Being a Secret Service agent—the best Secret Service agent, in my humble opinion—is who you are. And it's also one of the things I love about you. I couldn't ask you to give that up and still live with myself." She paused again.

The air had gone still in the room. Griffin's expression

was fixed and stoic.

Marin gulped in another breath and pressed on. "But if we continue this, whatever this is, I'd always want more than you're prepared to give. And that's not fair. To either one of us."

Griffin opened his mouth and then promptly closed it again. Marin ached to touch him again, to have him hold her against him.

"You're right," he finally said.

His words were like a sledgehammer to her heart, shattering it into a million pieces.

"Thank you for our honesty, Marin." He turned to head for the door.

"Promise me something, Griffin," she called out to his retreating back.

Griffin turned to face her. "Anything," he said.

The softly uttered word shattered her heart even further. Griffin was capable of so much love, if he'd only let himself.

"Be safe," she croaked out.

He nodded. And then he was gone.

Marin sat in the middle of the great big bed in the Queen's bedroom, tears streaming down her cheeks, trying to convince herself she'd just done the right thing by letting him go.

CHAPTER TWENTY-THREE

G RIFFIN WATCHED OUT the small window as the baggage cart snaked along the tarmac just as day was breaking. He blew out an exasperated breath. Why couldn't they hurry and get this plane's wheels up? Time was slipping away. He needed to get to Greece so he could bring down the ring of counterfeiters he'd spent nearly two years of his life chasing. And to free Elena.

Elena.

All these months, Griffin has thought of The Artist as some diabolical criminal, not some slave used by a conglomerate of gangsters. According to the agents at Homeland Security who'd briefed him last night, Elena was a twenty-five-year-old woman with the mind of a ten-year-old child. A gifted painter, she was a prodigy who was being manipulated by a gang of greedy thieves. Still, Salenko should have gone to the police to rescue his daughter. The string of dead bodies he'd left behind was unconscionable. Griffin wasn't rescuing Elena because of the bargain he'd made with the dead man. He was rescuing Elena because Marin had begged him to.

Someone slid into the seat next to him and Griffin was relieved to hear the chimes indicating that the exit door was now closed. When the plane began to push back from the gate, Griffin felt himself relax. The passenger beside him struggled with their seat belt.

Griffin reached over to help and he was stunned to see Leslie seated there. "What the hell?"

She grimaced as she tried to maneuver the bulky brace on her wrist. "Oh puh-leeze," she choked out. "You didn't think I was just going to hand you this collar. Come on, Griff, you know me better than that."

The flight attendants were reviewing the safety procedures as the plane taxied toward the runway. "Salenko fractured three bones in your wrist," Griffin argued. "You should be home nursing it."

"Relax. It's not my weapon hand." She shook a bottle of pills. "Besides, I've got enough of these to keep me happy during the ten-hour flight."

Griffin slammed his head back against the seatback. "You're nuts."

"Takes one to know one," she responded.

They sat in silence as the plane took off, dipping sharply several times before eventually reaching cruising altitude. Leslie unsuccessfully attempted to open the medicine bottle with one hand.

"Give me that." Griffin grabbed the container from her and pried the lid off.

Leslie swallowed the pill with a gulp of water from a bottle she'd tucked into the seatback in front of her. With a heavy sigh, she leaned her head back and closed her eyes. "Give me ten minutes and I'll kick your ass in cards."

"You shouldn't have come," Griffin repeated.

"I've got nowhere else to be," she said, her eyelids still shut.

"You have a young son who you haven't seen in five days."

He watched as she swallowed roughly. "He's still in Disney World with his father. Not that Daniel is spending time with him. He's at a bar association thingy. Daniel's parents are chaperoning."

"Ahh," Griffin said. "You're jealous because you wanted to go."

Leslie's eyelids snapped open. She had a tiger mom look in her eyes he only saw when she was arguing on the phone with Daniel. "I'm not jealous of Eileen and Bill. They are wonderful people who love Dylan and give him much needed support when I'm working."

Griffin cringed at her ferocity. "I'm sorry. That was out of line."

Her eyes were suddenly damp and she looked away quickly. "They won't be home until Sunday night," she murmured. "Plenty of time for me to capture the bad guys and still be back in New York to make my son's lunch for preschool on Monday."

He reached for her hand and gave it a squeeze. "But you'd rather work than sit at home alone."

"It figures you would be the one to understand." She sniffled. "You're the king at avoiding heavy issues by diving into a case."

He yanked his hand back. "What's that supposed to

mean?"

"Exactly what you think it means. You use your career to fulfill your emotional needs." She winked at him. "Not that I'm complaining about some aspects of your neurosis."

"I don't do that!"

"Really?" She arched an eyebrow at him, infuriating Griffin even more. "Then what are you doing on this plane?"

He felt like he was going to explode. "Apparently talking to a mad woman!"

Leslie had the gall to laugh. "Said the kettle to the black pot."

"I'm traveling to Greece to rescue a young woman who is being held captive for the purposes of forging money and valuable artwork," he said through gritted teeth. "In doing so, I'll be breaking up a conglomerate of counterfeiters and thieves that I've been chasing for well over a year."

"Pfft," Leslie said waving her arm brace through the air. "Interpol will be the ones doing the rescuing. You've already done the heavy lifting and solved the case. You didn't need to run all the way to Europe to finish this thing out. You could have talked the director out of sending you."

"Hey, Black Pot, you're on this damn plane, too!"

She laughed again. "Yes, but we've already established that I'm an emotional wreck. Of course, if you repeat that to anyone, I'll claim it was the drugs talking." Leslie sobered up. "You should be in New Orleans at that wedding, Griff."

Her soft words were like a sucker punch.

Griffin glanced out the window to avoid Leslie's prob-ing eyes. "You're definitely high," he mumbled as he stared down at the dark ocean dotted with fluffy white clouds.

Leslie sighed heavily. "She declared her love to you in front of a crowd of people," she said to the back of his head. "It doesn't get more real than that. And don't think that she spoke up then just because she had a needle shoved into her throat."

The image of Salenko's deadly syringe jabbed into Mar-in's perfect ivory skin caused his rage to ignite again. He clenched his fists tightly.

Leslie put her uninjured palm on top of Griffin's right hand. "That woman is perfect for you, Griffin. Don't let my or anyone else's failed relationships dictate how you live your own life. You have a real shot with Marin. There's something special there between you two and I'm pretty sure you know it. You can't give up on her like this."

"You don't know what you're talking about. I'm not the one who gave up," he snapped. "She is." He swallowed roughly remembering her parting words in the Queen's bedroom. "Marin *told* me to come to Greece to rescue Elena. She isn't interested in anything more than what we had the past week."

"Did she happen to mention why?"

Her question infuriated him more, because it conjured up the image of Marin naked, draped in the floral sheets of the big canopy bed. She'd looked so earnest, especially as she'd said the words that both set him free and cut him to the quick.

I'll always want more than you can give me. Being a Secret Service agent is who you are. I couldn't ask you to give that up and still live with myself.

"She said she didn't want to be involved with a Secret Service agent."

"Really?" Leslie wore a perplexed look. "Or is that just what you wanted to hear?"

Griffin was done listening to Leslie impersonate a cable network shrink. He ripped off his seat belt and went to crawl over her lap in order to reach the aisle. She placed her good hand on his arm to stop him.

"Just hear me out on one last thing and I'll let the subject drop forever," she pleaded.

He was tempted to pull out of her grasp, but his mother had raised him better than that. Leslie's eyes grew misty again as he hovered over her.

"If Daniel had looked at me just once the way you look at Marin, we'd still be together," she whispered.

MARIN ALWAYS LOVED how the big ballroom at the Chevalier, New Orleans looked when it was decorated for a wedding. She adored the ambiance the large alabaster chandeliers created when they washed the room in a warm glow. And the way the marble statues, set into arched vestibules in the wall, seemed to be bowing their heads in hushed prayer beneath their soft awning of individual spotlights.

On this particular Saturday afternoon, the staff had spared no expense in decorating for the owner's grand-daughter. The white on white tables accented with gold utensils and bronze bamboo chairs provided the perfect backdrop for the towering treelike centerpieces of peach Oceana roses. The crystal adorning each place setting sparkled in the late-day sun.

Behind the dais, sounds from Canal Street filtered in through the floor-to-ceiling doors that opened to the city. Marin wandered over to the table next to the dais and checked on her pride and joy, the wedding cake. Four of the five layers of vanilla cake were filled with a raspberry puree filling. The top layer Marin had baked herself, flavoring it with her cousin's favorite toffee. She'd covered the whole cake in cream cheese icing before decorating it with edible gold lace and pearls. A cascade of Oceana roses spiraled down one side, pooling at the silver base on which the cake stood proudly.

She lifted her hand to adjust one of the roses, trying not to aggravate the still tender skin on her palm. Marin hadn't done her injuries any favors by spending ten hours decorating her cousin's wedding cake. But the end result was worth it. And having something exacting to focus on helped to ease the residual pain—both physical and emotional—that Marin had returned home with.

Her family had blessedly given her space. Even more surprising, Ava had backed off her demand that Marin bring a date to the wedding. Her cousin seemed in a mellow mood leading up to her marriage ceremony. Marin was actually looking forward to celebrating with Ava and her new husband this evening.

"I thought I'd find you here," Ava said from across the room.

"Just making sure everything is perfect." Marin turned to face her cousin. "For your perfect—why aren't you dressed?"

Ava crossed the wide ballroom wearing a pair of faded, high couture jeans, a floral peasant blouse that flowed when she walked and stiletto-heeled Jimmy Choo's. Her long black hair hung down her back in glorious waves. She looked as if she was going to lunch with friends, not walking down the aisle of St. Charles Church in an hour.

"The wedding pictures are in forty-five minutes!" Marin exclaimed. "It took them that long just to get my hair into this ridiculous updo. You'll never be ready in time."

Her cousin avoided looking directly at Marin, instead ambling up to the wedding cake and admiring it like one would appreciate a statue in a museum, slowly tilting her neck from side to side.

"It's gorgeous," Ava said quietly. "You really are unbelievably talented."

Marin was starting to get a very bad feeling. "What's going on?"

Ava ignored the question. She picked up the silver cake knife from the table and proceeded to cut into the top layer of the cake.

"*What are you doing?*" Marin cried, her chest constricting painfully with each inch the knife slid into the cake.

"I'm having a piece before I go," Ave responded, matter-of-factly.

"Go?" Marin felt her face heat with anger. "What do you mean 'go'?" Except she had a sneaking suspicion she knew exactly what her cousin meant.

Ava dumped the slice of cake onto a plate and walked over to one of the tables where she snitched a dessert fork. As she put a forkful of cake into her mouth, her eyes slid closed.

"Mmm." A look of pure delight swept over her face. "Toffee." Ava's eyes were bright with tears when she opened them. "You made my favorite. For me?"

"Of course I did." Marin stomped her foot, the high heels she wore making her wobble on the plush carpet. "And I squeezed into a pair of Spanx to fit into this damn bridesmaid dress for you, too!"

Her cousin sighed as she slid into one of the chairs and speared another piece of cake. "You could say this is actually your fault."

"*My fault?*" Marin was so incredulous she could barely find the words.

"Last night, the president filled the family in on all the details of your adventure," Ava said around another mouthful of cake.

"My 'adventure'?" Marin's body began to shake. "Is that what you call getting kidnapped and nearly killed— *multiple times*? Say nothing of the fact that my 'adventure' was all *your fault*! If you hadn't demanded that I bring a date to your stupid wedding, I never would have given the creepy guy a second look and he never would have known I existed!"

Ava wore a serious expression when she looked up from her plate. "I didn't say it was a good adventure. But it changed you forever. You can't possibly look at life the same way after going through that. Life is short, seize the day, live for the moment, and all that. Right?"

Stunned, Marin sank into the chair next to her cousin's. "Something like that," she said softly. Except Marin hadn't exactly seized the day. Instead, she'd pushed the man she loved away.

"Life is too short to marry someone just because he's convenient," Ava explained, finally. "So, I'm seizing my day."

Marin picked up a fork of her own and nabbed a piece of cake off her cousin's plate.

"That's all Richard is to you? Convenient?"

"Don't get me wrong, Rich is a wonderful guy. He's my father's protégé, so I know he's smart and hardworking. But if I married him, my life wouldn't change all that much. I'd still be the same old Ava. Only then I'd be living in a different house with a different last name and a different man sheltering my life." Ava blew out a breath. "He'd be the perfect husband for any woman. Just not for me." She looked at Marin resolutely. "I'm not sure I'm invested enough in a relationship with him to kill another man in order to save Rich's life."

The cake caught in Marin's throat and she coughed.

"Since when is that a requirement for a woman to marry a man?" she choked out. "Besides, you don't have to love someone to save their life. It's just the decent thing to do."

Ave shot her the look she always gave Marin when she caught her in a lie. Then she put her fork down carefully. "Rich wants a society wife who'll stay home with the kids," Ava whispered. "What happens if I want more? What if I decide life with him and our children isn't enough? What's to stop me from just picking up and leaving?"

Marin's heart squeezed tightly. "So that's what this is all about." She reached over and took her cousin's hand. "You're not your mother, Ava."

"How do you know?"

Her cousin's words dumbfounded Marin because, really, she didn't know.

"You see," Ave said stubbornly. "That's why I have to go out there and live a little. Away from the protective cocoon of this family. And my father's Mini-Me. You followed your dreams. And look what happened. I want an adventure that will define me, too." Her face took on a faraway look. "And maybe I'll find that perfect guy who gets me like your Secret Service agent gets you."

"There's a world of difference between someone getting you and them wanting to give up a part of who they are to spend their life with you," Marin replied, blinking back tears.

"That's because I've been hit in the head with a hockey puck too many times and I needed to have it spelled out for me."

The sound of Griffin's voice behind them startled Marin and she jumped up from her chair. She turned to see him in his all too familiar pose, leaning nonchalantly against one of the room's pillars. Her mouth dried up at the sight of him in his tuxedo. The stark white shirt against his dark skin gave him that pirate look that made her knees feel like Jell-O. Every time.

"Griffin," she croaked.

"That's Griffin?" Ava murmured. "Hot. Damn."

He stepped away from the pillar and walked over to their table. Marin grabbed the back of a chair for support.

"What are you doing here?" she asked.

He gestured to his tuxedo. "I promised you an evening of chivalry, dancing, and meaningful glances. And I always make good on my promises. Especially for someone I owe my life to."

Sighing lustfully, Ava rose from her seat and sauntered over to Griffin.

"I'm her cousin, Ava." She stuck out her hand as she introduced herself.

"The bridezilla." Griffin wrapped his fingers around Ava's.

Ava shot Marin a look over her shoulder, then she mouthed the word "Wow."

Marin bit back a smile. She was still trying to figure out how and why Griffin was standing a mere two feet from her when he was supposed to be in Greece. Doing what he lived to do. Saving people. Taking down the bad guys.

"Technically I'm a *runaway* bridezilla, tonight," Ava

clarified. "And on that note, I think this is my cue to start running."

"Wait!" Marin lurched toward her cousin. While she wanted a private moment to question Griffin, she wasn't so sure she wanted Ava to leave her alone with him. Her heart was still too tender. "Where are you planning to go?"

Her cousin rolled her eyes. "Don't worry. I haven't completely slipped this family's leash. Grandfather is making me work at the Chevalier in London for two years. I'm his indentured servant until I pay back every penny"—she made air quotes with her fingers—"for the wedding-that-wasn't." Ava shrugged. "It's fair. Who knows? My adventure might be waiting in Europe for me." She wrapped her arms around Marin in a warm embrace. "I'll call you every day."

"Let's not go overboard," Marin teased.

"I'll miss you." Ava glanced over her shoulder at Griffin. "I'm guessing more than you'll miss me with that stud warming your bed," she whispered.

Marin hugged her cousin tightly, brushing her lips across Ava's cheek. "I really hope you find what you're looking for," she said around the lump in her throat. "But always remember that I love you. No matter what."

"Take this," Ava slipped a keycard out of the back pocket of her jeans and placed it on the table. "There's no reason to let the honeymoon suite go to waste since I'm paying for it with my blood, sweat, and tears. Seize the day!"

With a wink, she turned to leave the ballroom.

"Be good to her, special agent," Ava called from the doorway. "Because if you don't, I know people."

Griffin dropped his chin to his chest and let out a beleaguered sigh.

"She used to always want to play Thelma and Louise when we were kids," Marin explained for no other reason than to diffuse Ava's dramatic exit.

"Remind me never to introduce her to Leslie," he said with a grin.

Marin's breath hitched at the sight of his smile. She really needed to pull herself together.

"Elena?" she asked.

"Interpol rescued her about two hours ago."

"Interpol? Not you?"

He stepped closer to her so that their bodies were separated by inches. Griffin reached up and lightly traced a finger over her healing lip. Marin couldn't stop her sigh.

"It was pointed out to me by the other half of Thelma and Louise that I had already set Elena's rescue into motion and it was redundant for me to actually travel to Greece." He pulled apart the hands that Marin was wringing together and inspected each palm. "Besides, I had something more important to do. Like this." He pressed a gentle kiss to each hand.

Marin was embarrassed by the soft keening sound that escaped the back of her throat. Griffin's smile turned smug as he wrapped his arms loosely around her waist and pulled her in closer to him.

"And this," he said before tenderly pressing his lips to

hers. "And to tell you that you were wrong."

"About what?" she asked as her lips grazed his jaw. Not that she even cared what she was wrong about at this point.

"You said I couldn't give you what you wanted. But to be fair, you never gave me a chance to."

She pulled back to look into his eyes. Staring back at her was the passion guaranteed to always make her insides quiver. But there was vulnerability shining in them, too.

"When did you figure that out?"

He groaned before leaning his forehead against hers. "About an hour into a ten-hour flight. The *first* ten-hour flight."

Marin ran her hands up his back as she kissed his neck. "I could never ask you to give everything up."

Griffin lifted his head. "That's just it, you don't have to. I don't have to give everything up." He kissed the tip of her nose. "Yeah, my job is important to me, but I don't have to let it define me any longer. Not when I can be so much more with you."

A warm flush of happiness spread over Marin's skin. "Are you sure?"

"There are lots of jobs out there where I can protect people, Marin," he said. "But my first priority will always be protecting you."

She kissed him then. His mouth felt and tasted like home. And new beginnings.

"You were wrong about something else, too," he said when they came up for air.

Marin arched an eyebrow at him. "I don't think I've

ever been wrong twice."

Griffin didn't let her quip get by without another searing kiss.

"You were wrong when you said I didn't have to love you back," he said against her lips. "Because I do have to love you, Marin Chevalier. I can't *not* love you."

EPILOGUE

THE THREE BOHEMIAN cut-glass chandeliers hanging from the ceiling of the White House's East Room shimmered above tuxedoed butlers carrying silver trays of champagne flutes through the crowd. Standing at attention next to Gilbert Stuart's iconic painting of George Washington, Griffin tried to appear inconspicuous as he kept watch over the event.

"You do realize that you are a guest in the House this evening, Agent Keller," Admiral Sedgewick said when he joined Griffin along the wall. "You don't have to keep watch over the president. You are allowed to mingle."

Griffin hadn't laid eyes on the president the entire evening. Or the First Lady. He'd only had eyes for one person. A statuesque blonde in a stunning red gown who seemed to be floating around the room.

The admiral followed Griffin's gaze. The man's mouth turned up at the corners when he, too, spied Marin. "This was an amazing thing she did. Wes would be humbled by the collection the chef pulled together in his honor."

The late curator would be just one of many who were in awe of Marin's talents. In the absence of a permanent White House curator, Marin had been doing double duty as both executive pastry chef and steward of the mansion's vast inventory of artwork. Tonight's black-tie reception was the culmination of months of work.

She wanted to do something to recognize Wes's contributions to the White House. But this evening was about more than that. All he had to do was glance around the room and see the proud smiles worn by the family of Arnold, the Dupont's late doorman, as they mingled with the famous dignitaries in attendance. Or Seth's parents as they shook hands with President Manning. Tonight was primarily about Marin casting away much of the faultless guilt she carried around.

"She's got a big decision to make," the admiral murmured.

Griffin's head snapped around at his words. He stared incredulously at the man standing beside him. How did the admiral know? Griffin's fingers slid over the small blue pouch tucked inside his suit jacket. Griffin had only told one person about his plans. And that little imp had proven herself very reliable at keeping secrets. She had a room full of stuffed animals to prove it.

"The White House Historical Society would love for Chef Marin to take the job as the full-time curator." The admiral looked at him quizzically. "What did you think I was talking about?"

He was relieved when his parents joined them, so he didn't have to respond to the admiral.

"Oh, Griffin, what an amazing night," his mother said, her smile beaming. "I can't believe I'm actually here. I have to keep pinching myself."

"I'm glad you could come," he said as he leaned over and kissed her on the cheek. "You look beautiful."

"You should see our suite at the Chevalier," his father added. "Not too shabby. We may never leave. And to top it off, the president gave me a private tour of the presidential putting green. I can't wait until the guys at the club see the pictures."

"Don't forget to show the guys at the club the pictures of the White House pastry kitchen," Marin teased as she slipped into their circle. "I hope you tell them seeing it was your favorite part of the trip."

Griffin's father wrapped an arm around Marin just as his mother tucked her arm through Marin's on her other side. His chest squeezed at the sight of the most important person in his life enveloped by the two people he'd foolishly believed he would always love the most.

"That apple turnover was my favorite part of the trip," his father said with a wink. "I'm still trying to figure out how to get one to go."

"Oh, I think your son might be able to negotiate a sweet deal for you. Rumor has it, he's on very good terms with the executive pastry chef." Marin grinned at Griffin mischievously.

His mouth went dry just looking at her. She was positively glowing tonight. In six months, the physical wounds had healed. But the emotional scars were still lurking beneath the surface. There had been many nights when he had been awakened by her nightmares. But he was always there to protect her, to comfort her, holding her in her sleep. And if things went his way tonight, he always would be.

"Mr. and Mrs. Keller," the admiral said. "I don't believe you've had a tour of the West Wing. Would you be interested in seeing the Oval Office?"

Griffin's parents tried to appear cool about the admiral's offer, but he knew them well enough to know they were thrilled. His mom could barely contain her glee.

"We'll see you two later," she said with a wave as they followed the admiral out of the room.

Marin and Griffin were as alone as they could be in a room filled with over a hundred people. She sauntered closer until she was a scant inch from his body. With a sly smile, she reached up to adjust the angle of his tuxedo's bow tie.

"So how is my favorite G-Man tonight?" she asked softly. "The way you've been hugging that wall all evening, it looks like you miss being in the Secret Service. Are the cases at the Treasury Department not as stimulating as potentially taking a bullet for the president?"

He trailed a finger along her bare arm. Marin sucked in a breath at his touch.

"I love working at the Treasury," Griffin said. He wasn't lying; he did love working as a treasury agent. "Especially since my new job keeps me in DC with you. Tonight, I was 'hugging the wall' as you say so I could enjoy the scenery."

Marin tugged him forward by his lapels so that their

hips came into contact with one another. Griffin swallowed a rough groan.

"Nonsense," she whispered. "You weren't looking at any of the artwork. You've spent the past hour trailing me around the room with your eyes."

"The very definition of what constitutes artwork is in the eye of the beholder." He leaned forward and touched his lips to the tip of her nose. "And my eyes know what they like."

"Take me home."

Her sultry plea had his heart racing and the zipper of his pants causing him great pain. As much as Griffin wanted to take her up on her offer, he had other plans that needed to be executed first.

"We can't leave yet," he said. He maneuvered them out of sight behind one of the lighted ornamental trees. "Not while the dignitaries are still here."

She nipped at his jawline. "It's my party. I can leave whenever I want. And I want to go home. With you. Right now." Her eyes were bright with passion and Griffin was having a difficult time remembering where they were much less what his plans were.

"Take me home," she purred. "I promise I'll let you touch my artwork. I might even let you taste it."

Griffin was so bamboozled, he couldn't think straight. He took her hand in his and not so gently led her through the crowd toward the exit. Marin giggled behind him. Heedless of the marine guards and other Secret Service agents standing at attention in the massive Center Hall,

Griffin pulled Marin behind one of the marble columns and took her mouth in a demanding kiss. One Marin responded to with equal enthusiasm.

"Okay, you win," Griffin said when he came up for air. "Let's go home."

A child's giggle interrupted their flight toward the front door, however. Marin stopped in her tracks, turning toward the Grand Staircase. Dressed in a frilly nightgown, Arabelle sat halfway up the stairs, her fuzzy pink slippers clashing with the bright red carpet. Otto obediently waited at her side stoically enduring the feather boa his young playmate had wrapped around his neck.

"Arabelle," Marin said. "What are you still doing up?"

The little girl scrambled to her feet. "I'm going to bed right now. I just had to give Agent Keller a message."

Arabelle attempted a wink but failed miserably. She gave him a thumbs-up instead. Griffin stifled a laugh at the little girl's enthusiasm. Marin shot him a questioning glance when Arabelle and Otto disappeared around the corner.

Griffin tugged her toward the stairs. "Come on," he said. "We're sticking with the original plan. But that doesn't mean I don't want to admire your artwork later this evening."

"There's a plan?"

They rounded the corner leading up to the residence floor. "Yeah," he admitted, feeling a bit sheepish. "But I keep getting distracted by the scenery."

She smiled coyly as she squeezed his hand. Griffin led

her through the double glass doors at the top of the stair landing, across the Center Hall and into the Yellow Oval Room. Marin sighed with pleasure when she crossed the threshold.

"You do know this is probably my favorite room in the White House," she said.

"Mm. You might have mentioned it a few times."

Marin pulled her hand free and gravitated toward a colorful antique toy truck in one of the bookcases. She trailed a finger along its tire.

"Did you know this belonged to Calvin Coolidge's son? He died here in the White House." A melancholy look crossed her face.

Griffin quickly moved to intercept her before she explored more of the room. "Can I show you my favorite part of the White House?"

"I didn't know you had one." She tucked her hand under his arm as Griffin led them out onto the Truman Balcony.

The warm autumn breeze lifted the hem of her dress when she stepped over the threshold. A yellow harvest moon hung just above the Washington Monument, dotting it like a lowercase i Marin drifted over to the railing and sighed at the view.

"This is a wonderful part of the House," she said with a nod. "The view is stunning."

"Yes," Griffin said, his eyes firmly fixed on Marin. "It is."

She peeked over her shoulder at him. Her smile

dimmed when she saw the ice bucket of champagne and two glasses. Griffin's breath stilled in his lungs at her reaction.

"Griffin, we have to go. I think Aunt Harriet and Uncle Conrad have plans out here."

Chuckling with relief, Griffin closed the distance between them. "I had dibs on it first."

He wrapped his arms loosely around her waist pulling her body up against his.

"You did?" she asked.

"Remember when I told you I wanted you the first time I saw you in the pastry kitchen?"

Marin blushed and nodded.

"Well, I fell in love with you out here, on this balcony. On our first date."

"Are you sure it wasn't the ravioli?" she teased.

Griffin pretended to ponder her question, and she smacked him on the chest. His throat suddenly became clogged with emotion.

"This is where it all started," he said. "So it is where I wanted to make it official."

He pulled the velvet Tiffany's pouch out of his pocket. Marin's eye's widened, and her hands shook against his chest. The diamond ring sparkled in the moonlight when Griffin lifted it from the pouch.

"Marin Chevalier, I couldn't not kiss you. Just as I couldn't not love you. And I definitely can't not spend the rest of my life with you. Will you marry me?"

Years later, Griffin wouldn't remember what Marin

actually said. Just that with the stunning panorama of Washington DC behind her, she kissed him with reckless abandon and made him the happiest man alive.

THE END

THE MEN OF THE SECRET SERVICE SERIES

Book 1: *Recipe for Disaster*

Book 2: Coming Fall 2018

Book 3: Coming Spring 2019

More fantastic reads by Tracy Solheim

Smolder

Holiday at Magnolia Bay

It's going to be a Southern Born Christmas....

HOLIDAY IN MAGNOLIA BAY

After a mission goes terribly wrong, Navy Seal, Drew Lanham, is forced to take a leave from active-duty. Retreating to his godmother's beach house in coastal Magnolia Bay, Drew plans to spend the three weeks R&R licking his wounds and catching some rays while the nightmares from his failed op fade. What he doesn't count on is an encounter with a goddess rising from the sea. His interest is piqued and his body put on alert when he finds out that same woman may or may not be after his godmother's money.

Marine biologist, Jenna Huntley, has been searching her whole life for a place to call home and Magnolia Bay is that place. Everything is going as planned until the older woman's godson arrives. Suddenly, nothing is as it seems and Jenna's future is hanging in the balance, with a sexy warrior pulling all the strings. Her natural tendency is to help the damaged hero, but she's sworn off letting military men in her life ever again.

Will Drew and Jenna be able to put their pasts behind them and learn to trust their hearts long enough to enjoy their Holiday at Magnolia Bay?

Pre-Order Now!

ABOUT THE AUTHOR

Tracy Solheim is the international bestselling author of the Out of Bound Series for Penguin. Her books feature members of the fictitious Baltimore Blaze football team and the women who love them. In a previous life, Tracy wrote best sellers for Congress and was a freelance journalist for regional and national magazines. She's a military brat who now makes her home in Johns Creek, Georgia, with her husband, their two children, a pesky Labrador retriever puppy and a horse named after her first novel.

Thank you for reading

RECIPE FOR DISASTER

If you enjoyed this book, you can find more from all our great authors at TulePublishing.com, or from your favorite online retailer.

TULE
PUBLISHING

Made in the USA
Columbia, SC
28 April 2018